the Hope

**Also available from
Patricia Davids
and HQN Books**

The Amish of Cedar Grove

PATRICIA DAVIDS

the Hope

HQN™

HQN™

Recycling programs for this product may not exist in your area.

ISBN-13: 978-1-335-04152-4

The Hope

This book is lovingly dedicated to my brothers, Greg, Bob, Mark and Gary. I love you all. Maybe one more than the others, but I'm not going to say which one. The keys to the kingdom are mine. HA! HA!

CHAPTER ONE

"How long does it take to close a door, Faron?" Ruth Mast pulled her last cookie sheet out of the oven and glanced over her shoulder. Her son wasn't paying attention.

How many times had she asked him that same question? Hundreds? Maybe more. Ever since he was old enough to reach the doorknob, he had been gazing out the open door for one reason or another. Her throat tightened at the memory of him as a small boy waiting for his friends to arrive so they could walk to school, or for his father to come in from his evening chores. Now that Faron was growing up, he looked more like his father every day. "Faron?"

"I want to see if *Onkel* Ernest is on his way yet."

She assumed that would be his answer. He was eager to get going to the skating party, and his great-uncle Ernest was the only person missing. "He'll be here when he gets here. You're letting the cold air in."

Faron wasn't a child anymore, but he wasn't quite an adult. At seventeen he was occasionally oblivious to the needs of others, as only a teenage boy could be. He had come in from hitching up their horse. He might not be cold in his heavy overcoat, boots

and flat-topped black Amish hat, but she hadn't finished dressing for their outdoor trip. The last day of
February was sunny, but the breeze coming off the
snow-covered Kansas fields was still icy as it swirled
into the house.

She carried the hot pan to the table and began
transferring sugar cookies to a wire rack. The cold
draft continued to rush over her bare feet. "Faron,
please, close the door and watch for him out the window. My feet are freezing."

"Sorry." He shut the door and stepped over to gaze
out the window over the sink. "He said he had a surprise for me. I hope he gets here soon."

Her daughter, Ella, came in from the other room
with two large quilts in her arms. She was wearing
a dark blue dress with a matching apron and a white
kapp identical to the outfit Ruth had on. Ella was
Ruth's oldest child at twenty-one and she was leaving home at the end of the week. "*Onkel* Ernest will
be here the minute those cookies are cool enough to
eat. He has some special sense that tells him when
Mamm is finished baking."

Ruth chuckled. It did seem to be true.

Ella's new husband, Zack Hostetler, followed her
into the room holding two pairs of ice skates by the
laces and Ella's coat draped over his arm. Like Faron,
he was already dressed for the outdoors in a heavy
wool coat and hat. "I'll test a cookie for your *onkel*."

He reached for one, but Ruth batted his hand
away. "These are for the party."

"What difference does it make if I eat one here

or one there?" His exaggerated pout almost made her laugh. It was easy to see why her shy, bookish daughter had fallen for the charming fellow. And now he was taking her little girl away.

Ruth shook her metal turner at him. "The difference is I won't smack your hand at the party. Ella, it's up to you to teach your new husband some manners."

Ella grinned, her eyes full of love. "I sort of like him just the way he is."

He took the quilts from her and helped her into her coat. "And I love you just the way you are. I'll put these in the sleigh for you."

Ella didn't take her eyes off her husband. "I'll help you." The two walked out the door, smiling at each other.

Ella and Zack would soon be starting on their wedding trip. The skating party being held today was a farewell party for them. They would eventually settle in Jamesport, Missouri, with his family, after visiting other relatives and friends in Missouri and Arkansas for several weeks. Ruth hated to think they would be four hours away by hired car, but they promised to visit her at Christmas. They had been staying with her for two months, and she knew Ella was eager to have her own home. Only Ruth wasn't eager to see them go.

She suffered a sharp stab of jealousy. To be young and in love was a wonderful thing. She remembered the joy of starting her own home. The children had been Nathan's greatest gift to her.

Her husband had been taken from her much too soon. His death four years ago from a farming accident had rocked her world. She accepted that it was God's will, but there were times when she was lonely for the companionship and comfort of a spouse. Perhaps it was good that taking care of the farm was a full-time job and left little time to feel sorry for herself.

"I'll help you put the quilts in the sleigh." Faron mimicked his sister in a high voice. "As if a grown man couldn't handle the job. Getting married has turned my sensible sister's brain to mush. And Zack is no better."

"You'll do well to remember that in a few years," Ernest Mast said as he stepped through the door.

Ruth's mood immediately brightened. The children's great-uncle had that effect on everyone. A big jovial man in his midfifties, he was a clean-shaven Amish fellow who'd never married. He removed his black flat-topped hat and hung it on a peg by the door. His straight salt-and-pepper hair bore a permanent crease from it around his head. He was everyone's favorite uncle in Cedar Grove, Kansas—even those he wasn't related to by blood. Ernest was seldom seen without a fishing pole and always had a funny story to share. Together they were running the farm her husband left her, until Faron was old enough to take over on his own.

What would she have done during the dark days after Nathan's death without Uncle Ernest's fatherly advice and cheerful nature? It didn't bear thinking about.

Faron leaned against the counter with his arms crossed over his chest as he grinned at his great-uncle. "I'm in no hurry to wed. I may take after you and enjoy life as a single fellow. What's my surprise?"

"Have a little patience, my boy." Ernest crossed the room, snagged a cookie from the wire rack and bit into it. "Mmm, these are *goot*, Ruth."

"That is the only one you get," she said as she finished packing the napkins and paper plates on top of the container of fried chicken in her picnic basket. "Take this one out for me, Faron. I'll be ready in a few minutes. Do you have your skates?"

"Already in the sleigh." He took the basket and opened the door. "*Mamm!* Cousin Owen is here! Is that your surprise, *Onkel*? This is great!" He darted outside.

"Surprise," Ernest whispered as he slipped around her, snagged his hat and went out.

Ruth's shoulders slumped. She closed her eyes. Why Owen and why now? It was always hard to face her husband's unreliable cousin without resentment. She prayed for strength to offer him the kindness she knew was expected of her.

"Hello, Ruth. How are you?"

She straightened and faced the man who had disappointed her time and again. He held his black hat in his hands, turning it slowly. His thick brown hair had a little gray near his temples. He was only a year older than she was. He had always been good-looking, but his finely chiseled features had improved with age. His steel-gray eyes were as piercing as ever.

She swallowed hard. "I'm fine, Owen."

He raised an eyebrow. "Really?"

"What makes you think I'm not?"

"I'm here for one thing. Also, your daughter is leaving home. That girl's happiness is everything to you. You'll miss her more than you can say."

His understanding surprised her.

Ruth nodded and struggled to hold back sudden tears. "I will miss her, but that's what I get for sending her to stay with my parents for a month each summer. She fell head over heels for the boy who lives next door to *Daed* and *Mamm*. I'm glad I don't have to worry about Faron moving away. When he marries, he'll live here in Cedar Grove and raise his family on the land his father loved." She sniffled and wiped her watery eyes. "All right, maybe I'm not fine. Maybe I feel like crying."

He shook his head. "Not Nathan's Ruth. She is made of sterner stuff."

"You give me too much credit." Blinking back her tears, she raised her chin. "I'm glad you could make it for the send-off party even if you didn't make it to the wedding."

He looked down and stopped turning his hat. "I'm sorry about that. Something else came up."

"That always seems to happen where your family is concerned." She bit her lower lip. That wasn't kind. What was it about Owen that brought out the worst in her?

Ernest stepped through the door. "Are you ready? The children are getting restless."

Owen nodded. "I'm coming."

Ruth knew she shouldn't say anything else, but she couldn't help it. "Ernest, I'm so glad you and your mother are traveling with Ella and Zack to Missouri. It's a relief to know they have someone they can depend on in an emergency."

Owen settled his black hat on his head. "You made your point, Ruth. I'll be outside." The door banged shut behind him.

"Ruth, Ruth," Ernest chided as he came to stand beside her. "Let bygones be bygones. The boy has had a rough life."

"He isn't a boy anymore. He's forty-three, and my life hasn't been easy, either."

"True, but we do not question the will of *Gott*."

"I'm sorry. Forgive me." She decided to change the subject. "When do you expect to be back from your trip?"

"Haven't decided."

She smiled at him. "Why don't you take a long vacation? Faron and I can manage your farm and ours for a month or so."

"Funny you should suggest it. I've been meaning to talk to you about that." He snagged another cookie.

She playfully elbowed him in the ribs. "We'll discuss it after the party, and quit stealing my treats."

He rubbed his side, replaced the cookie and

glanced down. "Woman, where are your shoes? You'll catch your death going barefoot in the winter."

"I was getting ready, but I had to rush downstairs when the timer went off because I didn't want my cookies to burn. I'm going to finish dressing now." She started for the stairs but paused. "Don't eat any more of those."

She looked over her shoulder to see him snatch his empty hand away from the cookies and hold it behind him. He tried to look innocent. "I won't."

"I can count. I know exactly how many there were in that last batch."

He grudgingly replaced the one he'd already hidden behind his back. "Where is Meeka when I need to blame something on her?"

"I would hope your big white *hund* is guarding the farm and keeping the coyotes away from the sheep and chickens, but it's safe to assume she's sleeping on your front porch. That's the only place I've ever seen your dog." Ruth padded up the stairs.

"She makes rounds at night," he called out.

Ruth wasn't about to admit that the dog probably did much more than that. They hadn't lost a single lamb last spring or ewe this winter to predators. The dog was proving to be worth the money Ernest had paid for her.

Ruth sat on the edge of her bed and pulled on her thick gray woolen socks and fleece-lined boots. She rubbed the back of her neck to dispel the first twinges of a headache. Owen's sudden appearance wasn't going to ruin her enjoyment this afternoon.

She wouldn't let him. He wouldn't stay long. He never stayed anywhere for long.

She rose, grabbed her coat, bonnet and scarf off the hooks on the wall, then rushed back downstairs. Ernest was still waiting for her. She cast him a suspicious glance. "Why aren't you in the sleigh?"

"I was guarding the cookies you left out to cool." He licked his lips.

She brushed a few crumbs from the front of his coat and glanced at the wire rack. The same number of cookies remained so he must have taken some from the container on the counter. "*Onkel*, you should be ashamed of yourself."

"Sometimes it is better to ask forgiveness than permission."

She shook a finger at him. "One of these days that kind of thinking will backfire on you."

"Maybe, but I pray it won't be soon. Where are your skates?"

"I'm too old to skate. That's for the *kinder*."

"Don't be silly. I'm way older than you, and I'm not too old to go skating."

"That's because you never grew up." She transferred the last of the cookies into a plastic container after noticing two cookies were indeed missing, and sealed the lid.

"What's the point in growing up? Have you ever seen an adult having as much fun as the *kinder* do?"

"Maybe not but old bones don't heal as quickly as young ones."

"So true. Do you have everything?"

Pausing with her hands on her hips, she surveyed the kitchen. "I think so."

"Hot chocolate?"

"Martha is bringing that."

"She forgot the marshmallows at the last skating party."

"I packed some just in case." She pulled on her coat and slowly tied the ribbons of her bonnet beneath her chin. She was stalling. She didn't want to ride in the sleigh in Owen's company, but it couldn't be helped. "I've got everything."

"You are always prepared." He held open the door for her.

She stepped outside and stopped. Ernest was wrong. She wasn't prepared to see Owen Mast surrounded by her family chatting happily as if he belonged in their circle. She was the only one who didn't care for him. Her children loved him—as had her husband.

Owen Mast was her husband's first cousin. Owen had been thirteen when his parents and all but one of his siblings were killed in a buggy-and-car crash. He and his three-year-old sister, Rebecca, had survived. Rebecca had been sent to live with their mother's maiden sister, Thelma Stoltzfus, in Ohio while Owen had come to live with Nathan's family in Kansas. Owen and Nathan became as close as brothers, but Owen never forgot about his little sister. When he was old enough, he had gone looking for her.

She and Owen had been walking out together the summer she turned seventeen, but their relationship had apparently meant more to her than it had to him. He'd left town without a word to her. It was Nathan who'd told her Owen had gone to see his aunt and reunite with his sister. Later she'd learned his aunt had taken his sister and moved away before he arrived. No one knew where they had gone. Owen didn't show up at the farm again for another two years. Just in time to see her marry Nathan. Then he was gone again.

Nathan had been a man rooted in the earth and happiest on his farm; Owen was just the opposite. He could never stay on the farm for long. Not even when she had needed him the most. Her Amish faith required her to forgive him, but she couldn't forget the times he had let her down.

She knew Nathan had wanted his wife and his adopted brother to be friends. She owed it to him to try one more time.

She forced a bright smile. "I wish someone had mentioned you were coming, Owen."

Ruth slanted a glance at Ernest. His amused grin widened. "Slipped my mind."

She didn't find it funny.

Faron was beaming as he looked from Owen to Ruth. "Isn't it great to have Cousin Owen home?"

"Wunderbar," she said through clenched teeth, hoping Faron didn't notice her sarcasm but not caring if Owen did. Why was he here now?

"I asked Owen to help out with the farmwork while I'm in Missouri," Ernest said in a jovial tone that didn't quite ring true.

She nodded slightly. "I'm glad Owen was able to come, but Faron and I can handle things here, right, *sohn*?"

Faron's eyes shifted away from her as did Ernest's when she glanced his way. A hint of unease grew in the back of her mind. Something was going on.

"Where did you come from this time, Owen?" Faron asked brightly.

"Shipshewana," he said as if it were the next town over instead of hundreds of miles away in Indiana.

Faron's eyes lit up. "Did you see the Great Lakes? I want to hear all about it."

"Later," Ruth said with a sour look for Owen. The rare times he came to visit he filled her son's head with stories of far-off places and it was months before Faron stopped talking about seeing them for himself. Why couldn't the boy realize the best place in the world was right under his feet, on the land his father and grandfather had poured their blood, sweat and tears into?

She was afraid Owen would lure her son away from home and from her with his tales of travel and adventure. She couldn't let that happen.

"Your mother is right," Owen said. "We have a skating party to attend. We don't want the bride and groom to be late."

Zack and Ella grinned at him as they got in. The sleigh was a black vis-à-vis style with two maroon tufted bench seats that faced each other behind a raised seat for the driver. Faron scrambled up top and took hold of the reins. Ruth's black buggy horse,

Licorice, stood patiently waiting for the trip to start. Her harness was decked out with brass sleigh bells that jingled with her every move.

Ernest scooted across the front seat to give her room to sit. Owen held out his hand to help her in. She hesitated but had little choice except to place her hand in his. Why did he have to show up today when her emotions were already raw?

The strength of his touch sent her heart thudding wildly and triggered memories of their time together as teenagers. She thought she had been in love with him when she was a foolish seventeen-year-old. Only later did she come to realize it had been an infatuation and not the true, deep love she'd found with Nathan.

She pulled her hand away and slipped on her gloves. Owen could be charming, but he wasn't dependable, and she wasn't seventeen anymore.

RUTH WAS NOT happy to see him.

Owen hadn't expected she would be. That he hadn't stayed to help with the farm after Nathan's death had been the final straw in their uneasy relationship. He had returned to Cedar Grove this time at his uncle's invitation and with the intention of making amends, but Ruth wasn't going to make it easy for him.

He didn't agree with the plan Faron and Ernest had concocted between them. Faron intended to accompany Ernest and the newlyweds to Missouri and down into Arkansas. Owen understood that the boy wanted to see more of the country but springing it on his mother without warning wasn't the right way to go about it. Owen was happy for the chance to show Ruth she could depend on him to help while the men were gone, but he was pretty sure she was going to blame him for her son's idea to travel with Ernest.

Ruth settled beside Ernest. Owen stepped up and sat beside her in the rear-facing seat. She was sandwiched between Ernest and him. She spread a blue-and-white quilt over them. Owen pulled it across his lap, making sure she had enough to keep her warm.

Faron urged Licorice to a trot and headed down the snow-covered lane toward the county road. The sleigh bells jingled merrily as the horse trotted along and the sleigh runners hissed through the snow. Other than the muffled hoofbeats on the snowy road, they were the only sounds in the crisp air.

Within minutes Ruth's cheeks were red from the cold and wisps of her blond hair escaped from beneath her bonnet to flutter around her face. Her blue eyes sparkled in the sunlight. She looked more like a girl of twenty than a woman past forty. It was easy to see why she had captured Nathan's heart. He pushed aside the thought that she had once owned his heart, too, although he hadn't realized it until it was too late.

Zack and Ella began whispering with their heads together and their red-and-green quilt pulled up to their chins.

Ernest leaned toward Ruth. "Do you think they would notice if we jumped out and went back to the house?"

Ruth's lips curled in a small smile. "Only if we took the picnic basket with us. Then I'm sure they would come after us."

"So would I," Owen added. "You always were a *goot* cook."

She cast a narrowed glance his way. "As seldom as you've eaten at my table, I'm surprised you're any kind of judge."

He laughed, settled his hat lower on his forehead and folded his arms over his chest. "Always quick with that sharp wit. You haven't changed a bit, Ruthie."

Her eyes narrowed. "I don't imagine you have, either."

"You might be surprised."

"You won't mind if I don't hold my breath, will you?" she asked sweetly.

"Are you excited about the party?" Ernest asked Ruth, breaking into the tense moment.

"I am," Faron said before his mother could answer. "All my friends are coming. It should be loads of fun."

"Loads of fun," Ruth repeated with a wry smile.

"What are you going to do with all your free time after Zack and I leave?" Ella asked.

Ruth rolled her eyes. "I'm sure I will think of something."

Ella leaned forward. "You should consider marrying again."

Her comment caught Owen by complete surprise. He turned to stare at Ruth, waiting for her reply. He never imagined she would remarry, but there was nothing to stop her. She appeared as stunned by Ella's suggestion as he was.

Ruth shook her head. "*Nee*, for *Gott* already blessed me with my soul mate. I don't look to find another."

Her answer was what Owen expected. He didn't believe there was a better man than Nathan for her anywhere or even one half as good.

Ruth smoothed the quilt on her lap. "I won't be bored if you are worried about that, Ella. I'll enjoy having some free time. I certainly need to catch up on my letter writing. Besides, the two of you will bring me grandbabies to spoil in due time. Who knows, you may decide to move back to Cedar Grove and raise your family here."

"Don't hold your breath for that one, *Mamm*," Faron said.

"Why not?" She turned to look up at her son.

Owen rolled his eyes. Faron was about to ruin Ruth's day.

"Jamesport has a lot more going on than Cedar Grove will ever have. There are Amish-owned furniture factories and a homemade-candy store that does a lot of business with the *Englisch*. Some Amish there give buggy rides to tourists. Others own restaurants or sell baked goods and garden produce from their homes. They embrace the financial benefits that outsiders bring."

By the look on Ruth's face, Faron's obvious admiration for the distant community didn't sit well with her.

"And how do you know all of this?" she asked with a pointed look at Zack. Her new son-in-law shook his head no.

"Owen told me," Faron said brightly.

She turned her icy gaze in Owen's direction. "Owen did? I never would have guessed."

"He's done so many things, worked at so many different jobs. You know I like to hear his stories. He's almost as funny as *Onkel* Ernest." Faron looked back at his mother and stopped talking when he realized he'd said more than he should.

Owen was happy to shift the attention from himself. "No one is funnier than Ernest. He's more entertaining than a barn full of frisky kittens."

Ella and Zack chuckled. Ruth didn't appear amused.

Ernest leaned forward. "Speaking of cats, did I ever tell you about the time a mouse ran up my pant leg and a cat tried to follow it?"

"You have." Ruth turned her glare back on Owen. "Cousin Owen may be skilled at many trades, but farming is the finest profession an Amish man can undertake. To care for the land and animals is to care for *Gott*'s creations. To grow food for ourselves and for others is part of our Amish heritage," she said, still looking at Owen. "Don't you agree?"

It was a warning to stop filling Faron's head with ideas about seeing new places. "The best profession is the one *Gott* has planned for a man, the one a man can put his heart into. Don't you agree?"

Ruth's lips pressed into a narrow line.

"There are a lot of Amish farmers in the Jamesport area," Zack said to fill the sudden awkward silence.

"Mostly corn, I imagine," Ernest said.

"A mix of crops, about like here. Not as much wheat but plenty of soybeans, hay and some cotton."

"Cotton is a crop I've never tried, but ten years ago I wasn't planting soybeans." Ernest and Zack discussed crops and land prices for the next ten minutes. Ruth remained stubbornly silent.

The sun shone overhead with only a few gray clouds scuttling across the blue sky. The surrounding fields devoid of crops and blanketed in a foot of snow sparkled and gleamed so brightly it was hard to look at them without squinting. The air was chilly, but the sun felt warm on Owen's face.

When Zack and Ella began conversing quietly again, Owen leaned toward Ruth. "*Gott* has blessed us with a beautiful day for a sleigh ride and a skating party." He leaned closer and whispered, "Don't spoil it for everyone by pouting because I'm here."

Her eyes widened. "I am not pouting," she whispered back sharply.

"Aren't you? That's what I would call it."

After a minute, she relaxed. "It is a pretty day for a sleigh ride. *Danki.*"

He tipped his head slightly not quite trusting her sudden change of mood. "Thanks for what?"

"For reminding me to be grateful for *Gott*'s daily blessings. However, I was not pouting. I was simply lost in thought."

That was another thing that hadn't changed. Ruth was never wrong.

"My mistake. The forecast is for more snow tonight. I hope it doesn't start before we get home this evening."

She wrinkled her nose. "I'll be glad when spring gets here in spite of the fact that lambing makes it my busiest season."

The sound of a car approaching caught Owen's attention. Faron headed the horse toward the shoulder of the road as he muttered, "What is wrong with that fool?"

Owen leaned around to see what he was talking about. He saw a dark green car weaving toward them coming much too fast on the snow-covered road. "Hang on!"

His warning came too late. The car clipped the left rear side of the sleigh. The impact tipped the sleigh over flinging everyone out. He heard Ruth cry out and then silence as he hit the snow.

CHAPTER TWO

A SNOWBANK CUSHIONED some of Owen's fall. He sat up slowly, checking to see if anything hurt. It didn't. He brushed the snow from his head, found his hat and looked around. Faron was already trying to calm the spooked horse to keep her from pulling the overturned sleigh farther along the ditch. Ernest sat at the edge of the road dusting off his coat. Zack was helping Ella to her feet. They both seemed unharmed. Ruth lay on her back a few feet away from Owen. She wasn't moving.

Fear made his already rapidly beating heart pound wildly. He floundered through the snow to her side and dropped to his knees, fearful of what he would find.

Please, Lord, let her be okay.

She moaned softly. She was alive. Relief made his head spin. He grabbed her hand. "Ruth, are you all right? Ruth, speak to me."

Her eyes fluttered open. "What happened?"

He sank back on his heels as he gave silent thanks for the Lord's mercy. "A car hit us."

"Is everyone okay? Faron? Ella?" She tried to sit up and groaned.

"Everyone is on their feet except you and Ernest. Can you stand?"

"I think so."

As he helped her up, she grimaced and fell against him. He kept a steadying arm around her. "What's wrong?"

"My knee. I must have twisted it." She took several deep breaths, then nodded. "I'll be fine. Was anyone in the car hurt?"

"I reckon not. They didn't stop."

Her mouth dropped open. "They drove away without seeing if we were injured? I can't believe that."

"I think the driver was drunk," Faron said, leading Licorice toward them. He had unhitched her from the sleigh. Her brass bells jingled as she tossed her head and sidestepped in agitation.

"Did you see who it was?" Ernest asked as he got to his feet.

Faron shook his head. "It happened so fast. The sun was glaring off the windshield. I saw the car weaving as it came toward us and then I was flying through the air. I didn't recognize the car, either."

Zack and Ella joined them. "*Englisch* teenagers out for a joyride." Zack looked as furious as Owen felt.

"Did you see them?" Ruth asked.

"*Nee*, it's only a guess on my part," Zack admitted.

"A good one, I think," Faron said as he checked over the horse. She quieted as he ran a soothing hand over her neck and down each of her legs.

"We're all okay thanks to *Gott*'s mercy." Ella gripped her husband's hand.

Owen realized he was still holding Ruth. For some reason he couldn't move away from her. The sight of her lying motionless in the snow was burned into his mind. He straightened her bonnet and brushed the snow from her coat. "Are you sure you're okay?"

"I'm shaken up." She tried to step away from him but cried out and crumpled as her leg gave way.

Owen caught her before she fell and held her tight against him. "You aren't okay. What's wrong?"

She grimaced. "My knee doesn't want to hold me up."

Ella rushed to her side, moving Owen out of the way. "Zack, bring one of the quilts over here."

He spread the blue one on the roadside and helped Ella lower her mother to sit on it.

Ernest came to stand beside Owen. "Are you okay, my boy?"

Owen stuffed his hands into the pockets of his coat and hunched his shoulders. "I'm fine."

Was he?

Holding Ruth brought back a long-repressed memory of the last time he'd had his arms around her. He had been taking her home in his buggy after a singing. He'd stopped the horse at the end of her father's lane and asked if he could kiss her. She had nodded shyly. It was an awkward, amazingly sweet kiss. The effect it had on him had scared him half to death. At eighteen he hadn't been ready for the kind of commitment she deserved. He was an orphan with nothing to offer except a farmhand's pay and a little sister waiting for him to come get her and make a home for them both. As much as he cared for Ruth, he believed she would be better-off with someone else.

He should have talked to her after that night, at least said goodbye, but he never found the courage. Fear that he wouldn't be able to leave if she asked him to stay kept him from seeing her. He headed to Ohio a few days later but before he left he had encouraged Nathan to ask Ruth out. Nathan was the kind of man she deserved. It turned out he was right about that. Nathan had been her soul mate.

Owen had gone to collect his sister from their aunt in Ohio. Only she wasn't there. He'd spent the next twenty-five years trying to find her.

How different would his life be if he had stayed on the farm and kept seeing Ruth instead of running away from his feelings for her?

It was a pointless question. Rebecca was part of the reason he'd left. Although he'd finally found her two months ago, she was also the reason he had to leave Cedar Grove again in a few weeks. It didn't give him much time to make amends with Ruth, but he was determined to try.

Owen pushed the memory of their kiss to the back corner of his mind, where it belonged.

RUTH DIDN'T UNDERSTAND the look in Owen's eyes as he stared at her. He looked confused, almost sorrowful. The sound of another vehicle approaching drew everyone's attention to the roadway. A blue tractor pulled up beside them and stopped. The Cedar Grove Amish, like most Kansas Amish, were allowed to own and drive tractors. They could even drive cars or trucks for work, but they weren't allowed to own them. Ruth recognized Joshua King. His wife, Laura Beth, and her sister Sarah were riding in an open trailer behind the tractor. "Is everyone all right?" Joshua asked.

Sarah scrambled out of the trailer and raced to Ella. The two girls had been friends for years. Sarah hugged her and stepped back. "I couldn't believe my eyes when we saw that car hit you. Is anyone hurt?"

Ella looked around in amazement. "We all seem to be fine except for *Mamm*. She hurt her knee."

Ruth waved aside everyone's concern. "It's nothing. I twisted it, that's all. It's already feeling better."

Ernest stepped up to the large tractor tire to speak to Joshua. "The only casualties seem to be the sleigh and the picnic basket. A sad, sad loss if you ask me."

Ruth realized the contents of the sleigh had been strewn along the ditch. Her wooden picnic basket hadn't survived. It lay in splintered pieces. Many of her food containers had spilled, including the one with her cookies. They lay scattered along the edge of the road.

Joshua got down and helped his wife out of the trailer. She held his one-year-old son, Caleb, in her arms. The boy looked like an adorable stuffed toy in his blue snowsuit, white knit hat and white mittens.

Joshua had left the Amish as a young man but

returned the previous spring with his infant son. A widower, he met and married Laura Beth Yoder not long afterward. He now farmed and operated a large engine repair business with his neighbor Thomas Troyer. Joshua looked back in the direction the car had taken. "I witnessed the accident if you want to report this to the sheriff."

Ruth glanced at her family. They all shook their heads. She turned to Joshua. "We will not. It's not our way. We forgive the driver and pray that he or she sees the error of their actions."

Joshua took a deep breath. "It's not my way now, either, but it's hard to let something like this go. I guess I was in the outside world too long. Let's see if we can get your sleigh upright."

Owen and the other men went to examine the vehicle. Sarah began to gather up the scattered belongings. Ernest soon joined her.

"You are welcome to ride with us," Laura Beth offered.

"*Danki*. We will if the sleigh is badly damaged. I can't believe how your little one has grown. I can remember when Faron was that age. It seems like only yesterday."

Laura Beth nodded. "We can't keep them little forever, no matter how much we would like to do so."

The two mothers exchanged knowing smiles. Laura Beth kissed Caleb's forehead. "I've learned never to take a day for granted."

The sound of the men righting the sleigh made Ruth turn in that direction. After a brief consultation,

Owen and Faron hitched up the horse again. Ernest came to hand Ruth the containers that hadn't spilled.

She smiled at him. "You were wise to sample the cookies before we left the house."

He chuckled. "I rescued some of them and put them in my pocket for later." He glanced down at her feet. "At least now you have the perfect excuse not to skate."

She shook her head at his foolishness. "My blessings never cease."

Ella finished her examination of Ruth's knee. "It isn't dislocated. I think you should be fine if you stay off it for a day or two. If it doesn't get better, you should have Granny Weaver look at it."

Martha Weaver, the bishop's mother, was eighty years old and known affectionately as Granny Weaver to everyone. She was a healer who used herbs and plants to treat the maladies of the community, but she was also quick to tell her patients to see the doctor if their illnesses were beyond her skills.

Ruth looked at Owen as he came to stand beside Ernest. "Can the sleigh be used? We are making the guests of honor late for their party."

"The back runner is bent. The floorboard is cracked and the storage box behind the rear seat is shattered. Licorice is fine, but the sleigh won't pull as easily for her."

Ella patted her mother's hand. "Zack and I will ride with the Kings."

"We will follow you to make sure you arrive in one piece," Joshua said.

Two more tractors pulling trailers loaded with Amish family members stopped beside them. Owen and Joshua explained the situation. No one else reported seeing the car. The women in the groups were quick to offer their assistance to Ruth. Embarrassed by being the center of attention, Ruth wanted to hide beneath her quilt. Instead she urged her friends and neighbors to go on ahead and not let the incident spoil the day. The women helped her to the sleigh.

Faron mounted the driver's seat. He looked over his shoulder. "Ready to try again?"

Ruth nodded. "It was a beautiful day for a sleigh ride when we started out. It still is a beautiful day. I have always loved riding in the sleigh. We seldom get snow that lasts long enough to enjoy a ride like this. It would be a shame to miss it."

Ernest sat in the rear seat facing Ruth. He piled the rescued food beside him, leaving Owen no option but to sit down beside Ruth. She quickly shifted over, leaving as much distance between them as possible. She couldn't be sure, but she thought she caught a glimpse of pain in his eyes before he looked away.

Had her words and actions today truly hurt his feelings? Shame doused her anger. She needed to live the forgiveness her faith required and not simply give lip service to it. She would be polite to him no matter how hard it was.

IF RUTH COULDN'T bear to sit beside him, it didn't bode well for the coming weeks. He was back to help with the farm. The main problem would be getting her to accept any help from him. Ruth was stubborn enough to work herself to the point of exhaustion rather than admit she needed him.

Owen was saddened by the chasm that seemed to stretch between them. Would he be able to regain her respect or was this going to be a wasted effort on his part? He knew he'd let her down, but he wanted a chance to prove he'd changed. He longed to be part of the family again if only for a few weeks.

"Here's hoping the rest of the day proves to be less exciting," Ruth said with a smile that looked forced.

"Agreed," he said. She gave him another half smile and looked away.

The rest of the trip to Henry Shetler's farm was uneventful. The horse was able to pull the sleigh, though it wobbled back and forth because of the bent runner. The pond where the party was being held was less than a quarter of a mile from Henry's house. Already there were automobiles, tractors and buggies parked along his lane. Everyone in the community, *Englisch* and Amish alike, had been invited to see off the newlyweds.

Betty Shetler, Henry's wife, came out of the house to greet them. "We heard what happened. It's just terrible the way some people drive with no regard for anyone else on the road. Faron, drive on down to the pond so your mother doesn't have to walk. Henry and the children are there getting things ready for her."

Faron drove through the farmyard and out into the pasture. Ruth looked at Owen. "I wonder what she meant?"

He shrugged his shoulders. "I reckon we'll find out."

Faron pulled Licorice to a stop beside several picnic tables set up together. Fifty-five-gallon steel drums had been cut in half and served as four fire pits located along one side of the pond. The shore had been lined with a dozen hay bales where skaters could sit and rest without taking off their skates. A group of youngsters were already speeding across the ice with happy shouts to one another. By the first picnic table was a rocking chair with a footstool in front of it. Henry was spreading a blanket over it. He beckoned to them. "Bring her over here."

Owen got out to help her down. Ruth put her hand on Owen's chest. "I am not going to sit in a rocker with my feet up like some ancient *grossmammi*. I can hobble to a picnic table and sit there."

Martha Weaver came up to the side of the sleigh, leaning heavily on her cane. A tiny woman with gray hair and black piercing eyes behind rimless bifocals, she seldom minced words and everyone was a little in awe of her.

"Don't expect this ancient grandmother to crawl under a picnic table to look at your knee, Ruth Mast. What are you waiting for, Owen? Pick her up and carry her to the chair. Faron, take your animal back to the barn. I don't want horse apples decorating the snow by these tables. Ernest, you stay out of the way. Get a move on, Owen. I'm not getting any younger." She stomped away, forgetting to lean on her cane.

"You heard Granny." Owen swept Ruth up in his

arms. She instantly stiffened. Faron turned the horse around and went back across the pasture at a fast trot.

"This is ridiculous," Ruth whispered in Owen's ear.

He could have kissed Granny for insisting he carry Ruth. "I don't know, I kinda like it."

"You would enjoy making me look like a fool."

"*Nee*, I enjoy watching folks take care of you instead of the other way around." He deposited her in the rocking chair. Granny Weaver shooed him out of the way. One of the Shetler children produced a folding stool for Granny and a large brown bag.

Granny looked up at the crowd gathered around her. "You men go find something else to gape at. No respectable woman wants a bunch of thickheaded fellows staring at her limbs."

The men immediately left the group. The women drew into a tight circle around Ruth and Granny. Owen lingered nearby. He heard Granny muttering but couldn't make out what she was saying until she asked for her bag. "Arnica cream with peppermint oil is what you need. Stay off your feet for a day at least. If it hurts to walk, rest with it up on a pillow. If it doesn't hurt, use it but take it easy."

Owen was thankful Granny didn't think it was serious enough for Ruth to see a doctor. Faron came up to him carrying all their skates by the laces. "How is she?"

"Okay as far as I can tell. Do you think we can keep her on the couch with her leg up on a pillow for a day or two?"

"If Ella and I both sit on her, maybe."

Owen smiled. "I hope it doesn't come to that."

"Do you want your skates?" Faron asked, holding out Owen's pair.

"Sure. That's why we came." They walked down to the edge of the pond and sat on an empty hay bale.

"Can I ask you something, Cousin Owen?" Faron took off his boots, pulled on his skates and began to lace them up slowly.

"Sure." Owen followed his lead, waiting for the boy to work up the courage to talk about whatever was on his mind.

"What did you think about Ella's suggestion earlier today?"

"It's been a long day. Which suggestion?"

Faron glanced up. "When she said *Mamm* should think about getting married again."

Owen frowned. "I thought your mother answered her. She said she isn't looking for another husband."

"I know what she said, but don't you think it's time?"

Owen concentrated on lacing his own skate. "It doesn't matter what I think. Love isn't something you can find at the drop of a hat. It's something that finds you."

"Ella and I have been talking about this."

Owen didn't care for the direction the conversation was taking. Faron stopped talking when several young women skated in front of them. Once they were out of earshot, he met Owen's gaze. "You could ask her to marry you. Ella and I wouldn't object. That way the farm would stay in the family like *Mamm* wants."

"She wants you to carry on farming your father's land."

"I know, but I'm not sure I want to be a farmer. Will you at least think about it?"

Owen couldn't believe they were having this conversation. "I could never replace your father in your mother's eyes. Besides, she doesn't like me very much and I'm only going to be here for a few weeks."

Faron tied a bow in his laces and stood up, wobbling slightly. "That's what I said, but Ella made me promise to ask."

"I hope you two haven't said anything to your mother about this." He held his breath, waiting for the answer.

"Nope. We decided to talk to you first. Can I ask you something else?"

"Okay."

"You liked seeing new places and traveling, didn't you?"

"I went to a lot of places because I was trying to locate my sister Rebecca. You know that, right?"

"Sure, *Mamm* and *Daed* told us all about how you were separated after your parents died and she was sent to live with your mother's sister while you were sent to live with *Daed*'s family. Then your *aenti* sort of vanished and took your sister with her."

"Your grandmother was sick when I came to live with them. She didn't think she could take on two extra children at that time. When she got better, she wrote to Aunt Thelma telling her she was able to take Rebecca. Thelma refused to give her up. She moved away without telling anyone where she was going. I guess she was afraid of losing Rebecca."

"But it was exciting to see new places, wasn't it? I mean, nothing ever happens in Cedar Grove."

Owen took a deep breath and blew it out slowly. "I guess it was exciting."

Faron's eyes brightened. "I knew you'd say that. Want to race?"

"Maybe after I get the hang of being on skates again. It's been a while."

"I remember watching you and *Daed* race. You always won, so don't pretend you couldn't beat me with both hands tied behind your back."

Skating was the only thing he ever did better than Nathan. "Maybe I could beat you, but to say so would be boasting and show I lack *daymoot*."

"I've never heard anyone question your humility. I'm glad you're back. I hope you stay a long time." Faron skated away without waiting for Owen to answer him.

"I second that remark." Bishop Weaver had come up behind Owen. "It is *goot* to see you again. What is this I hear about a drunk driver colliding with your sleigh?"

"There was a collision, but I can't be certain the driver was drunk."

"Could anyone identify the driver?"

"No one saw who was behind the wheel or recognized the car. It was dark green."

"If it was one of our *youngees* I would like to know about it. The sheriff has asked for my help in reporting underage drinking and driving so that our youth can be educated on the dangers during their *rumspringa* years. I don't normally believe in involving the *Englisch* law, but I feel Sheriff McIntyre has the best interest of our people at heart."

"It could've been one of our teenagers being reckless in a borrowed car, but unless he or she comes forward we will likely never know."

"I fear you are right. Enjoy your afternoon. I'll go check on Ruth." The bishop turned and walked away.

Owen skated out into the center of the pond and made slow circles on the ice. Ella and Zack skated past him, holding hands. The skaters and picnickers were a mixture of Amish and non-Amish having fun, visiting with each other and enjoying a break from the dreary winter days. The Amish children in the area attended a public school and often remained friends with their *Englisch* classmates years after they left school.

Several races were getting underway by age group. Henry enlisted Owen's help to judge at the finish line. An hour later Owen left the ice and made his way to where Ruth sat wrapped in a blanket and sipping hot chocolate while she visited with her friends.

"We've come up with something to occupy Ruth's free time," Betty Shetler said.

Julie Temple, one of the two teachers at the public school, clasped her hands together and grinned. "She'll do a wonderful job."

"At what?" He looked at Ruth.

"They want me to become the community scribe for *The Diary* newspaper and for *Family Life Magazine*."

He nodded as he thought over the idea. "Gathering information on families and reporting those things in the Amish publications might suit you. I know you enjoy gossiping."

All the women groaned. "It's not gossip," Julie said sternly. "It's news. This community has been underrepresented and it's time we let other Amish settlements know about our accomplishments as well as our troubles."

Owen noticed Ruth grimace as she moved her leg. He could see she was in pain even if she wouldn't admit it. "I think it's a *goot* idea. Now I would like to take the new scribe home if she is ready."

Granny Weaver nodded her agreement. "See that she stays off that leg for at least a day."

"What about Faron, Zack and Ella? Are they ready to go?" Ruth looked toward the ice. Faron and Ernest sat with their heads together on one of the hay bales.

"Joshua and I will see that they get home when they are ready," Laura Beth said.

Owen smiled at her. *"Danki."*

"Owen, how long are you staying in Cedar Grove?" Julie asked.

"I'm just here to keep an eye on Ernest's farm while he is gone."

He couldn't stay longer. An unexpected letter had arrived from his sister a week ago. In it she said she was coming to see him in Shipshewana on the fifteenth of April. Letters were the way Amish families notified each other of their visiting plans. It wasn't unusual.

What was out of the ordinary was the lack of a return address on the envelope that had been mailed from Columbia, Missouri, and the last two lines of her note.

I need your help. Don't tell anyone.

CHAPTER THREE

RUTH WATCHED AS Faron left Ernest's side and jogged up to her with his skates in his hand. "*Mamm*, after talking it over with Owen and *Onkel* Ernest, I've come to a decision."

"That sounds serious," Granny said with a grin for Ruth.

Faron drew himself up to his full height. "I'm going to Missouri and Arkansas with Ella, Zack and *Onkel* Ernest for a month."

Ruth couldn't believe the words coming out of her son's mouth. She was acutely aware of the women surrounding her and listening intently. "If you are trying to be funny, Faron, you aren't."

"I'm serious. I can experience the outside world during my *rumspringa* and I want to see new places and meet new people before I consider taking my vows."

Ruth drilled Owen with her gaze. "Did you tell him to do this?"

"*Nee*, I… He took my words wrongly."

"Oh, I just imagine how wrongly he took them." She didn't want to have this conversation in front of the women of her church. "We'll talk about it at home."

"There's nothing to talk about. I'm going."

"Faron, I can't spare you for a week let alone a month. The lambs will start arriving in three weeks. We have a lot of work to get done before then." He didn't know how important this lamb crop would be. She never discussed the finances with him and she wouldn't in front of so many people. Family business was private business. It was prideful, but she didn't want others to know she was having trouble meeting her bills or that she might lose some of her land.

Faron waved aside her objection. "Owen will be here to help you. You don't need me. I'm going. You can't change my mind."

She was trapped by the number of people around her. She had to moderate her tone as she felt sure Faron knew when he'd chosen such a public place for his announcement. How long had he been planning this? "We'll talk more about this when we get home. I'm ready to go now."

She had a lot more she wanted to say to her son and to Owen about his interference. Her worst fear was coming true. Owen's stories were finally luring her son away from her.

"Joshua is taking Ella, Zack and me home later. I'll tell Ernest you're ready to go and bring the sleigh down." Faron hurried off. It seemed her son wasn't eager to have that conversation.

A short time later Ruth was seated in the sleigh, facing Ernest while Owen drove them home. The blue sky had vanished behind a wall of gray clouds advancing from the north. Fat snowflakes began swirling down. Ruth waited for Ernest's cheerful teasing to start, but he was uncharacteristically silent.

"I think you and Owen had better explain yourselves," she said in a tight voice.

Ernest sighed. "Don't blame Owen. He had nothing to do with this."

"Except to fill my son's head with stories of the amazing, far places he's visited. No wonder the boy wants to leave home." She glared at him up on the driver's seat.

"Maybe he wants to leave because his mother never lets him out of her sight," Owen snapped back.

"Don't quarrel, you two," Ernest said. "Ruth, you have kept a tight rein on Faron. I know you needed him on the farm, but you could have let him stay with your folks a time or two when you sent Ella to stay with them every summer."

She looked away. "You should have consulted me before telling him he could travel with you."

"If I had asked, you would have said no."

She glared at him again. "Better to ask forgiveness than permission, right?"

Ernest shrugged as a tiny grin curved the side of his mouth. "Something like that. Face it, the boy wants to go. You could forbid it and he would stay until he found a way to go by himself. This way I'll be able to watch out for him and you can worry less. Don't you think it is the best solution, Owen?"

"Leave me out of this. I agreed to take care of the farm while you were gone. That's it."

"Ruth and I farm together. That means you will have to give her a hand with anything she needs."

"I won't need any help from him." She turned to stare at the snow-covered countryside.

"False pride is a sin, Ruth. Not asking for help when you need it is prideful," Ernest reminded her.

She drew a deep breath as she recognized the truth in his words. "Do you know anything about sheep, Owen?"

"I count them when I can't get to sleep," he drawled.

She held out her hand to Ernest. "Really? This is the man you expect to work day and night at my side when the ewes start birthing?"

"Owen knows as much about sheep as I do. He's worked on sheep farms in Ohio and Illinois. Haven't you?"

"It doesn't matter. Face it, she doesn't want my help."

"Because you'll leave when I need you the most. That's what you do." She fought back tears as her old resentments surfaced.

He pulled the horse to a stop and half turned on the seat to face her. "I won't leave this time, Ruth. You have my word."

She wished with all her heart that she could believe him. She folded her arms across her middle. "I won't lie. I'm not sure I can believe you, but my faith says that I must trust that you mean what you say."

"I do. And it is my faith, too." He turned around and got the horse moving again.

"It has been a hard winter," Ernest said. "It has

been tough on the livestock. Such long cold spells make for good skating but not for healthy animals. We're running low on feed for the cattle and the sheep. You will have to buy hay until the grass greens up."

"Why haven't you told me this before?" Ruth demanded.

"I saw no point in having both of us concerned."

"Who should I approach about it?" Owen asked.

"Bob Navarro at the feed store," Ernest said. "He'll know who has extra feed on their hands. Ask at the next church service, too. Amish farmers generally charge less than *Englisch* do but most of the *Englisch* in our area are *goot* honest people. I'll write out a list of names."

Ruth scowled at Ernest. "I can give him the names of the people we do business with. If we must manage the farm together, I expect to remain in charge."

"Never doubted that for a second," Owen said under his breath, but she heard him.

The wind was picking up. She pulled the brim of her bonnet down to keep the snow from hitting her face. "I hope that Faron and Ella have started for home. This seems like it could get nasty."

Owen turned into her driveway and drew the horse to a stop in front of the house. Ernest got out. "I'll take care of the horse."

"Joshua's tractor won't have any trouble getting here. Joshua and Thomas have promised to have a look at the sleigh and help me make repairs." Owen got down and held out his hand to help her out of the sleigh. She had no choice but to lean on him as she hobbled on one foot.

"See," Ernest said brightly. "Things are never bleak when we have friends to help us. The two of you will do fine without Faron and me."

She glanced at Owen. He didn't comment. Ernest's bright smile faded. "I have to go check on my mother. She hasn't been feeling well."

"Take the sleigh," Ruth said. His mother lived in a small house at the edge of town.

"I'd rather take my tractor. I plan on spending the night with her. Owen will stay with you until the *kinder* get home."

"I don't need anyone to stay with me."

"Okay." Owen stepped away from her, leaving her teetering on one leg.

"At least get me in the house." She closed her eyes so she wouldn't have to see him smirk.

"Don't let her send you away, Owen," Ernest said firmly.

"I won't."

He lifted her arm over his shoulder and hooked one arm around her waist. "It's hard to ask for help. I know that only too well," he said in a low voice, leaving her to wonder what he was referring to and wishing she wasn't curious about anything in his life.

OWEN HELPED RUTH inside and over to her sofa in the living room. She pushed away from him and sat down without looking at him. *"Danki."*

"That almost choked you, didn't it?"

She untied her bonnet and pulled it off. "I don't know what you mean."

"Having to thank me for anything. I'll take your bonnet and coat. No point in telling me you can manage, I know you can but I'm here so I might as well make myself useful."

She slipped out of her coat and handed it to him without comment. He motioned for her to stretch out. "You should lie down and put your leg up."

"I'll be fine here until my children come home. You may go."

"I have my orders. I'm staying. Save your breath."

She pressed her lips into a tight line and folded her arms across her chest. He brought her a pillow for her leg and one for her head from a cedar chest in the corner. She jerked the pillows out of his hand and arranged them without his help and then flipped a knit throw from the back of the sofa across her legs. Ruth's annoyance was palpable.

He took a seat in a nearby chair and waited uncomfortably for his relief to arrive. He watched the clock tick quietly on the mantel.

"Where are you off to next?" she asked, surprising him.

"Back to Indiana when Ernest returns in a month."

"The longest you ever stayed here was for two weeks."

He tipped his head to stare at her. "Ruth, I lived in Cedar Grove from the time I was thirteen until I was eighteen."

"I remember how old you were when you left."

"Do you?"

"Of course." She looked away.

He sighed. "I never apologized for that, did I?"

"It doesn't matter. It was a long time ago."

"It does matter, and I am sorry. I should have had the courage to tell you I was leaving instead of taking off and letting Nathan be the messenger."

"As I said, it was a long time ago, but it wasn't the only time you left when you were needed."

"I know I've let you down in the past, but I promised Ernest I'd take care of his place and help you until he returns. I won't go back on my word."

"Faron will change his mind about leaving when he's had a chance to consider it properly. You won't have to stay on our account, and we can look after Ernest's place, too. If Faron does leave, which I'm sure he won't, I can hire a man to help me. Someone I know I can…" Her words trailed away.

Trust? Depend on? Was that what she was going to say? She didn't want him around. She couldn't have made it any clearer. Maybe it had been a mistake to think he could patch things up between them, but he wasn't willing to give up after only one day. Ruth was nothing if not stubborn, but he could be stubborn, too.

He leaned back and chuckled.

It wasn't the reaction she was expecting. She glared at him. "What's so funny?"

"I'm here until Ernest returns, Ruth. You can't get rid of me with a few well-placed insults."

She huffed and turned her back to him. "I didn't insult you."

"Ah, but you wanted to."

The newlyweds arrived half an hour later with Faron. He stood with his hat off in front of his mother. "I'd like to talk about my plans in the morning."

Ruth nodded. "You know my feelings, but I agree we both need to sleep on it."

Owen picked up his coat and hat. Ernest's farm was less than a quarter of a mile from Ruth's place.

Ella slipped off her coat. "Zack will drive you home in the buggy."

Owen shook his head. "Take pity on poor Licorice. She's most likely already asleep in a warm stall after her trying day."

"Very well but bundle up. The weather is getting bad."

He left on foot, but a hundred yards from Ruth's house he wished he hadn't been so insistent. The wind was blowing harder and the snow was piling up in growing drifts. It wasn't a fit night out for man nor beast. As if to prove his point, he found Meeka, Ernest's big guard dog, lying across the corner of the porch out of the wind. Instead of coming out to greet him, she whined repeatedly.

"I know it's a cold night, but if I had a coat as thick as yours, I don't think I would mind it. Great Pyrenees dogs can happily live in much colder climates than this."

He opened the door of the house. "Come in for a bit." She still didn't get up. He closed the door without going in. Something was wrong. Was she hurt?

He walked toward her. She sat up and growled low in her throat. She had never done that to him before. "Are you sick, girl?"

She looked back at something in the corner and whined softly. Over the wind he heard what sounded like a sobbing child. "What have you got there, Meeka? Let me see."

He came closer. There was a child in an Amish bonnet and bulky winter coat trying to bury herself beneath Meeka's thick fur. Where had she come from? Why was she here? He looked around. Where were her parents?

He bent and held out his hand. "Hello, little one. You must be cold out here. Come into the house and warm up."

The child stared at him fearfully over Meeka's back. He held out his hand. "It's okay. I won't hurt you."

She shook her head but didn't say anything. Meeka growled again. He could pick the girl up and carry her into the house, but he wasn't sure Meeka would allow him to do that. She was in her protective mode. Maybe what he needed to do was convince the dog to come in. He racked his brain over who the child might belong to. He didn't remember seeing her at the party.

He went in the house and returned a few moments later with two pieces of baked chicken breast left over from supper the previous night. He tossed one to the porch floor in front of the dog. She sniffed it once and gulped it down. Owen smiled at her. "*Goot hund. Goot* dog."

He held out the second piece of chicken as he pushed the door open. "Come on, Meeka. Come in."

As the dog walked slowly toward the door, the little girl clung to her side and shuffled along with her. Owen tamped down his impatience. Somewhere people had to be frantically searching for this child. In weather like this, even the searchers were at risk.

Meeka stretched out her neck and took the chicken. She licked his fingers and stepped closer. He ran a hand over her massive head and scratched behind her ear. Her tail began wagging. "See? Meeka likes me. I won't hurt you. Come in the house and get warm."

Meeka padded inside and crawled onto Ernest's couch. The amount of white dog hair on the blue cushions was proof she'd been there many times before. The little girl, who looked to be only three or four years old, climbed onto the couch and positioned herself with Meeka's head in her lap. She was shivering. Her round face featured a pug nose, ruddy red cheeks and a bow mouth, but her lips were chapped and tinged with blue. Wisps of dark curly hair escaped from her *kapp*.

He knelt beside the dog and spoke to the child in a calm voice. "I'll turn up the heat. Would you like a blanket?"

She nodded once. He went to the spare bedroom and pulled a brown-and-cream-colored quilt off the bed. She held out both hands when she saw it. He was making progress. He took off her wet mittens and rubbed her hands between his to warm them despite Meeka's low growl. The dog sounded less threatening, but he didn't know her well enough to be sure she wouldn't bite him. "Lean forward and I will tuck this around you."

She hesitated and he thought she would refuse but she bent over and laid her face on the top of Meeka's head. He draped the throw around her and she pulled it tight. He smiled at her. If he could just gain her trust maybe she could tell him more. "Would you like something hot to drink? It won't take me long to make hot chocolate."

He received a tentative nod and rose to his feet. He laid a hand on his chest. "I'm Owen Mast."

She tipped her head slightly. "Owen?"

"That's right."

"Owen is safe."

"Yep. You're safe here. What's your name?"

"Grace," she replied in a tiny voice and clutched Meeka's head again.

"What's your last name?"

"I can't say," she whispered, putting a finger to her lips.

That took him aback. Why couldn't she give her last name? "Can you tell me where you came from?"

"Outside."

He pushed aside his frustration and kept his voice calm. "Before you went outside, where were you? Does your family live close by? Where's your mother?"

"Mommy's sleeping."

"Sleeping at your house?"

She shook her head no.

"Where is your father?"

"Gone."

"Okay, what's his name?"

She shook her head. "I can't say. When is *Mamm* coming to get me?" She pressed her face into Meeka's fur.

"I don't know."

"She'll be here soon?"

"I hope so, but she may have to wait until it quits snowing."

"What if she's scared?"

"Are you scared?" he asked, dropping to her level.

She nodded. He smiled gently. "Don't be scared. *Gott* is with your mother and with you."

He stood up. It seemed he wasn't going to get much information out of her. He went into the small kitchen, filled a pan with milk from the fridge and put it on the stove to warm. Ernest, like all the members of Bishop Weaver's church, was allowed to use propane to heat his home and run his appliances. Owen was thankful he didn't have to stoke a fire and wait for the stove to heat up.

He walked to the door and looked out into the growing storm, hoping to see searchlights or hear shouting. He heard only the wind. How far had she come? How could he let her family know she was safe if she couldn't tell him more than her first name?

"Is your mommy sleeping at your *grossmammi*'s

house?" he asked, thinking Grace might have been staying with grandparents or other family in the area.

Again she shook her head no. "I'm hungry."

What could he fix her to eat? "Okay, I'll find something for you." He added the cocoa and sugar to the milk, stirring it before taking it off the heat. He searched through Ernest's kitchen cabinets and came up with bread, peanut butter and marshmallow creme. "How about some church spread?"

She nodded eagerly. One problem solved. He mixed the peanut butter and marshmallow creme together in a small bowl with some sugar and then spread the mixture thickly on a slice of bread, the way the treat was usually served at the noon meal following prayer services.

He carried the sandwich to the sofa. Meeka raised her head hopefully. He held the food out of her reach and ordered her off the couch. To his surprise, the dog got down and moved to lie in front of the doorway, still watching him intently. "How old are you, Grace?"

Grace held up three fingers before she took the food from him gingerly.

"Do you have brothers or sisters?" Were there other children lost in the storm?

She shook her head as she bit into the sandwich. He went back to get her hot chocolate, filling a mug half-full and adding extra milk to cool it enough for her to drink. When he returned to the sofa, she was finishing the last bite of her sandwich. He handed her the mug and she drank it eagerly.

He went to the door again and looked out into the night. What should he do? He had no idea who she was. He needed someone who knew the families in the community. Ruth and her family were the closest. He hated the idea of dropping this problem in Ruth's lap after the day she'd had. She was likely to bite his head off the minute he stepped through the door.

He heard a noise behind him and turned around. Grace had dropped her mug as she bolted off the sofa and raced to wrap her arms around his legs. "Don't leave me."

"Take it easy." He dropped to his knees beside her.

She let go of his legs and wrapped her arms in a choke hold around his neck. "Please don't go, Owen."

He pulled one arm loose. "I'm not going anywhere, Grace. I was trying to see if your folks are out looking for you. I won't leave you."

"Promise?" she asked in a tiny voice.

His heart twisted with pain. He had promised his little sister when she was no older than Grace that he would come back for her and never leave her again. He hadn't been able to keep that promise.

"I won't leave you until you are safely back with your family. I promise." This one he would keep.

CHAPTER FOUR

A DOG'S DEEP-THROATED barking roused Ruth from a restless sleep. She sat up in bed, not sure if she was dreaming. The dog barked again. It sounded like Meeka was right outside the house. Ruth swung her legs out of bed, grimacing as her knee protested the move. She hobbled to the window and looked out. A huddled figure was crossing her lawn with a large bundle clasped to his shoulder. Meeka bounded around him.

Ruth lit her lamp and limped to her bedroom door. In the hallway she knocked on Faron's door. Zack poked his head out from across the hall. "What's going on?"

"There's someone outside."

"Who is it?" Ella asked from beneath her husband's arm.

"I don't know. That's why I want Faron to go see who it is."

"I'll go," Zack said.

She waited until Zack appeared fully dressed a few minutes later. She heard a voice downstairs as Zack stepped into the hall. It sounded like Owen. She made her way to the stairwell. Zack stood beside Owen at the bottom of the steps. Owen held something in his arms. Ernest's massive dog stood beside him.

"Owen, what is going on?" she asked.

"Ruth, you shouldn't be up with your injury. We can handle this. Zack, tell Ella I need her help."

Ruth started down the stairs. "No one's going to send me to bed in my own house until I know what you are doing here. Granny Weaver said that I could walk if it didn't hurt." It did hurt, but not so badly that she couldn't negotiate the stairs by leaning heavily on the railing.

Owen carried his burden to her sofa and laid it down. He pulled back the corner of the brown-and-cream quilt and she saw a little girl's face. Confused, she looked to Owen for an explanation. "Who is she?"

"I was hoping you knew. She was huddled on the porch behind Meeka when I got to Ernest's place. I have no idea how long she'd been there or where she came from. Meeka probably saved her life by keeping her warm."

Ruth pressed a hand to her heart. "Her family must be frantic."

"That's what I thought, but I don't know who they might be. Do you?"

Ruth was sure she had never seen the child before. "She must be visiting someone in the area. She can't have gotten far in this weather. We should check with the closest families."

Ella came down the stairs, followed by Faron, who was yawning and rubbing his head.

They all gathered around the sleeping child. Ella gently pulled back the quilt. The girl was wearing a *kapp*, a long winter coat and snow boots that were too big for her. "I don't know her." She looked up at Faron. "Did you see her today at the skating party?"

"I didn't pay any attention to the *kinder*. She could have been there."

The child's eyes fluttered open. She took one look at Faron and started screaming at the top of her lungs. The dog stepped forward, barking fiercely. Faron hopped backward.

"Meeka! You know Faron," Ruth said and ignored the dog. Meeka's head and tail drooped. Ruth sat down by the child, who had scrambled up and was huddled in the corner of the sofa.

Owen held out both hands palm first. "It's okay, Grace. No one is going to hurt you. These are all my friends. We're going to help you find your family."

Grace's eyes darted from face to face. Meeka crawled onto the sofa and lay in front of the child in a gesture of protection.

"Can you tell us where your *mamm* is?" Ella asked.

"Mommy's sleeping" came her faint reply.

Ruth leaned closer. "Sleeping where?"

Grace shook her head and buried her face in Meeka's ruff.

"That's all she would tell me," Owen said. "That and her father is gone. I couldn't get a name out of her."

"I'll hitch up the buggy," Zack said. "Ella and I

will go to the farms west of here. Faron, you can take the tractor. Check the farms east of here. Owen, do you think she could've come cross-country?"

"It's possible. No one would walk into the wind and snow if they didn't need to. A child certainly wouldn't. I'll go get Ernest's buggy and check the farms north of here." He turned to go.

Grace scrambled over Meeka, jumped off the sofa and threw her arms around his leg. "Owen, don't go. You promised."

He detached her and knelt beside her, holding on to her shoulders. "I have to find your *mamm* and *daed*. They will be worried about you."

Tears welled up in her eyes and ran down her face. She flung her arms around his neck, nearly choking him. "Stay. You promised."

Zack wagged his eyebrows. "I guess we will check the farms north, east and west of here."

"I'll make coffee." Ruth limped toward the kitchen but paused in the doorway to look back.

Ella sighed. "Try to get the child back to sleep, Owen. She looks exhausted."

He nodded and sat down in a chair with the child still clinging to his neck. Ruth's family went upstairs to get dressed. She went to the kitchen and soon heard them head out the door.

Ruth set the coffee on to perk and came in to sit across from Owen. Grace's eyelids were drooping lower, but she continued to fight sleep.

"I said I didn't want more excitement. Did you forget that?" Ruth asked softly.

"I didn't know who else to bring her to." He looked at her with worried eyes.

She halfway expected him to leave the child with her and bolt out the door. "You did the right thing bringing her here. My feelings about the dog aren't as generous."

"You try to drag Meeka outside. This is her stray lamb, and she's guarding it with her life."

"A stray, frightened lamb."

He gazed at his charge. "Yeah. I can't blame her. I know how scary it is to be left alone."

Was he thinking back to the deaths of his parents and how he felt when he was a child separated from his only family? She didn't want to feel pity for him. He wasn't a child anymore and he had turned his back on the family that took him in. And on her.

He looked at Ruth. "Is that coffee ready? I think she's asleep."

He laid Grace on the sofa, and she didn't stir. Meeka stretched out on the floor in front of her with her head on her paws.

Ruth poured them both some coffee and filled a kettle with cider to warm for her children when they returned. She settled at the kitchen table, took a sip of coffee and considered who Grace might belong to. "Bishop Weaver's oldest son, John, is home for a visit. He has four children if I remember right."

"How about the other church district? Could she belong to them?"

"Maybe, but that district is more than ten miles

from here. I don't see how she could have walked that far."

He rose and went to look out the door. It seemed he was learning bad habits from her son. "Don't let all the warm air out."

He sent her a sheepish look. "Sorry. I keep thinking of her poor parents looking for her in this storm. I pray their faith sustains them. Meeka, come here. Time to go home." The dog raised her head but stayed put.

"Owen?" They heard Grace's sobbing call from the other room. They both walked in. Ruth went to Grace and tried to pick her up, but Grace wanted nothing to do with Ruth. She pushed her away and held out her arms to Owen.

Owen lifted her into his arms. "Don't be rude to Ruth. She's okay."

"I want you." She laid her head on his shoulder and circled his neck with her arms.

"Okay, I've got you." He proceeded to walk about the room, soothing her.

Ruth grudgingly admitted to herself that he was good with the child. Patient and caring, he allayed Grace's fears and held her until she fell asleep again. After laying her down, he returned to the table to sit opposite Ruth.

The silence stretched between them. He finished his coffee and put the empty mug down.

"Care to tell me how much trouble the farm is in?"

"I am doing well enough."

"Honest answer?"

"Ernest made it sound worse than it is. A good lamb crop will let me pay off my debt this year. The land will be free and clear for Faron to take over when he's ready." She bit her lip. Why had she mentioned her debt? That wasn't like her. Perhaps the accident had shaken her up more than she'd realized.

Owen frowned slightly. "I thought Nathan inherited a clear title to the land."

"He did." She folded her arms across her chest. "He took a loan against the farm in order to expand our flock shortly before his death. I wasn't experienced enough with sheep to manage them. Our losses were high the first two years after his passing." It went against the grain to admit she had failed in the beginning, but she had learned from her mistakes.

He hung his head for a moment and then looked her in the eye. "I should've stayed to help you after the funeral. I'm sorry I didn't."

It was something of an apology even if it was years late in coming. She tried to brush it off as unimportant instead of painful. "I didn't expect you would stay. Fortunately, Ernest stepped in to give me a hand. He purchased half the sheep so I wouldn't default on the loan payment that first year. Half the sheep still belong to him. He was the one who said we needed a guard dog. Meeka has cut our losses from predators substantially since she arrived last spring."

"I'm here now, and I will help in any way I can."

He sounded sincere but she knew him too well. She shook her head sadly. "We both know you'll be moving on when the mood strikes. Maybe not right away, but I need someone I can depend on. Not a fellow who has a record of disappearing at the drop of a hat."

Especially when things got tough. She didn't want to depend on him and have him take off before Ernest returned.

He didn't reply, and she was glad. There was nothing he could say that would convince her he had changed. Two weeks was the usual length of his visits before moving on. Maybe he would stay for the whole month, but she would be shocked if he did.

The outside door opened and Faron walked in. His eyebrows and eyelashes were crusted with snow. Ruth turned in her chair to face him. "Did you learn anything?"

"Nothing useful. None of the farms I stopped at knew anything about a missing child. Perhaps Zack and Ella are having more success."

"Sit down. I've made some coffee, or would you rather have some hot spiced cider?"

He sank onto a kitchen chair. "Don't go to any trouble, *Mamm*."

"No trouble. I put some cider in the kettle a while ago. I know Ella prefers it to coffee."

"So do I. You don't need to wait on me. I can get it."

Owen put a hand on Faron's shoulder. "Both of you sit still. I'll get it."

Faron looked toward the living room. "How is she?"

Ruth followed his gaze. "Fine as far as I can tell but she gets upset if Owen is out of her sight."

"I have that effect on a lot of women." Owen winked at Faron as he set a mug of steaming cider on the table in front of the boy.

Faron chuckled. Ruth didn't.

It was another thirty minutes before Ella and Zack returned with the same story. No one they spoke to at the neighboring farms was missing a child.

"What do we do now?" Faron asked Owen.

That her son looked to Owen for the answer surprised and annoyed Ruth. She was surprised again when Owen turned to her. "What do you think we should do?"

"Nothing until morning. Then we will take her to Bishop Weaver. He may know what family she belongs to."

"If he doesn't?" Ella asked.

"Then we will continue to check with neighbors both Amish and *Englisch*. There are a few former Amish in the area who have Amish nieces and nephews." Ruth spoke to everyone. "Take off your coats. No one is going out again tonight."

Ella pulled off her coat. "I'll make us some hot cider. I don't know about anyone else, but I am chilled to the bone."

"It's already warming on the stove," Ruth said.

"Bless you." Ella fixed a mug for herself and Zack.

"We should notify the sheriff," Zack said. "Remember the story of the two Amish children kidnapped from their roadside produce stand? The *Englisch* law was able to find them."

Ruth's eyes widened. "You think she may have been kidnapped?"

Owen held up one hand. "We are getting ahead of ourselves. There's no point in jumping to conclusions. We will seek more answers tomorrow and hopefully reunite Grace with her family."

"The two of you should stay here tonight," Ella said. "You don't want to take her out into the cold again. I'll make up cots for the two of you. Owen, try to convince the dog to go home."

"I have tried. She won't budge more than a few feet away from Grace."

Ruth wasn't sure what to say. She didn't like the idea of having Owen stay in her home, but she had to agree with Ella. It would be cruel to send them back out into the storm. She wouldn't do that to Owen, let alone a frightened lost child. "Zack and Faron, bring down the cots from the attic. Owen, you and Grace can sleep in the living room. Ella, the spare linens are in the closet in the upstairs hallway."

Ella smiled at her mother and crossed her arms. "I know where everything is, but nothing will get done until you are sitting down with your leg propped up. I can see it is swelling again."

Ruth had little choice but to do as she was told. Once she was seated on the sofa with a pillow under her knee, Ella, Zack and Faron trooped upstairs.

"I hate to put you out like this," Owen said.

"You aren't putting me out," she said quickly.

"You would rather I went back to Ernest's house."

"What I prefer doesn't matter. It's Grace I must think about. She seems to need you close by to feel secure. Besides no one should be out in this kind of weather."

OWEN KNEW WHAT Ruth was thinking even though she didn't say it. The child might need him nearby to feel secure, but his presence had the opposite effect on Ruth. He waited until the men brought down the cots and then transferred Grace to one of them.

Ella tucked her in. "Poor baby. What a terrible time she has had."

"We've all had a hard day," Ruth said. "I'm going to bed. Ella, can you help me up the stairs?"

"Of course." She handed the rest of the linens to Owen and took her mother's arm. Zack and Faron followed behind the women as they went upstairs.

Owen made up his own cot and lay down. As tired as he was, sleep was a long time coming. His mind kept replaying his conversation with Ruth and he wondered if she was right. Would he feel the need to move on and disappoint her again? He wanted to prove her wrong, but he honestly wasn't sure he could. Staying where he wasn't wanted might prove to be a bigger challenge than he could overcome. Ruth didn't believe he could do it. She didn't want him around, and she clearly didn't trust him.

Sometime later someone nudged his arm. He opened one eye. Meeka stood beside him, her tongue hanging out as she panted in his face. He tried to push her aside, but it was like trying to move a furry boulder. She whined once and glanced toward the front door.

"I'm going to guess this means you want to go out." She padded to the door, where she waited for him.

He glanced at the clock on the mantel. It was nearly five in the morning. He rubbed his face with both hands, then glanced toward the other cot. Grace slept quietly with her fingers curled beneath her chin. Meeka whined again. He was afraid she would start barking and rouse the house. "Okay, I'm coming."

He crossed the room and opened the door to let the dog out. The storm had blown itself out. The fresh snow glistened as the moon slipped in and out of the clouds passing overhead. The yip of a coyote broke the absolute stillness of the night. Meeka bolted away, growling ferociously as she bounded across the snow. He listened for the sound of an ensuing fight but didn't hear anything. Apparently her size and fearless charge were enough to discourage the would-be predator. He closed the door. At least he and Ruth's family wouldn't have to worry about Meeka blocking their attempts to take care of Grace.

Wide-awake, Owen considered going back to his cot but decided he might as well get started on the chores waiting for him at Ernest's place. There were cattle and horses to be fed along with the poultry and pigs. The temperature drop would have frozen the stock's watering tanks. They would have to be chopped open and he'd need to gather the eggs before they froze in the nests. He quietly folded up the bedding and left it at the foot of his cot. Grace was still sleeping peacefully.

He pulled on his boots, coat and hat before he realized he should leave a note telling Ruth where he'd gone. In the kitchen he found a piece of paper and a pen. He scrawled his message and placed it beside the coffeepot, knowing Ruth or Ella would be up early to start breakfast. Once he was finished with the chores, he would take Grace to Bishop Weaver's farm and find out where the child belonged. He was hopeful he could fulfill his promise to Grace today and reunite her with her family.

Stepping into the living room, he checked to make sure Grace was still sleeping. Then he went out into the cold dark morning.

CHAPTER FIVE

RUTH ROSE AND got dressed while it was barely light outside. It had been a short night, but she was in the habit of getting up early. She ventured down the stairs slowly. Her sore knee felt worse than it had yesterday, but she wasn't going to stay in bed. She readied herself to have an argument on the subject with Owen or Ella, but the only one she found up was Grace. The child sat on the floor in front of the outside door with a look of utter dejection on her tearstained face. She clutched the quilt Owen had wrapped her in when he brought her to the house.

Ruth's heart went out to her. "Oh, Grace, what's wrong?"

The child looked up. "Owen left me."

Surely not. Ruth glanced toward the living room and saw Owen's cot neatly made up. She was annoyed that he had decided to leave the child with her without a word but more than that, she was disappointed. He had sounded so sincere when he said he was here to help, but her feelings weren't the issue. Grace needed comforting.

Ruth eased herself down to sit on the bottom step

so she was close to the child's level. "I'm sorry Owen has gone."

"He promised to stay with me." Fresh tears welled up in her eyes.

The urge to pick the child up and hug her was overwhelming but Ruth didn't think Grace was ready for that. She looked about to bolt. "Don't cry, Grace. I think we will both be happier without that old Owen underfoot. I'll take care of you until we find your family. Are you hungry? Would you like some breakfast?"

Grace shook her head. "I want my *mamm*. I want Owen. I want Meeka."

Ruth hadn't noticed that the big dog was missing, too. She heard footsteps behind her and looked up to see Ella coming down. "What's going on?" Ella asked.

"Grace is upset because Owen isn't here. I'm trying to convince her to eat some breakfast with us."

"Where is Owen?"

"I don't know, and I don't think I care." Ruth levered herself to her feet and tried to pretend she spoke the truth. "He rarely tells anyone where he's going when he pulls one of his disappearing acts."

"He wouldn't take off without a word. Aren't you being hard on him?"

Ruth shrugged one shoulder. "I don't think so. He is the way he is."

Ella walked around her mother and held out her arms to Grace. The child scooted backward until she was against the wall. "Go away. I want Owen. I want my *mamm*."

"No one is going to hurt you," Ella assured her.

Grace buried her face in the quilt she held. Ella stepped back.

Ruth shook her head sadly. "I don't understand why she is so attached to Owen. She only met him last night."

"She was lost and frightened. He rescued her. I'm not surprised she sees him as her hero." Ella held out her hand to the child. "I'm sure Owen will be back soon. Why don't you come have some breakfast while you wait for him?"

Grace got to her feet but ran back into the living room and huddled under her quilt in the corner of the sofa.

Ruth frowned at Ella. "You shouldn't tell her that Owen will be back when you have no idea where he is. Check with Faron to see if Owen spoke to him."

Ella hurried up the stairs and returned a short time later. "Faron hasn't seen Owen this morning."

"Of course not. I don't know what Ernest was thinking when he asked Owen to stay and take care of things while he was gone." Ruth headed to the kitchen intent on making coffee.

"I'm sure there's a perfectly logical reason he isn't here." Ella intercepted Ruth and pulled out a kitchen chair. "Sit and put your leg up."

"I'm fine." She tried to go around her daughter.

Ella moved to block her way. "You can sit and put

your leg up, or I will call Zack and Faron to come down and carry you back to your bedroom."

"All this fuss over a sprained knee. It's nothing."

"I heard Granny tell you not to walk on it if it hurts. I can see by your limping that it does hurt."

"All right. Fetch me a pillow and I will put it up on another chair. Satisfied?"

Ella grinned. "I think this must be the first argument with you that I have won."

"Don't let it go to your head. I'm still your mother."

Ella chuckled as she went into the living room and returned with a pillow. She positioned it on another chair and carefully propped Ruth's leg up. "How is that?"

It did feel better. "This will do for a while but there is much work to be done. I can't sit around all day."

"You have two willing children and a new son-in-law who can take over any chores for the next two days."

Ruth's mood soured. "Apparently Faron doesn't want to do farm chores anymore."

Ella gave her a disgusted look. "That isn't true, and you know it."

"It's all Owen's fault. He has filled Faron's head with nothing but foolish tales of travel and adventure since the boy was old enough to sit on his knee."

"We all enjoyed Owen's stories. You can't blame Faron's wanting to experience life outside Cedar Grove on Owen's influence alone. I talked about how much fun I'd had in Jamesport when I stayed with *Grossmammi* and *Grossdaadi*. Maybe it's my fault."

Ruth chose to save her breath. It seemed Ella didn't want to hear anything bad about Owen. Ella picked up the coffeepot along with a piece of paper on the counter.

The outside door opened letting a blast of cold air into the room. Ruth looked over her shoulder. Owen stepped inside, closed the door and pulled off his hat. "It isn't snowing but it sure is cold." He grinned widely as he hung his hat on a peg beside the doorway and slipped out of his coat. "Good morning, Ruth. Good morning, Ella."

"Where have you been?" Ruth demanded.

His smile faded. "Doing the chores at Ernest's farm. Didn't you see my note?"

"I was too busy trying to console Grace." She crossed her arms over her chest and glared at him.

A frown creased his brow. "I'm sorry. I was hoping she'd stay asleep until I got back."

"Well, she didn't."

"Where is she?"

Ruth jerked her head toward the living room. He walked out of the kitchen.

"There is a note." Ella waved it toward Ruth. "I think you owe him an apology."

Ruth huffed but stayed quiet. Owen hadn't bolted this time but that didn't mean he was going to remain and help through the entire lambing season. She needed Faron to stay home.

"Admit it, *Mamm*. You were wrong this time."

After a brief internal struggle, Ruth had to accept that Ella was right. She did owe him an apology. Her intention to be kind to Owen had flown out the door at the first opportunity. "I will ask Owen's forgiveness and show more charity toward him."

By leaning to one side, Ruth could see the sofa through the archway into the living room.

Owen sat down on the couch. The little girl remained huddled under the quilt. "Hello, Grace. Did you miss me?"

At the sound of his voice, Grace pulled the blanket off her head. "You didn't leave me." She scrambled up and threw her arms around his neck.

He patted her back. "Of course I didn't. I went outside to feed the animals and hurried back as quick as I could. I'm sorry you were scared."

She drew back and cupped his face between her hands. "You need to be under my foot."

He tipped his head to the side. "Okay."

"I'm hungry now."

"I have the cure for a hungry girl," Ella announced. "How do pancakes sound?"

Grace leaned close to Owen's ear and whispered something. He laughed. "*Nee*, I'll have my breakfast with you, but Meeka is not going to have pancakes with us. She's outside doing her job taking care of the sheep."

He lifted Grace in his arms and strolled into the kitchen. Ruth sat upright, moved her leg off the pillow and stood up. "I'll scramble some eggs and make toast."

Owen took a seat at the table and settled Grace

onto the chair beside him. "Should you be up walking on that knee?"

Ella gave an exasperated sigh. "I got her to sit down for a few minutes. I may have to tie her to a chair for the rest of the day."

"I'm perfectly fine," Ruth said between clenched teeth.

Owen seemed to take the hint and changed the subject. "It's too cold to take the tractor over to the bishop's place this morning. Grace and I will take your buggy if you don't mind, Ruth. It will be warmer. Do you have some bricks you can heat up to keep our feet warm?"

"Of course. What time are we going to leave?"

"I thought I'd go about nine o'clock, but there's no need for you to come with us."

"I'm as interested in finding out where Grace belongs as you are. There is also something I wish to discuss with the bishop."

Owen quirked an eyebrow. "Faron's plans?"

"I hope the bishop can convince Faron to remain at home."

"I wouldn't get my hopes up if I were you. It's your buggy, so if you wish to ride along it's okay with me. What about you, Grace? Is it okay if Ruth comes along with us?"

Grace seemed to think it over for a moment, then she said, "Okay, but don't get under her foot. She doesn't like that."

Ruth saw comprehension dawn on his face. He

chuckled as he stared at her. "Ruth doesn't like having me underfoot, is that what she said?"

Grace paused as she considered his question. "She said we would be happier if you weren't underfoot, but I wouldn't be happy."

As his intense gaze remained focused on her, Ruth felt the heat rising in her cheeks and knew she was blushing. "You can't fault me for being honest."

He assumed a look of complete innocence. "I didn't say anything."

"Maybe not but I know what you were thinking."

"She's a mind reader," Owen whispered to Grace.

Grace tipped her head to one side. "What does that mean?"

"It means she is always right because she believes she knows what other people are thinking."

Looking impressed, Grace closed her eyes. "What am I thinking now?"

Ruth glared at Owen. "You're thinking that Owen should stop poking fun at me."

Grace cupped her hand by Owen's ear. "That's not right."

His eyes twinkled with suppressed laughter. "We know she can be wrong, but you will never ever get her to admit it."

Footsteps coming down the stairs announced the arrival of Faron and Zack. The two men came into the kitchen and took seats at the table. Faron took his place at the head of the table. Zack took a seat beside Owen.

Faron frowned at Ruth. "You should be resting that knee. Ella can manage breakfast for us all."

Exasperated Ruth planted her hands on her hips. "Will everyone quit fussing at me about my knee?"

Grace leaned close to Owen again with a worried look on her face. "I think she's mad at us."

He patted her head. "She isn't mad at you."

Grace cupped her hand close to his ear. "Are you sure? She looks mad." Everyone heard her loud whisper. Zack and Faron choked back their laughter.

Ruth reined in her annoyance and smiled at the little girl. "I'm not angry with you, Grace."

"Does that mean you're mad at Owen?" Grace asked.

Ruth kept a smile on her face with difficulty. "I'm not angry with anyone, but I do wish everyone would stop pestering me about my knee."

Grace tipped her head to the side. "Does it hurt? What happened?"

"It only hurts a little. I fell out of our sleigh yesterday." She didn't think the child needed to know the circumstances.

Grace shook her finger at Ruth. "You should be more careful. That's what my *mamm* always says." Her face grew sad. "I miss her. Owen, can we go find her?"

"As soon as we finish our breakfast, we will do just that." He glanced at Ruth, and she nodded.

She didn't need to be a mind reader to know what he was thinking. He was praying his words would prove true.

OWEN DROVE RUTH'S horse and buggy down the county road toward the bishop's farm. The road was rough and filled with snow-covered ruts. Grace sat securely between Ruth and Owen, but he was concerned about the jolting Ruth was receiving on her injured leg. She remained quiet with her jaw tightly clenched. Was it because she was in pain or unhappy because she didn't like his company? Either way the ride was made in strained silence. Snow began to fall again in large fat flakes that drifted down gently.

Owen stopped the horse in front of the bishop's house. He lifted Grace out of the buggy and then went around to help Ruth down. She was trying to lower herself carefully when he intervened by grasping her waist and lifting her easily to the ground. Her hands grabbed his shoulders. A bolt of awareness shot through him as he looked into her eyes.

She was a remarkable woman. Tough and capable but still soft and feminine. His hands lingered at her waist until he noticed her frown of displeasure. He stepped away as he tried to pretend helping her out of the buggy was simply a common courtesy, but his racing pulse was anything but normal. He forcefully reminded himself that he had returned to make amends for his past behavior. Any attraction he felt toward Ruth was strictly off-limits. He needed to keep those emotions bottled up for the next month.

The bishop came out of the house. "Good morning. We weren't expecting visitors today. Owen, Ruth, is something amiss?" His mother, Martha, came out to stand beside him.

Grace, who had been hiding behind Owen, peeked at them.

Owen stepped to one side. "I found this young girl on Ernest's porch when I returned home after the skating party. Her name is Grace, but she hasn't been able to tell us who she belongs to or who she is visiting in the community. We're hoping you can help us locate her family."

"We know they must be frantic," Ruth added.

The bishop stroked his gray beard with one hand as he studied Grace. She stepped behind Owen again. "I don't recognize her. *Mudder*, do you know who this child belongs to?"

Granny Weaver shook her head. "I've never seen her before in my life."

"We are at a loss," Ruth said. "We checked with all the families near our farm and no one is missing a child."

"Most extraordinary." The bishop gestured toward the door. "Won't you come in out of the cold and sit down while we puzzle this out? You would think there would be a loud hue and cry over a child that is gone missing."

"That is exactly what we thought," Owen said as he stepped inside the bishop's home. The kitchen was large and airy with pale wood cabinets, spotless blue-and-white linoleum on the floor and plain white paint on the walls. Dual propane gas lamps with light blue shades hung over the oak table in the center of the room. The scent of pine cleaner lingered in the air.

Grace kept her face hidden against Owen's leg

even when they were inside. He laid a hand on her head. "The weather was so bad last night that I'm sure she couldn't have walked far."

"Won't you sit down?" Granny said. "Can I get you some coffee?"

Owen and Ruth both shook their heads. "We just finished breakfast," Ruth added as she sat down.

The bishop took a seat and leaned forward in his chair to address Grace. "Can you tell me where you come from?" She didn't say anything.

Owen added what he knew. "I was able to learn that her name is Grace and that her mother was sleeping. That's all I know about her. She told me she came from outside."

Granny Weaver smiled at Grace. "I have some snickerdoodle cookies in the kitchen. Would you like one?"

Grace looked up at Owen. He nodded. "It's okay. You can have one."

"Have a seat at the table," Granny said as she crossed the kitchen and lifted the top from a cookie jar on the counter.

She placed two cookies on a plate and set the plate on the table. Grace climbed onto a chair beside Owen and bit into a cookie. She gave Granny a bright smile. "These are *goot*."

"If you have checked all the nearby farms, I think the best thing to do is to notify the *Englisch* sheriff," the bishop said. "I'll go make the call. I think you should wait here, if that is agreeable."

Ruth nodded. "We'll wait. Hopefully Sheriff McIntyre can provide us with the answers we need."

Bishop Weaver rose from the table, put on his hat and coat, and went outside. Owen knew the small white shack that served as one of the Amish community phone buildings sat a quarter mile down the road.

Owen got up and walked to the window. It was snowing heavily now. He considered what the involvement of an outsider would mean. If the sheriff knew who Grace belonged with that would be wonderful. Owen could keep his promise to Grace and see that she was returned to her family. If the sheriff didn't know where she belonged, would he take Grace away, or would he leave her with Owen even though they weren't related? Owen had no way of knowing. *Englisch* and Amish ways sometimes ran contrary to each other.

He glanced back to see Ruth watching him. "Do you know the sheriff well?"

"Marty? I do. He was the police officer in Garnett who arrested one of our neighbors, Joshua King, last spring. It turned out to be a mistake. Marty later went out of his way to make sure people knew Joshua was innocent. He and Joshua became friends after that. Marty ran for sheriff last fall at Joshua's urging and won."

"He's considerate of our ways," Granny added.

Owen was relieved to hear that. Grace finished her cookies and came to stand beside him. She tugged on his pant leg. "Can we go find my *mamm* now?"

He sank to his heels and brushed a few cookie crumbs from her chin. "We are going to need some help to find her. The bishop has gone to get more people to help us look. We have to wait until they get here."

Granny went to a cabinet and pulled out a large box. "Grace, do you like to play with puzzles?"

Grace nodded. Granny smiled at her. "Why don't you show Ruth how to put a puzzle together while I make us some hot chocolate?"

Grace gave Ruth a funny look but climbed up onto a chair beside her at the kitchen table. Granny laid out the pieces of a wooden puzzle in the shape of Noah's Ark and then looked at Owen. "Would you like some coffee now?"

"I believe I would." He sat down beside Grace and listened to her explain to Ruth how to match up the puzzle pieces. Ruth dutifully obeyed her instructions and soon had all the animals arranged inside the ark.

The bishop returned twenty minutes later. His hat and coat were covered in snow. "The sheriff will be here in a few minutes. He hasn't had a report of a lost child. He's having his office contact some of the neighboring towns."

They didn't have long to wait before the sheriff arrived in a black SUV with gold lettering along the side. Marty McIntyre was younger than Owen expected him to be. He didn't look much over thirty. He had serious gray eyes and a ready smile for the bishop and his mother. The bishop introduced Owen and Grace.

She immediately buried her face in Owen's side when the sheriff turned his attention to her.

Owen patted her head. "Don't be frightened. This is a friend. He's going to help us find your family."

The sheriff sat on a chair and leaned forward to speak to her. "Howdy, Grace. I'm Sheriff McIntyre. I'm here to help. Can you tell me your last name?"

She shook her head. The sheriff looked at Owen. He shrugged. "I did ask her that last night. She said, 'I can't say.' I thought that was odd. All I've been able to find out is that her name is Grace, she's three, has no siblings and that her mommy is sleeping."

The sheriff's eyes narrowed. "'Can't say' as in she doesn't know or that she isn't supposed to tell?"

"Your guess is as good as mine."

Sheriff McIntyre smiled at her. "Grace, why can't you tell us your last name?"

She looked at Owen. "It's okay. You can tell the sheriff," he urged.

"*Mamm* said no." She pressed her lips together.

Sheriff McIntyre tried a different tack. "Whose house is your mommy sleeping at? Is it your house?"

"She's in the car," Grace said without making eye contact.

The sheriff's eyebrows shot up. "Your mother is sleeping in a car?"

"Uh-huh."

"Is the car at someone's house?" Ruth asked.

Grace shook her head. Owen leaned down to look in her eyes. "Can you show us where the car is?"

Grace's eyes filled with tears. "I don't know where it is. It's lost."

"Is there anyone else with your mother?" the sheriff asked abruptly, his tone full of concern. "Was the car running? Could you hear the engine?"

"*Nee*, it stopped. She's all alone. I want my mommy." Grace burst into tears.

Owen lifted her into his arms to console her. He caught the sheriff's worried look. It was echoed in Ruth's eyes. If Grace's mother had spent the frigid night in a car, she could be in serious trouble.

The sheriff rose to his feet. "I'll get a search party started right away."

CHAPTER SIX

RUTH LISTENED AS the sheriff spoke into the radio fastened to his shirt, giving rapid commands in a succinct voice that conveyed the urgency of the situation. He glanced at Owen. "See if she can tell you what color the car is. We'll start a grid search at Ernest's farm since that's where Grace first showed up."

Owen lifted Grace onto his lap. "Can you tell me what color car your mother was in? Think hard. It's important."

Grace shook her head. "I don't know."

"Was it red? Was it black? Maybe it was a green car?" Each of Owen's questions was answered with a vigorous shake of her head. Finally, Owen patted her back and looked at the sheriff. "Sorry we can't be more help."

The sheriff took a deep breath. "That's okay. Was your mother driving or was someone else driving you?"

"*Mamm* was."

"So she's alone," the sheriff said as he stood. "Time is of the essence now." He headed for the door.

The bishop was already pulling on his coat. "I will meet you at Ernest's place with as many men as I can gather."

Owen stood up with Grace in his arms. "I'll ride with you, Bishop. Ernest may be home by now. If he's not, I'll take his buggy and join you. Ruth, take Grace back to your place." He tried to detach her from his neck, but she screamed at the top of her lungs and hung on more tightly.

"It's all right, Grace," Ruth said calmly. "Let Owen help these men look for your mother."

Grace wasn't having any of it. She kept sobbing. "Don't leave me."

Finally Ruth stepped back. "Let's take her back to my place, Owen. We can send Zack and Faron to help with the search."

She could see Owen wanted to take part, but realized upsetting Grace wasn't doing any good. "Okay."

When they reached the buggy, he helped Ruth in while maintaining his hold on Grace. It was snowing heavily. The sheriff drove off with his blue lights flashing. The bishop backed his tractor out of the shed and followed him. Ruth picked up the reins. Owen didn't object.

Once they were out on the county road, Ruth urged Licorice to a faster pace. "If Ernest is at home he's going to be surprised by his visitors."

"Seems odd to think he doesn't know what's going on yet. He doesn't even know about Grace arriving on his doorstep."

"He'll take it in stride." She glanced at Owen.

He managed a halfhearted smile. "I can't wait to hear the stories *Onkel* Ernest spins out of this."

"Let's pray they have a happy ending."

Grace still clung to Owen. He shifted her weight to a more comfortable position. "I have already been doing that."

Grace finally grew calm when she realized Owen wasn't leaving her. She left his lap to sit between them. The rest of the drive was made in silence.

Faron must've been watching for them. He came out of the house as soon as Ruth drew Licorice to a halt. He opened the driver's-side buggy door. "Did you learn anything?"

"We did." She let her son assist her out of the buggy. "Put Licorice away and come back to the house as quick as you can. I'll tell you about it then."

His eyebrows rose but he led the horse away without another word. Owen followed Ruth into the house. They both took off their coats. Owen helped Grace take hers off, too. The child began rubbing her eyes. Ruth caught Owen's gaze. "Someone looks like they could use a nap. Why don't you take her up to my room, where it's quiet?"

She didn't want Grace to overhear the plans to search for her missing mother. Owen nodded and carried the child upstairs.

Ella and Zack stopped their game of checkers and waited for Ruth to sit down in her chair. A few minutes later Faron came in. "Okay, what did you learn that you didn't want to repeat in front of Grace?"

Ruth told them what she had learned. "When the sheriff started questioning Grace, she said her mother was sleeping in a car that wasn't running."

They all exchanged perplexed looks. Zack was

the first to realize the significance of Grace's statement. "A stalled car would be a very cold place to spend the night. Especially last night."

Ruth sighed. "Exactly. Was she really asleep or is that what a three-year-old would assume? The sheriff is setting up the search party at Ernest's place."

Zack and Faron looked at each other. "We'll go," Faron said as he got to his feet. "What about Owen?"

Ruth shook her head. "Grace won't let him out of her sight."

"The poor child," Ella said. "She must be terrified of being left alone again. I can't imagine what she went through last night before she found shelter."

"Too bad Meeka can't tell us what happened," Faron said. "After all this wind there won't be any footprints to retrace." The men started for the door.

Ella shot to her feet. "Wait. I'm coming with you. I can get hot coffee and hot food going for the searchers in case they need it."

That her children were eager and willing to help swelled Ruth's heart. *We raised them right, Nathan.*

Ella turned back before she left the room. "How is Owen holding up?"

"Maybe he's not happy about having a child to look after but I assume he's fine."

Ella rolled her eyes. "How can you assume that when he lost his entire family at a young age? He has to know what Grace is going through being separated from her mother." She left the room, shaking her head.

Shame brought a lump to Ruth's throat. She hadn't

given much thought to Owen's feelings. To do so meant examining feelings of her own. About him. She wasn't ready for that, but she could treat him with more kindness.

She climbed the stairs to check on Grace—and on him. She paused with her hand on her bedroom door. The soft sound of singing came from inside. She eased the door open a little. Owen sat in the rocker by the window where she liked to do her needlework. He had Grace cradled in his arms as he rocked gently to the tempo of the song. It was an Amish lullaby that she had sung to her children. He was staring out the window and didn't notice her. *"Schloof, bobbli, schloof,"* he sang. "Sleep, baby, sleep. Your father tends his sheep. Your mother shakes the dreamland tree. And from it falls sweet dreams for thee."

She thought Grace was asleep, but the child reached up and patted Owen's cheek. "Can you take me home now?"

"I wish I could, but I don't know where your home is."

"Sing me the song again."

He started the song over as he continued rocking. It was a side of Owen she never expected to see. Ruth quietly closed the door and went into the spare bedroom, where she opened a trunk that contained some of Ella's and Faron's outgrown clothes. She had kept them for the grandchildren she hoped to have one day. Ruth pulled out a small dress she thought she could alter to fit Grace and went downstairs.

In the kitchen she decided to start a meal that

would be ready whenever Owen came down. She pulled a ham from the refrigerator and began slicing it into a pan. Deciding what she would say to Owen was a much harder choice.

OWEN LAID GRACE on the bed and pulled the quilt up over her shoulders when she finally fell asleep. He stood watching her for a while. She was so young and so innocent. She couldn't understand what was happening and why her mother wasn't with her.

He had understood his parents and siblings weren't coming back when they were killed, but his little sister hadn't been old enough to grasp the finality of their deaths. She had asked him time and again when they would come home. Rebecca had clung to him much the same way Grace was doing. He'd felt responsible for Rebecca and it had torn his heart in half when she'd been taken away from him.

He wanted to join the search for Grace's mother, but he wasn't going to leave Ruth with a distraught child if Grace woke up and found he was gone. He couldn't do that to either of them.

He left the bedroom door open and went downstairs. He could hear Ruth in the kitchen. He walked to the front door and stepped out onto the porch. It was still snowing heavily, but the north wind was driving it sideways now. It wouldn't take long for the east-west roads to begin drifting shut. Visibility was already down to a quarter of a mile. The blizzard-like conditions would soon make searching for Grace's mother impossible. He prayed she had already been found. He stared into the whiteness, hoping to see the sheriff's car approaching but nothing was moving except the snow.

The door behind him opened. "You'll catch your death without a coat on out here."

He turned to see Ruth with a thick dark red shawl clutched around her shoulders standing in the open doorway. "At least I'm not letting all the warm air out of the house."

"If you are worried about my heating bill, then come inside." She turned around and he followed her.

"Any sign of them?" she asked hopefully.

"Nothing. Something smells *goot*."

"I heated up some leftover ham to make sandwiches along with tomato soup if you want some." She headed toward the stove. "Do you like cheese and mustard on your ham?"

"Cheese and mayo if you have it." He couldn't put his finger on it, but something seemed different about Ruth.

"That's the way Faron likes his, too." She sent a small smile in his direction and turned back to the stove.

Something was different. She was being nice. He stepped to the cabinet. "I'll get the plates and bowls."

"Danki."

He pulled a platter from the cabinet and handed it to her. She began filling it with slices of steaming ham.

"Would you like your bread toasted?"

"Don't bother."

"It's no bother. I like mine that way."

"Okay, sure." She was definitely being nice. He waited until she had the meal on the table and sat down. He bowed his head to say the silent prayer before meals. He looked up when he was finished. She glanced up, smiled. "Can I get you anything else?"

"This is fine." He ate his sandwich and tried to figure out what had changed. When he finished his coffee, she got up and poured him another cup.

"Ruth, what's going on?"

"What do you mean?" She kept a smile on her face as she carefully placed the pot on the table.

"You're acting odd."

Her smile slipped a little. "I'm simply being kind."

"I know and, believe me, that is odd."

"It's *odd* for me to show a guest in my home kindness?" Any trace of her smile vanished as her voice rose.

"It's unusual for you to be nice to me."

"Owen Mast, how can you say such a thing? I have never in my life been anything but civil to you."

He put his elbows on the table and laced his fingers together. "I remember one evening when you were far more than civil."

Her cheeks bloomed fiery red. "I haven't the faintest idea what you are talking about."

He knew he shouldn't, but he couldn't help himself. "It was a pretty spring evening. You had on a blue dress that matched your eyes. We were riding home from the singing at the Yoder farm. We stopped at the end of your father's lane." He winked at her. "I remember it in great detail."

She raised her chin. "Then your memory is as flawed as the rest of your character."

He leaned back in the chair. "That's better. That's the Ruth I know."

"And to think I was feeling sorry for you."

"Ah! Now the truth comes out. Why would you feel sorry for me?"

"I have no idea."

He shook one finger at her. "Lying is wrong."

She glared at him. "Ella was concerned that Grace's missing mother would bring back troubling memories for you."

"Ella has always been sensitive to the needs of others."

"And I'm not? Is that what you're saying?"

She was fun to rile, and he enjoyed teasing her. Maybe too much so. Spending time with her was getting easier. He was starting to look forward to their skirmishes.

"That's not what I'm saying at all. You pour your heart and soul into caring for your family. You are a good mother, but pity the person who gets between you and your cubs. You need to cut the apron strings."

"So you decided to slice them for me?"

"I had nothing to do with Faron's plans. I know you don't believe that, but it's true. When Ernest wrote and asked me to take care of the farm while he was gone, I thought it was an unusual request from him, but I was glad to help. He's never needed me before. I thought maybe he was in poor health or something. As soon as I arrived and heard Faron was going with him but hadn't told you yet, I knew the two of them had cooked it up between them."

Owen watched Ruth mull over his comment. "I can't believe Ernest would go behind my back to plan this."

"You might want to lay the blame at Faron's door. He is a good boy. He didn't want to leave you short-handed, but this was his chance to see something of the world. I know you don't think I'll be much help, but I'm flattered that Ernest and Faron assume I will be. Faron is better off traveling with Ella, Zack and Ernest to look out for him. If you forbid him to go this time, he may decide to strike out on his own someday. When a fellow does that, it's hard to come home and admit you made a mistake."

"Is that why you never came back?"

"I came back lots of times."

"But you never stayed. Why not?"

He looked down at his plate. "There was never anything to keep me here, and I had to find my sister." He looked up and forced a smile. "Besides, I liked seeing new places and meeting new people. I reckon I was born with a wanderlust."

"Somehow I don't think that's the whole truth," she said softly.

He couldn't meet her gaze.

"THIS IS HARD for you, isn't it?" Ruth asked, watching the emotions play across his face. She didn't want to feel sorry for him but she did.

"For me? You mean because of my sister?" He rose and went to stare out the window.

"Are you still searching for her after all these years?"

He looked around at her. "I found Rebecca two months ago."

Ruth was stunned. "Owen, that's wonderful. Why didn't you tell us? Where did you find her?"

"She was living in an Amish community in Indiana."

"You don't sound excited. You've been searching for her for twenty years."

He turned to face her. "Twenty-five years. That was when my aunt Thelma stopped writing to your mother-in-law and moved the first time."

"How did you find her?"

"I met an Amish woman in Ohio who knew Thelma. She said she had seen Rebecca working at a diner in Shipshewana, Indiana. I went there as soon as I could."

"Two months ago. About the same time as Ella's wedding?"

"That's right. I'm sorry I missed the ceremony, but I didn't feel I had a choice. I asked the manager at the diner if he knew a woman named Rebecca Mast. He didn't but he said Rebecca Stoltzfus worked for him. Turned out that she had the week off. I took a job at a construction place in town and rented an apartment. I was low on funds at that point, so I had to get work. I hung around the diner the day she was supposed to return. I knew as soon as I saw her that Rebecca

Stoltzfus was my sister. She looked so much like our *mamm*. I waited until her shift was over and spoke to her as she came out of the building."

"She must've been stunned to see you after all that time. What did she say?"

He pushed his hands into his pockets. "Not much. She had no idea who I was. Rebecca was only three years old when we were separated. I never considered that she wouldn't remember me. She didn't recall my promise to come and get her. She thought our aunt was her mother and that she was an only child. Rebecca said Thelma passed away five years ago."

Ruth leaned back in her chair. Sympathy pushed aside some of the bitterness she felt toward him. "I'm sorry, Owen. How terribly sad for you. But now that she knows she has a brother she'll keep in touch, won't she?"

"I gave her my address. I left her Ernest's address and yours. I told her about him and about you and your family. I thought she would be happy to know she wasn't alone in the world. She didn't seem interested in learning more. She brushed me off, said she had somewhere to go. She seemed, I don't know, frightened or something. I told her I'd be back the next day after her shift was over again. When I returned she was gone."

Ruth frowned. "Gone? What do you mean?"

"The restaurant manager said she came in early and gave her notice but didn't say why."

"She didn't leave word for you?" Ruth was astonished.

"*Nee.* She didn't seem to want anything to do with me. I don't even know why. I thought maybe she didn't believe my story. I was crushed. She was all I had left. Our parents, our sister and our two brothers were taken away in the blink of an eye. I was holding Rebecca on my lap when the car struck our buggy. I don't know how we survived."

"It was *Gott*'s mercy."

"I didn't see it that way. I used to wish He had taken us altogether. I thought it was cruel to leave Rebecca and me behind. I wasn't old enough to take care of her. That's what the bishop said when he sent her to stay with our aunt. Thelma said she couldn't take care of a boy my age, so I was sent to stay with Nathan's family. I just wanted my family back. That's why I was so determined to find Rebecca."

"Owen, I'm so sorry." She didn't know what else to say.

"Talk about a wasted life," he said bitterly. "I left the family that wanted me, to search for a sister who didn't remember me and the aunt who was afraid I would find her. I crisscrossed the country following every lead to Amish settlements no matter how small, trying to track down my aunt's whereabouts. I guess she feared losing the little girl she'd come to love. I only wanted to make sure Rebecca was safe and happy."

"What did you do after that?"

"I stayed in Shipshewana. I hoped I would run into her if I remained in the area. I didn't but I got a letter from her a short time later. There was no return address. The postmark was from Columbia, Missouri." He rubbed his palms on his pant legs.

"That's something. What did her note say?" Ruth sensed he wanted to say more but she heard Grace calling for him.

He went to the stairs. "I'm down here."

Grace made her way down one careful step at a time until she reached the bottom. "I took a nap."

"*Ja*, you took a *goot* nap. Now what shall we do?" Owen took her hand and led her into the kitchen.

Ruth folded her arms across her chest. "First some lunch for you. Do you like ham sandwiches?"

The child nodded eagerly, and Ruth led her to the kitchen. Owen followed and leaned against the counter watching her.

Grace ate her sandwich and downed a glass of milk in record time. She sat back with a sigh, wiping her milk mustache off with the back of her hand. "Now what should we do?"

"I have an idea," Ruth said. "I think you need a bath and some clean clothes. How does that sound?"

"Okay, come on. I like baths." Grace slipped off her chair, grabbed Owen's hand and pulled him toward the hallway that led to the bathroom.

He stopped and held both hands in the air. "I'm going to turn you over to Ruth for this one."

Grace looked around Owen at Ruth and then beckoned him to lean down. She cupped a hand to his ear. He listened and nodded. "*Ja*, you are safe with Ruth. She knows all about giving little girls a bath."

To Ruth's surprise Grace smiled at her and held out her hand. "Okay."

Shocked but not wanting the child to change her mind, Ruth took her hand. She looked at Owen. "What did she say to you?"

"She asked if you were a safe one."

"A safe one? What do you think that means?"

"I'm not sure. I just agreed. At least she isn't screaming for me."

"Yet." Ruth followed Grace down the hall but looked back. "Don't go far."

HAPPY TO TURN Grace over to Ruth without a fuss, Owen breathed a sigh of relief. It was short-lived. He went back to the window, hoping to see the storm was letting up. It wasn't. Had they found Grace's mother yet? Was she okay? He didn't want to consider the worst. Grace needed her mother. He knew what it was like to wake up from a nightmare and not have anyone to comfort him. He missed his mother to this day.

What had the child meant when she asked if Ruth was a safe one? She had said something like that to him the night he found her.

It was easy to assure her Ruth was a friend once he knew what she needed to hear. Ruth would care for Grace as if the child were her own. He didn't doubt that for a second. Maybe one day Ruth would see him as a friend again. He hoped she would.

Owen hadn't told anyone about locating his sister until now, not even Ernest. Ruth seemed to understand how painful his sister's initial reaction had been for him. It was hard not to share the cryptic wording of Rebecca's letter with Ruth, but he couldn't betray his sister's trust.

Over the sound of the wind outside he caught the drone of a tractor engine. He opened the door and stepped out onto the porch. The snow flew sideways past the house, driven by a fierce north wind. A drift was already forming next to the steps. Ernest's tractor appeared out of the blowing snow followed by Faron on Ruth's tractor. Ella and Zack were huddled behind him. Ernest had a long gray scarf tied over his hat to hold it on with one end covering his mouth and nose. Everyone's clothes were caked with snow.

Faron stopped to let Ella and Zack off at the house and then drove his tractor down to the shed beside the barn where Ernest had stopped. Owen looked but didn't see the sheriff's vehicle on the lane. Ella walked up the steps and stopped in front of him.

Owen's heart sank when he saw the expression on her face.

CHAPTER SEVEN

"THE SHERIFF CALLED off the search," Ella said. "There's no sign of a stranded car near Ernest's place."

It wasn't good news but at least it wasn't the worst. Owen stepped aside so Ella and Zack could go in. He waited for his uncle and Faron to cross the yard. If the visibility got much worse, he would be forced to string a rope from the house to the barn to keep the family members and himself from getting lost going out to do chores.

Faron bounded up the steps. Ernest climbed them slowly. Owen grasped his elbow to help him up the last step and guided him to the door. Inside the house, water was already puddling on the entryway floor as the snow melted from the searchers' clothing.

Ella hung up her traveling bonnet, straightened her *kapp* and looked around. "Where is Grace?"

"Ruth is giving her a bath," Owen said.

"Without you? How did she manage that?" Ella asked.

"We found the friendship key. Apparently if you tell Grace that someone is safe, she accepts that person as a friend without any fuss."

Ernest untied the scarf beneath his chin making

his black hat look like Ella's bonnet. "I leave you alone for one night, Owen, and look at the crisis that unfolds."

Owen chuckled. "I'm not taking the blame for this one, *Aenti* Ernest."

Ella giggled. "It does look like you're wearing a bonnet."

"He makes a homely *fraw*," Faron said.

Ernest kept a straight face as he pulled off his hat with a flourish. "Both Henry and Otis Shetler asked to walk out with me before they realized who they were talking to, so I'm not that homely."

The chuckles died away as the seriousness of the situation returned. "We searched as much of the roads as we could manage," Faron said. "If the car is drifted over, we may not see it until the weather warms up next week. She may not even be on one of the roads. She could have turned into a field without realizing it."

Ella helped Zack slip out of his coat. "If she got out of the car and tried to follow Grace there's no telling where she could be. Hopefully she found shelter."

"The best thing we can do now is pray for her," Zack said.

Owen gestured toward the window. "Does anyone know how long this blizzard is supposed to last?"

"Another two days is what the sheriff said. I'll get some towels to mop up this mess." Ella walked down the hall.

"What about your flock, Faron?" Owen asked.

"Do they have enough feed to last a couple more days?"

Faron nodded. "I filled the hay feeders the day before yesterday. We may have to dig some of the sheep out of the drifts when this is over but they should be fine for a few days. We started changing over to Icelandic sheep the year before last. They are a hardy breed and don't mind the snow."

Owen tipped his head. "Icelandic sheep? I've never heard of them."

"They are a new breed in the US, but they've been in Iceland for more than a thousand years. They have a double coat and are a lot less trouble at lambing time. We have about fifty head now."

"We still have thirty Dorset ewes," Ernest added. "I like the look of them better than those shaggy Icelandic critters. Sheep should be white and wooly, not muddle colored with coats like a floor mop."

"Those Icelandic critters get ten times as much for their wool as your Dorsets bring, and their meat is better, too," Ella said.

Ernest wasn't done. "They are far more expensive than my sheep. The price your *daed* paid for them was outlandish. If your *mamm* doesn't recover their cost with this year's crop of lambs she's going to lose the land your *daed* mortgaged to buy them."

"Won't the church help her if things get that bad?" Owen asked.

Ernest shook his head. "The church takes care of their own if sickness, accidents or a disaster strikes, but a bad business decision is the responsibility of the person who made it. A man or woman learns as much from their mistakes as their successes."

"That's why I'm not going to fail," Ruth said, coming into the room with Grace bundled in a large towel in her arms. "My Icelandic sheep will pay for themselves this year if your Dorset sheep don't upset the basket by losing too many ewes and lambs this spring. Not to mention your dog cost as much as one of my ewes. I assume by looking at your faces that you don't have news to share."

"Where's my *mamm*?" Grace asked the question none of them wanted to answer.

"We don't know," Owen said gently. "But we'll keep looking."

Ella laid towels on the floor to soak up the snow-melt. "The weather has made it too difficult to continue today, but Owen is right. We'll keep looking as soon as we can."

"Meeka is doing her job. We haven't lost any sheep so far, have we?" Ernest returned to the sore spot Ruth had touched on.

She grinned at him. "Meeka has done a wonderful job and even brought us one more lamb than we were expecting." Ruth transferred her smile to Grace.

Grace eyed Ernest with distrust. "I don't like him."

"Grace, this is my *onkel*. His name is Ernest Mast," Owen said, gesturing toward the older man.

Grace switched her gaze to Owen. "Ernest is safe."

"That's right," Ruth said, glancing at Owen. He shrugged.

Grace narrowed her gaze at Ernest. "I still don't like him."

Everyone laughed. Ernest looked crushed. Ruth patted the girl's back. "You have taken him down a peg or two. He's used to being everyone's favorite jokester. Let's go try on your new dress and see how much I need to alter it. Everyone, there is ham for sandwiches in the kitchen. Owen, Grace and I have already eaten."

Ruth carried the child up the stairs. Zack looked at the rest of the family. "I reckon there's nothing to do now but wait for the weather to clear."

With a murmur of agreement, the group split up, with the youngsters heading for the kitchen. Ernest remained. "Why do you think the child doesn't like me? *Kinder* always like me."

"Grace is an odd child." Owen thought she would be relieved to know Ernest was one of the "safe ones," whatever that meant. It seemed it took more than the password to become her friend. "Once she gets to know you she'll be as delighted with your company as I have always been."

"Maybe so. Her appearance here is mighty strange. Why would a mother let her child get out of the car in such bad weather? Especially one as young as Grace. None of it makes sense. If the child left a vehicle she couldn't have gone far. We should have found it."

"Maybe Meeka brought her from farther away than we assumed."

"The only way I see that happening is if the child climbed on the dog's back."

"She's your dog. Would she allow Grace to do that?"

"Meeka has strong protective instincts. Maybe. Why don't you ask Grace how Meeka led her to the house?"

"I'll do that when she comes down."

Owen heard the door open upstairs and Grace came hurrying down the steps. "Owen, see my dress? It's new. Ruth made it for me."

She stopped at the foot of the stairs to turn around. Her damp curly hair had been tamed into two braids. The dress was dark blue, loose and reached her ankles. Ruth had made a long apron of the same color to cover it. Grace patted her bare head. "Ruth is going to make me another *kapp* to wear when my hair is dry."

"You look very clean and tidy," Owen said, and he knelt in front of her. "Can I ask you a question about Meeka?"

"Is she here?" She peered around him.

"She is still outside guarding her flock of sheep. When you came to *Onkel* Ernest's house, did you walk there by yourself?"

"It was cold. I couldn't see a house. Meeka scared me when she came out of the snow. I was crying. She licked my face and I wasn't scared anymore. She was warm when I hugged her."

"Did you walk beside her all the way to the house?"

She nodded. "It took a long time."

What was a long time to a three-year-old? Owen looked up to see Ruth descending the stairs. "Did you learn anything new?" she asked.

Owen shook his head. "Not really."

Ernest rubbed the back of his neck. "I've put in a long day. I'm going to get a bite to eat and head home."

"Stay the night," Ruth said. "We have room for you, if you don't mind a cot."

"All right. Honestly, I'm tired enough to sleep standing up."

Ruth led Grace into the kitchen to fix her something to eat. After supper the family returned to the living room, where Faron and Zack began a spirited game of checkers. Ella found a children's book and lay down on the floor beside Grace to read to her in front of the fireplace. Ernest settled in a recliner nearby to read the newspaper, but he was soon asleep and snoring gently. Ruth settled in the second recliner and pulled her knitting from a basket beside the chair.

Owen found a suitable piece of wood in the wood box and began working on it with his penknife. The sound of the wind outside was muted by the sturdy house, but he could still hear the hiss of the snow hitting the windows. Outside the storm was raging but inside all appeared calm. The quiet was deceiving. They all were thinking of the young mother lost somewhere out there, separated from her little girl.

He whittled on his piece of wood between watching Ruth's knitting needles flashing through the gray yarn and Grace's sleepy yawns. Every once in a while, Ruth would look in his direction and then quickly look away. What was she thinking?

For the first time since he came to Cedar Grove as an orphan, Owen wished there was nothing to pull him away from Nathan's family. He was comfortable among them, almost as if he did belong. But it was impossible to ignore his sister's letter. He'd read it so many times he knew it by heart.

Owen,
As you must have guessed I was shocked to learn of your existence and our relationship. I'm sorry I couldn't stay to visit with you but something important came up. I'm returning to Shipshewana on April 15. I'll tell you what has happened then. I need your help. Don't tell anyone.
Yours in Christ,
Rebecca

He'd be going back to Shipshewana to meet Rebecca next month and he had no idea when he would return to Cedar Grove.

Of course he was thankful Rebecca had reached out to him. The only conclusion he could draw from her letter was that she was in trouble of some kind. She needed his help. He would do whatever he could for her. All he'd wanted in life was to find her and become a family again. Maybe when he did see her he could convince her to come meet Ruth and Ernest.

He glanced at his uncle asleep in the chair. Ernest was the linchpin that had kept Owen from drifting completely away from Ruth and the children. Ernest had always insisted that Owen let him know where he was. Each time Owen stopped in one place long enough to earn the money needed to move on, he had mailed a postcard or letter to let Ernest know where to reach him. That was why he had given Rebecca Ernest's address.

His uncle was a better storyteller than a writer, but he passed on some of the everyday news of Cedar Grove in his letters. He wrote outlandish fishing stories mixed with snippets about the weather and farm prices, but he always ended his letters the same way.

Ruth and the children are doing fine. They would love to see you.

Until his last letter. It had been uncharacteristically brief.

Owen,
I must be away from the farm for a few weeks. Can you look after the place for me? Ruth is going to need help, too. Please come as soon as you can.

It was the only time his uncle had asked anything of Owen. He would've come even if Ernest hadn't said that Ruth was going to need help. When Owen arrived at his uncle's farm it had been a relief to find his uncle was simply taking a long-overdue vacation with his mother and that Faron planned to go along. Owen had been upset to learn Ruth wasn't privy to Faron's plan. He knew she wasn't going to like it and he'd been right. He also knew she would blame him.

He willingly faced her ire because he wanted to make amends for his absences in the past. He needed to prove to Ruth and Ernest that they could depend on him. In a way, he had to prove to himself that he was dependable, that he wouldn't let Ruth down the way he had failed her in the past.

He should've stayed to help Ruth after Nathan's death. His uncle Karl, Nathan's father, had been in poor health by then but he wasn't about to give up control of the farm and he was too stubborn to admit he and Ruth would need help. He'd given Owen a letter from a bishop in Indiana who wrote that Thelma Stoltzfus was a member of his congregation along with a girl named Rebecca. Karl had urged Owen to go at once. He knew what finding Rebecca meant to Owen and how many times Owen had missed them by a few weeks or even days.

Leaving Karl to explain the situation to Ruth, Owen had taken the next bus east. Two days later he had arrived in Elkhart, Indiana, only to discover that the woman in question wasn't his aunt. She had merely been an Amish woman with the same name who had a daughter called Rebecca. As soon as Owen realized he'd made the trip for nothing he should've gone back, but he hadn't. That had been his real mistake.

Ruth put her knitting aside. "I'm going to turn in. Don't wake Ernest. He often sleeps in that chair when he stays over. Owen, do you need anything?"

"I'll be fine."

The rest of the family bade him good-night and left the room. Ruth remained. She held out her hand. "Grace, it's time to go to bed. You can sleep in my room, if you like."

Grace shook her head. "I want to stay with Owen."

He put aside his knife. "I'll fix up her cot again. Good night, Ruth, and thank you for all you have done for her."

"Think nothing of it."

She left the room and he tossed his wood shavings into the fire. After making up Grace's cot, he tucked her in and returned to his chair to stare into the fire. He heard his uncle shifting his position and looked over at him.

"Ruth is a good woman," Ernest said, followed by a deep yawn.

"I've always known that." She kept a fine house, ran a farm and raised two children after laying her husband in the ground. She was remarkable.

"Didn't you court her when you were teenagers?"

"We went to a few singings together. That was a long time ago."

"Maybe, but I still remember my first love, and I'm a lot older than you. The heart doesn't forget even if that girl marries someone else."

Owen shifted uncomfortably in his chair. "I never said she was my first love. She picked the right man.

You can't dispute that. I had nothing to offer her. Nathan had a farm and a passion for the land."

Ernest grunted. "It's not what a man has in this world. It's what he makes of it. You left because you were afraid of loving and losing her."

Owen's jaw dropped. "How could you know that?"

"Because I know you. Don't get me wrong, Nathan was a *goot* decent man. He loved Ruth. They had a *goot* life together, but she would have had a fine life with you, too. The trouble with you, boy, is that you never believed you deserved happiness. You still don't. You're scared of it. Well, you're wrong. *Gott* has given you a chance to change that. Don't mess it up this time."

Ernest turned his head to the side and closed his eyes. "You'd better get some sleep."

Owen sat glued to his chair by his uncle's words. What would his life have been like if he hadn't left at eighteen? Would he and Ruth have made a life together? Had the search for his sister been an excuse to cover his own feelings of unworthiness? Was he afraid of loving others because he feared losing them? In his heart he knew it was true. It was a sobering thought.

Owen put his head back and stared at the ceiling. Everyone he loved had been taken away in the blink of an eye except Rebecca, and he hadn't been able to hold on to her. How could he hope to find love and happiness when it might be snatched from him again?

He cared about Ruth, but he couldn't allow his

emotions to go beyond that. The search for his sister might have been an excuse to leave before, but she was the very real reason he would have to leave again. Until he knew Rebecca was safe and happy, he couldn't think about his own future.

OWEN SLEPT FITFULLY that night and rose before anyone else was up and about. He had coffee brewing when Ruth came down. She scowled at him. He figured she wasn't used to someone taking over her kitchen.

"Don't you like the way I make coffee?"

He shrugged. "It's all right." Her eyebrows shot up and he laughed. "Of course I like your coffee. I'm just trying to repay your kindness. How is the knee?"

"Better," she admitted grudgingly.

"I wish the weather was better."

"It sounds like the wind has backed off."

"I think you're right but it's still snowing." If nothing else, they could talk about the weather.

Ernest came into the room, scratching his head and yawning. "Morning. The coffee smells *goot*."

"Have a seat and I'll get some breakfast started if Owen will move aside."

Owen bowed and stepped away from the stove. "Be my guest."

The rest of the family trooped in after a few minutes along with Grace, who sat down beside Owen at the table. Ella joined her mother at the stove. They soon had sausages and eggs ready along with toast and thick white sausage gravy.

After a silent prayer they began passing platters to each other. "Do we have a plan today?" Faron asked.

"Wait out the worst of the storm and then check on the flock," Ruth said. "It will be a good time to make sure the lambing pens in the barn are ready to go."

"What about, you know." Faron nodded toward Grace.

"We'll resume that as soon as we can," Ernest said quietly. "For now we have chores waiting in spite of the weather."

Owen turned to Grace. "I have to help with chores outside and you have to help Ruth with the chores inside. I'll be back soon. Okay?"

Worry clouded Grace's eyes. "You'll come back?"

"As soon as my work is done. Ruth needs your help until then."

"Okay." She agreed but she didn't look happy about it.

Owen grinned. *"Goot."*

RUTH LET OUT the breath she'd been holding. At least Grace wasn't hysterical at the thought of him being out of her sight. Maybe the child was getting over her fear of others.

After the meal, Faron and Owen went outside to work. Grace helped clear the table and carried some of the dishes to the sink. Ruth thanked her with a quick hug. Zack went out to bring in more firewood while Ella opened the door to the cellar where all of last summer's produce was stored. *"Mamm,* did you have anything in mind to fix for lunch later today?"

"Bring up some of the meat we canned and more potatoes. We'll make beef stew." Ruth placed the last plates in the sink. "Then we might make another dress for Grace."

Grace grinned and clapped her hands.

"And a black *kapp*. They don't show the grime as quickly." Ella nodded toward the child, who had a smear of strawberry jam on the side of her face and on her new white *kapp*.

Ruth wet a washrag and cleaned Grace's cheek. She dabbed at the stain on the *kapp* and grinned at her daughter. "You're right. You make a couple of black ones, and I'll make another white one. I like the way the white looks against her pretty hair."

"It's not how we look that makes us pretty," Grace said in a solemn voice. "It's how we act."

"I'd bet your mother taught you that," Ella said with a knowing smile for Ruth.

Grace nodded once. "She did. I miss her. When is she coming to get me?"

Ruth gathered her close in a hug. "I don't know, but *Gott* is with her, so you don't need to be scared."

Grace wrapped her arms around Ruth's neck. "That's what Owen told me."

"Then for once, Owen was right," Ruth murmured against the child's hair.

FARON AND OWEN soon had the horse, chickens, cows and sheep fed and made sure they all had open water in the stock tanks by chopping through the ice with an ax. Unless the temperature climbed above freezing they would need to be opened again in the evening. Zack entered the barn, picked up the three-legged stool and a pail and went to milk the family's two cows. Faron nodded toward the back of the building. "Come see what we've done since you were last here."

He opened a door to an addition on the rear of the barn. "This is our new lambing shed." He gestured toward the ceiling. "I put in a skylight so we have natural light for the lambs and ewes during the day. On hot days it can be opened for ventilation. We have gaslights for working at night. As you can see, it's got all the comforts of home. Propane refrigerator for keeping colostrum and milk substitute handy, a small stove to warm bottles and keep it comfy in here for humans and lambs. There's also a couple of cots I've never used, but *Mamm* sometimes stays out here."

Owen surveyed the little pens on either side of the main aisle. "Do you often have this many sick newborns in here?"

"The small pens are for the orphan lambs and for getting an ewe to adopt one if she has lost hers or only has one. We sometimes treat sick ewes in here, too."

Ernest walked in. "Getting the tour?"

Owen looked over the number of pens. He had worked herding sheep, but he'd never helped with lambing. "Do you get a lot of orphans?"

"We don't lose many ewes," Faron said, "but an ewe with twins or triplets will sometimes only nurse one. We put an ewe that's lost her baby in with the rejected or motherless lamb and hope she'll accept it. Sometimes it works, sometimes we end up bottle-feeding it."

Ernest slapped Owen on the shoulder. "Sometimes we end up bottle-feeding a dozen or more. I gotta say I love that part. Nothing is cuter than a newborn lamb. They melt your heart. Think you can do this?"

"If I say no will you leave Faron here?"

Faron scowled at Owen. "I'm going. If you don't want to do this, I'll find someone else."

"Then I guess I can do it." Owen turned and walked out of the barn into the larger sheep pens. Only a few animals stood around the hay feeders. They were coated with snow but didn't seem to notice it sitting on their thick wooly backs.

The snow was becoming lighter, but the wind had kicked up again, blowing the snow that had already fallen across the pasture and forming drifts along the fences.

"If this keeps up we'll have to dig out some sheep for sure," Ernest said, holding on to his hat as he stepped out beside Owen. "They huddle together and get drifted over with snow. They can eat the snow for water and paw down for old grass to nibble but if the snow gets too deep they can smother."

Owen pulled his collar tight. "I pray Grace's mother isn't out in this weather."

"The sheriff and our neighbors will resume the search once it clears. We'll find her. Until then she is in *Gott*'s hands."

The two men walked back into the house. Grace came running up to Owen. "You came back."

"I told you I'd be back." He slipped out of his coat and picked her up. "What are you doing?"

"Ruth is making me another dress, and Ella is making me a black *kapp* 'cause I'm messy."

"Sounds about right." He put her down, and she raced back into the living room. He followed more slowly.

He and Ernest were stuck here until the weather cleared. He knew Ernest didn't mind but Owen had no idea how he was going to get through another day of Ruth's silent displeasure.

Faron laid aside the supplies he had been assembling for the lambing shed. "Owen, tell us about Maryland."

Owen caught Ruth's sour look, but she didn't say anything. He considered declining but decided there was nothing wrong with sharing his experiences. It didn't mean he was encouraging Faron to travel to the East Coast. "Maryland is a pretty place. Lots of history, from sailing ships to the first railroad, grand old houses. The coast is marshy in places. If you ever go to Maryland, you have to have the crab cakes. They are amazing."

"People eat crabs in their cake?" Grace made an ugly face. "That sounds yucky."

"My thoughts exactly." Ruth continued hemming the dress she had completed for Grace.

"I've often wanted to try fresh seafood," Ella said, jumping into the conversation.

"Maybe we can extend our wedding trip to visit the Gulf Coast," Zack suggested.

"Oh, could we?" Ella's eyes lit up at the thought.

"I don't see why not."

Faron sat back in his chair. "Now I am going to be jealous. Where else have you been, Owen?"

Owen proceeded to tell them about his trip to the Amish communities in Maryland while he was looking for his sister. He didn't share the heartbreak of each dead end of his search. No one wanted to hear his sad story. He managed to keep them entertained until lunchtime. For a while it seemed that even Ruth was interested in his tales, but he thought perhaps he only imagined it.

After lunch Ruth retreated to her bedroom upstairs, and he didn't see her for the rest of the day.

THE STORM KEPT everyone indoors for another day, but it finally blew itself out during the night and daybreak brought the return of sunshine. Before long the snow was melting off the roof, forming long icicles and puddles in the yard. Even with the warmer temperature Owen knew it would be two weeks or more before all the snowdrifts were gone.

After breakfast Ernest began putting on his coat. "I should get going. I have chores waiting at my place and I have to check on Meeka. Zack and Faron, come over to my place when you can. I'm sure the sheriff will be out once the roads are plowed by the county maintenance worker."

"I'll come with you," Ella said.

Owen stood up. "I'll ride back to your place with you and help with the search. Ruth, do you mind keeping Grace? I know she'll be better off here than with two old bachelors."

"I'd be happy to look after her."

Owen cupped Grace's chin in his hand. "Be *goot* for Ruth."

He turned and started toward the door. Grace rushed after him and tried to pull her coat off the hook. "I'm going, too."

He took her hand. "*Nee*, I want you to stay with Ruth. She'll take good care of you."

"I wanna go with you. I stay with you until you find my *mamm*. You said so. You promised."

"I know what I said but Ruth is much better at taking care of a little girl. Ernest and I will look for your mommy today. Until we find her you should stay here."

Tears welled up in her eyes and she threw her arms around his leg and sobbed, "Don't leave me."

Ernest let out a low whistle. "I see what you've been up against. You should stay here with the child. You don't mind having him and the child another night, do you, Ruth? I'm sure the bishop would approve."

Owen turned his gaze on her. She opened her mouth and snapped it shut. She clutched her hands together in front of her apron and spoke through stiff lips. "Owen is welcome for as long as need be."

Owen knew it was an outright lie. She did mind but she was compelled by her faith to extend aid to any member of the Amish church who came to her door. Even unreliable Owen Mast. He lifted Grace into his arms and chuckled. "I'll bet those words left a bitter taste."

He eagerly waited for her comeback.

CHAPTER EIGHT

RUTH HEARD THE amusement in Owen's voice and wished she could call back the invitation. He might find humor in this situation, but she didn't. A dozen retorts ran through her head, but she swallowed them all unspoken and patted herself on the back for her restraint. "My only thought is for the welfare of the child. She seems to need you, although I can't conceive why that is."

He looked disappointed by her response. "Her attachment is not my doing."

"I'm not suggesting it is, but I do find it odd."

Ernest slapped his hat on his head. "Faron and I'll make a quick count of our sheep so we know how many are missing. I'll see the two of you tonight. Until then, play nice, children." He laughed as he went out the door.

"Sometimes that man really annoys me." Ruth limped into the kitchen. "I'm going to need more bread."

Owen followed her, still holding Grace. "I find him refreshing. Is your knee hurting again?"

"It's the least of my troubles." She began pulling

out pans and clanking them on the counter with more force than necessary.

"Is there anything Grace and I can do to help?"

She spun around. "Stay out of my kitchen."

Grace had her arms around Owen's neck. "Is she mad at us again?"

He looked into her worried eyes. "The thing you have to understand about Ruth is that she pretends to be mad at us, but she is really only mad at herself."

Ruth fisted her hands on her hips. "What is that supposed to mean?"

"It means exactly what I said. Are you mad at Grace?"

Her expression softened. "Of course not. I'm delighted that Grace can stay with us for a while."

"Are you mad at me? Be truthful."

"You're putting me on the spot."

"Tell Grace the truth. Are you mad at me?"

"Oh, I guess not. I'm upset with the situation and don't pretend you don't know why."

He managed a sad smile for Grace. "Ruth is upset because she likes me a little, but she doesn't want to admit it and she doesn't want me to know."

Grace tipped her head to the side as she looked up at him. "Why not?"

He fixed his gaze on Ruth's face. "Because it makes her feel disloyal to someone we both loved. The sad thing is, he always wanted us to be friends."

He smiled at Grace. "Let's go in the other room and play a game."

After he walked out of the kitchen, Ruth sat down

at the table feeling as if all the air had been pulled from her lungs. He was right. When had Owen learned to know her so well?

She slowly pushed to her feet and followed Owen into the living room. He was on the sofa with one of the children's books Ruth kept on hand to entertain the *kinder* of her friends when they came to visit. Grace was leaning against him to see the pages. He looked up and waited for Ruth to speak.

It took her a moment to find her voice. "You are right about one thing."

"One thing? I'm right about a lot of things. Which one do you mean?"

Ruth rolled her eyes. "I don't know why I bother."

She turned to leave but his voice stopped her. "I'm sorry, Ruth. I was trying to be funny. It didn't come across that way. What you have to say is important to me. Go ahead."

She took a deep breath. "My husband did want us to be friends. You are right about that. He thought a great deal of you."

"I loved him like a brother. There was very little I wouldn't have done for him. I know it must not seem like that to you, but there were reasons I couldn't stay on after the funeral."

"It doesn't matter. The past can't be changed," she said quickly.

Had she judged him unfairly? It went against the teachings of her Amish faith to judge any man, and yet what a man did was more important than what a man said. Owen had a poor record of dependability in her eyes. "Only *Gott* can see into the hearts of men and women. He is the ultimate judge of our thoughts and actions."

"He knows my only intention is to aid you while Faron and Ernest are gone. If you can put the past aside, do you think we can become friendly if not friends for the weeks that I'll be here?" There was a look of pleading in Owen's eyes that belied the calm tone of his request.

She studied his face for a long moment. She would need help and she couldn't afford to pay a hired man. Not if she was to make a decent profit on the lambs.

Was it a mistake to trust him? What choice did she have? She finally nodded. "I can do that."

He smiled. "*Danki*. That means more than I can say."

Ruth relaxed and the knot between her shoulders eased. It was only for a few weeks, and then Owen would be gone again and Faron would be home with his foolish need to travel out of his system and her life would return to normal.

Grace sat up straight. "Come listen to the story, Ruth. This is the good part where all the animals come to the ark."

Ruth grinned at her. "What animals came to see Noah?"

Grace tipped her head. "How do you know his name is Noah?"

Owen chuckled. "I think she read this book to Ella and Faron many times when they were little."

Grace seemed impressed. "I think there were

elephants and camels and horses, but I don't know why he let the spiders on. They're yucky."

"I agree. I think he could've left the mice off, too. I don't like mice."

Grace's eyes grew round. "Mice are very quiet. In our game, *Mamm* says I have to be quiet as a mouse and she's always happy when I am."

"What game is that?" Ruth asked.

"The safe place game," Grace whispered.

Ruth and Owen exchanged puzzled glances. He leaned forward a little to meet Grace's gaze. "I've never heard of that game. How do you play it?"

"You show me the safe place. Then you say, 'Go to the safe place,' and I do."

"This is a game you played with your mother?" Ruth asked.

Grace nodded. "Every day. Sometimes at breakfast. Sometimes at night. She tells me to go to the safe place and I run, run, run and hide."

"What do you do in the safe place?" Owen asked.

Grace pressed both hands to her lips. "I'm quiet as a mouse, even if I hear yelling."

Ruth wasn't sure what to make of Grace's story. "Did you hear yelling very often?"

"Sometimes. I stay quiet in the safe place until *Mamm* comes to get me. She says I'm the best mouse ever."

"I'm sure you must be," Ruth said as she glanced at Owen.

"Wanna play?" Grace asked hopefully.

"Sure. What makes a good safe place?" Owen asked.

Grace wiggled down from the sofa and studied the room. She walked around it once and then proceeded out into the hall. Ruth and Owen followed her. In the bathroom she opened the door on the vanity and looked inside. She stood up and smiled. "This might be a good safe place."

"Okay, now what?" Owen asked.

Grace pointed out the door. "We go in the other room and you tell me, 'Go to the safe place.'"

They followed Grace as she went back to the sofa and sat down. She picked up her book and began to turn the pages. Owen and Ruth sat down on each side of her. After a moment, Owen said, "Grace, go to the safe place."

Grace dropped her book and ran out of the room. Ruth heard the bathroom cabinet open and close. She looked at Owen. "What sort of game is this? You've been to many other Amish settlements. Is it a kind of hide-and-seek?"

"I don't think so. I've never heard of it. To me it sounds as if Grace's mother was fearful something would happen to her child or maybe there was something she didn't want Grace to see."

Ruth shook her head in disbelief. "That is not the way Amish folk live their lives. *Gott* is our protection. We must accept the good and the sorrow in this world without question, for He allows it according to His plan and not ours. His goodness and mercy give us strength. What mother teaches her child to hide at all hours of the day or night?"

"A better question might be what is she hiding

Grace from? When I first asked her what her father's name was, she whispered, 'I can't say.' I thought it was odd at the time, but that could be who her mother wants to hide her from."

"An abusive husband?" Ruth frowned as she digested that thought. She wasn't naive. It was rare in their community, but she knew abuse happened in both the *Englisch* and Amish worlds. "I'm afraid we're just guessing. Do you think this is something we should tell the sheriff?"

He nodded. "I do. If Grace's mother is hiding from someone, that may be why we haven't found her."

"How do we contact the sheriff?"

"He will be back to see Grace before long."

"How do you know that?"

"Unless they find her mother today, Grace is the only one who knows where her mother is. I figure he will question her again, hoping for some new clue."

Owen's prediction proved to be true. Ruth's family and the sheriff returned a little after one o'clock. Melting snow had turned the gravel and dirt roads into slush. Everyone was peppered with mud thrown up by the tractor tires.

The sheriff took off his hat when he stepped inside. "Afternoon, Ruth. Is it okay if I speak with Grace again?"

"Of course. She's in the living room with Owen. Any sign of her mother?"

"Nothing." He walked away. She explained to her family about Grace's strange game. No one knew quite what to make of it. Ruth nodded toward the kitchen. "I have food ready for you. Are you going out to search again?"

"We are," Zack said. "I hate the idea of leaving tomorrow with this mystery unsolved and that poor woman still missing."

"I agree," Faron said.

"You can always postpone your trip," Ruth suggested. "Or forget it altogether and stay home."

"We did talk about it," Ella said.

Ernest hung up his hat. "We have covered every road, lane and farmyard for five square miles without any sign of a stranded car. What the searchers really need is warmer weather. If I thought there was a chance of finding her, I'd stay, but I'm beginning to believe she isn't out there."

Ruth held her hands wide. "Grace didn't fall from the sky. Her mother has to be somewhere."

"Or maybe she drove away," Faron said.

"What an appalling thing to suggest." Ruth couldn't believe Faron would say such a thing. "You think she put her child out in a snowstorm and then drove off and left her? I can't believe that."

Ella brightened. "That's what I said to the sheriff."

"And what was his reply?" Ruth asked.

Ella sighed deeply. "He says it happens."

Ruth shook her head at the sorrow in the world. "If that is true, there are parents who need our forgiveness and our prayers. For themselves and their children. How very sad. Go in and get something to eat. I'm going to see what the sheriff has to share."

OWEN LOOKED UP from his place on the sofa as Ruth entered the room. She was visibly shaken. He started to get up, but she quickly composed herself and came in to sit beside Grace, who was putting a puzzle together at a table by the window. The sheriff sat opposite the child. Owen relaxed but kept an eye on Ruth as well as Grace.

"I was just wondering if Grace remembered anything else about the night she arrived," the sheriff said, turning his trooper's hat slowly around in his hands. "Let's start at the top, Grace. Where were you when you and your mother got in the car?"

"I told you." She kept her eyes down.

"My memory's not so good. Why don't you tell me again?"

"We were at home."

"Do you remember the name of the town?"

"Not in town. On *Grossmammi*'s farm but she isn't there. She's in heaven."

"What's your grandmother's name?" Sheriff McIntyre laid his hat aside and pulled a notebook from his pocket.

Grace tipped her head to the side. *"Grossmammi."*

"Did she have a last name like Granny Weaver?" Owen asked.

Shrugging her shoulders, Grace held her hands wide. "I don't know."

The sheriff closed his eyes. "Did your mother have blankets or quilts in the car? Did she have a suitcase?"

Grace shook her head.

"Where was she planning to go on this trip?"

"I don't know."

"Were you going to the grocery store or to visit someone?"

Grace sighed with exasperation. "I don't know." Owen could see she was getting upset.

The sheriff softened his tone. "I'm sorry, Grace, but I have to ask these things. Anything you can remember might help. Did your mother often take trips in the car?"

"*Nee*, she drove Pansy and the cart."

The sheriff perked up. "Who is Pansy?"

"Our pony. She's black-and-white. *Mamm* says I'm too little to drive her, but I think I could do it."

The sheriff looked up from his notepad and smiled at her. "Did the car belong to your mother?"

She gave him a don't-be-silly look. "Amish can't own cars."

"That's right. Did it belong to a friend of your mother's?"

Grace's expression turned guarded. "Not a friend."

"Okay, the car didn't belong to a friend. Who did the car belong to?"

She got down from her chair and came over to whisper in Owen's hear. He glanced at the sheriff. "She can't say."

The sheriff's eyes narrowed. "Isn't that what she told you when you asked her father's name?"

"It is." Owen leaned toward Grace and whispered, "Did the car belong to your *daed*?"

Tears spilled down Grace's cheeks. "I can't say. I want to go home now."

"Honey, you don't have to say. Just nod if it's true."

She crawled into his lap and buried her face against his chest as she nodded. He patted her back. "It's okay. This is the right thing to do. It may help us find your *mamm*."

"I want her to come get me. I don't want to stay here anymore. I want to go home," she mumbled against his shirt and began crying.

"I think that's enough questions for now," Owen said.

The sheriff looked disappointed. "Just one more and I'll leave. Grace, did you and your mommy take the car the same day you ended up here?"

She sniffled and peeked at him. "I think so."

The sheriff smiled at her. "That is a big help, Grace."

Ruth held out her arms to the child. "I'll take her upstairs. I think she's ready for a nap."

Owen handed her over and waited until the pair left the room. Then he turned to the sheriff. "Is it really helpful?"

"There are no databases on missing Amish women or teens. It's rare that we even hear about missing children. Not all Amish communities are as comfortable sharing information with the law as this one is. I sent out alerts to law enforcement near the Amish settlements in Missouri and Kansas. So far nothing. If the Amish don't come to the law for help, our hands are tied."

"What about contacting the Amish directly?"

"How? There are hundreds of Amish communities in the US. Only a few have telephone listings."

"I have contact information for 122 Amish bishops." Owen got up and walked to where his coat hung in the entryway. He withdrew a small book from an inside pocket. He removed his sister's letter from it and tucked the letter back in his coat pocket. Then he returned to the living room and held out the book to the sheriff.

"I spent more than twenty years searching for my little sister and my aunt. Wherever I went I collected the names and addresses of other local bishops. I wrote to them all. These should be current unless one of them has passed away. Becoming a bishop is a lifetime appointment. One more thing. Grace has this game she played with her mother where Grace has a special hiding place. She scurries to it when her mother told her to and didn't come out until her mother asked her to. She found her own safe place here under the sink in the bathroom."

"That's odd." He took the address book from Owen. "This could be useful, thank you. It doesn't sound as if Grace's mother had a good relationship with the child's father. Did he loan her the car, or did she take it? If it was the latter, maybe her dad reported his car as stolen, even if he didn't report his child and her mother missing."

"How does that help you? There must be thousands of cars stolen across the US in a year."

"There are but now we have a date to match up

with any report. That will narrow the field considerably. If we concentrate on the ones closest to us, say within a day's drive, and within twenty-four hours of when you found Grace, I think we can find the dad. Maybe he can tell us where Mommy went."

"You don't think she is out there in her car?"

"It's possible the car is buried under a drift, but I'm starting to doubt it."

"Are you calling off the search?"

"Not yet, but after that storm and the frigid temperatures, the odds of finding her alive are shrinking by the hour." The sheriff settled his hat on his head and went out.

Owen was still sitting in the living room when Ruth came down. She sat in her recliner by the fireplace but didn't take up her knitting.

"Is something troubling you?" he asked after a few minutes of silence.

"All of it troubles me."

"I understand what you mean. The weather is warming up and the snowdrifts will be melting in a few more days. I'm guessing we will find her car at that time if not before."

"Poor Grace. She has been through so much. Did you tell the sheriff about her safe place game?"

"I did before you came in the room. That is partly what leads him to think the father is the one who may be at the bottom of this."

"I hope that isn't the case."

"So do I, but if Grace's mother had anyone else to

go to she wouldn't have ended up out here in a community of strangers."

"We shouldn't give up so easily," Ruth said, rising to her feet. "I'm going to join the searchers if you are okay with watching Grace."

"I'm fine with her. Are you taking the buggy?"

"I thought I would take the sleigh."

"We never got the back runner fixed."

Ruth slapped a hand onto her cheek. "Oh, that's right. So much has happened since then I've forgotten about our accident. Do you think Grace's mother could have been the one who crashed into us that day?"

"It's worth considering. No one saw the driver. The car was swerving before it hit us. What if the driver was sick and not just some teen out joyriding?"

Ruth nodded. "It's worth mentioning to the sheriff."

"You're right. At least we know the color of that car and which way it was headed."

Her eyes widened. "It was headed toward Ernest's farm. There is only one more farm past his on that road, then it loops around a portion of the lake and reconnects with the highway out west of Garnett. If you hurry maybe you can catch the sheriff before he leaves. I can't move fast enough."

"Your sharp mind makes up for your limited mobility."

"Flattery from you? That's different."

"Think of it as a long-overdue compliment." He rushed out the door before she had time to utter a comeback.

Outside he saw the sheriff with the map spread on the hood of his SUV. Around him were four Amish men, including the bishop, and three *Englisch* fellows. He recognized all of their faces from the skating party, but the tall Amish man with a new short beard was the only one whose name he could remember. He was Joshua King. Meeka came up to Owen wagging her tail and began nosing his hand. She whined and grasped it in her mouth. He shook her off.

Joshua stepped over to the side so Owen could view the map.

"How is the little girl doing?" Joshua asked.

"Pretty well, all things considered." The dog grasped his hand again. "Meeka, stop it." He moved her back with his knee.

"Laura Beth will be relieved to hear that. She and her sister Sarah have been concerned about the child. Tell Ruth if there is anything she needs she has only to ask. Now that the weather has taken a turn for the better I'm sure they'll be over to visit."

"They will be welcome. Sheriff, there is something I neglected to tell you. Before the skating party, Ruth's sleigh was hit by a car that didn't stop."

The sheriff frowned. "You're just now reporting a hit-and-run?"

"The decision was mine," said the bishop. "No one could identify the driver. The sleigh wasn't badly damaged. I saw no point in troubling you."

"With everything else that happened later it slipped my mind," Owen admitted. "It wasn't until

Ruth pointed out that the car was headed toward Ernest's place that we thought there might be a connection."

The sheriff turned back to the map. "Show me where it happened."

Joshua pointed a finger to the spot. "About there."

"You saw it? What time was that?"

Joshua looked at Owen. "I saw it happen, but I was too far away to see the driver. The car was weaving back and forth before it hit Ruth's sleigh. It didn't even slow down. It just kept going. It was about two o'clock."

Owen nodded. "I think that's right. It was a dark green car. I don't know the make or model. Faron might be able to tell you."

"I'll take a look at the sleigh. If we are lucky there may be some paint transfer from the car."

"It's in the shed beside the barn." Owen pointed out the building. The sheriff walked off.

Ruth came out of the house with Ernest. Owen left the group to harness Licorice and hitch her to the buggy. He led the horse out of the barn and up to the house. The searchers on tractors, four-wheelers and pickups pulled out of the yard one by one.

The sheriff came back to Owen. "There's a streak of dark green paint on the side of the sleigh. I'll have my lab people collect a sample." He got in his vehicle and left.

Owen opened the buggy door to help Ruth in. She took his hand without hesitation and stepped up. Once she was seated, he leaned in. "Be careful out there. It will be dark in a couple of hours. Don't go walking onto any snowdrifts. The crust might not be strong enough to hold you. You could sink up to your neck before you knew it. I know you. You'll be out searching before long. Which way are you going first?"

"Toward the lake."

"Do you have a *goot* flashlight?"

She opened the compartment on the dash, pulled out a yellow one, pointed it at his face and switched it on. He flinched away from the intense light and put up his hand. "*Goot* enough?" she asked with a hint of humor in her voice.

"A simple *ja* would have worked."

"It wouldn't have been nearly as convincing."

He blinked until the spots in his vision cleared. "It will be in the future."

That made her smile. Hope grew in his heart. If they could part as friends when his time here was up, he'd be a happy man. He wouldn't stay away so long next time. Seeing her smile lifted his spirits. "If you aren't back by seven o'clock, I'll come looking for you."

Ruth picked up her reins. "Don't fuss. Licorice knows her way to the barn."

"Make sure you're with her when she gets here." He closed the door and stepped back, wishing with all his heart that he could accompany her. He understood her need to be doing something. He felt the same way. He turned on his heels and went back into the house. But until Grace was comfortable staying without him he wasn't going to traumatize her more.

He had promised to look after Grace. His purpose for coming back to Cedar Grove was to help Ruth any way she needed. Even if that meant being a baby-sitter when he wanted to join the search.

Inside he slowly climbed the stairs and peeked into Ruth's room, where she had put Grace down for her nap. The bed was empty.

"Grace?"

She didn't answer. He checked the other rooms but didn't find her.

He went downstairs. "Grace, where are you?"

Hopefully she wasn't playing the safe place game in a spot she had decided was better than the bathroom cabinet. He checked there first. No Grace.

He headed for the kitchen but stopped in the entryway when he realized her coat and her boots were gone. He opened the front door and went to the end of the porch. "Grace, answer me!"

There was only silence.

CHAPTER NINE

RUTH WAS LESS than a quarter of a mile from the house when she noticed Licorice begin limping. She pulled the horse to a stop and got out. The mare didn't want to put weight on her right front foot.

"Easy, girl. Let me have a look." Ruth patted the horse's neck, praying it wasn't anything serious. Licorice was her only buggy horse. She lifted the animal's leg. It took her only a moment to assess the trouble. There was a stone wedged between the hoof and shoe.

She released Licorice's leg and rubbed the horse's cheek. "This is an easy fix. I'm glad it's not a thrown shoe or worse."

Ruth fetched a hoof pick from the toolbox under the front seat. She thought she heard a voice in the distance. She listened closely but didn't hear anything else. After removing the offending stone, she put the pick back in the box and walked to the rear of the buggy. She listened intently and heard a shout this time. It sounded like Owen repeatedly calling for Grace. What was wrong?

She ignored the pain in her knee as she rushed to climb in the buggy and turn Licorice around. When she reached the yard, she saw Owen hurry out of the barn. She drew Licorice to a stop beside him. "Owen, what's wrong?"

He helped Ruth out of the buggy. "I can't find Grace anywhere. I've looked all through the house, even the cellar and attic."

"What about her hiding place?"

"That's the first spot I checked. Her coat and boots are missing, too. I thought she must've come outside. Maybe she got in one of the vehicles that were here with the sheriff."

"To hunt for her mother. She might do that. Let's be sure that she isn't here before we involve anyone else."

"I was going to search the barn when I heard you drive in."

"Go ahead. I'll search the henhouse and Faron's workshop."

They met up fifteen minutes later. Ruth could see how worried Owen was. He cared deeply about Grace and so did she. More than she had realized. Ruth shaded her eyes to gaze out into the pasture. Nothing moved. "Why would she suddenly decide to leave the farm?"

She wasn't expecting an answer, but he grasped her arm. "Meeka. The dog was here earlier."

"I haven't seen her since I got back. Was she in the barn?"

"She wasn't."

"Meeka! Here, Meeka," she yelled. The dog didn't appear. Owen walked away from Ruth and began searching the ground.

She realized what he was looking for. Tracks. She began walking in the opposite direction. There were a few paw prints in the snow but no little boot impressions until she reached the side of the house. "Owen, over here."

He hurried to her side. They discovered Grace had left by the back door and followed the dog toward the sheep pasture behind the house. With a clear trail in front of them they picked up the pace until Ruth began limping heavily.

Owen stopped. "What was I thinking? You can't go traipsing through this snow-covered, uneven ground. Can you make it back to the house?"

"I can but I'm not going back."

He rolled his eyes. "How did I know you were going to say that? Wait here a minute."

"If you walk away and leave me, I will just follow you."

He turned around and gave her an odd look. "Is that a promise? Never mind. I'm not leaving you. I'm getting you a walking stick."

"Oh. *Goot* idea." She knew her cheeks were red, but she hoped that he attributed it to the cold. It was just like him to suggest she cared enough to go running after him. She didn't now, but she had considered it at one time. A long time ago when she was a brokenhearted teenager who didn't understand why he'd left without saying goodbye.

She shook off the memory of those days. When he finally left this time all she'd feel would be relief.

He grinned. "I have them sometimes."

"What?" She realized she had lost the drift of the conversation.

He tipped his head. "*Goot* ideas."

She crossed her arms. "I'm sure YOU think they are *goot*."

He chuckled and turned away to trudge through a snowdrift by the fence where a lone tree stood. He broke off a thick dead branch, pruned a few of the smaller stubs with his pocketknife and brought it back to her. "See if this helps."

It made keeping her balance easier. "*Ja*, this is better."

She thought he would make another smart remark, but he simply walked on ahead. She struggled to keep up with him, but she wasn't about to admit it was too difficult. Little Grace was out here somewhere and could easily become lost in the unfamiliar landscape even if she had Meeka with her.

Every few minutes Owen stopped, cupped his hands around his mouth and called out Grace's and Meeka's names. Ruth noticed he spent longer than necessary listening for a reply. She suspected he was simply giving her time to catch up and rest before he started again.

They were nearing the creek when Ruth stepped in a hidden hole and went down face-first into the snow.

He was at her side in an instant. He knelt next to her, lifted her in his arms and began gently brushing the snow from her face. "Are you hurt? Is it your knee?"

She struggled to sit up by herself. He released her. She began removing clumps of snow from beneath her coat collar. "I'm fine. Embarrassed, cold and foolish, but otherwise fine."

"You don't appear foolish to me," he said softly.

She looked at him in surprise. "I don't?"

"I see someone determined and amazing" was his soft reply. There was no trace of humor in his eyes.

Speechless, she got to her feet, brushed off her coat, took the walking stick he handed her and set out again. She was still trying to come up with a reply when she heard a dog bark ahead of them. She looked over her shoulder. "That's Meeka."

Owen ran past her. When she caught up with him, he was kneeling beside a large snowdrift with Grace clasped to his chest. Meeka stood beside him. The dog greeted Ruth with a single deep woof and began digging in the snow.

Relief made Ruth weak, but she managed a stern tone. "Grace, you should never, ever run off like that. You have to tell someone where you are going. You frightened us both."

Grace clung to Owen's neck as she peeked at Ruth. "Are you mad at me?"

"We are both upset with you," he said. "This was very bad. What made you come all the way out here?"

"Meeka wanted to show me where *Mamm* is." Grace let go of Owen and began to dig in the snow beside the dog.

Owen snagged her around the waist and pulled her away. "Let me do it, Grace. You and Ruth go stand out of the way so Meeka doesn't cover you with snow."

"But I want to help. *Mamm*, can you hear me?"

Ruth knew exactly why Owen didn't want Grace to help. He was afraid of what she would see. She took Grace from him and moved away.

MEEKA KEPT DIGGING and barking. Owen knelt beside her and began digging into the drift with his hands. He desperately wanted to find Grace's mother, but not like this. There wasn't a vehicle under the drift. It wasn't tall enough to hide a car, although it was wide and long. Had she left her car and tried to follow Grace on foot only to fall victim to the cold and snow in Ruth's pasture less than a half mile from Ernest's house?

Meeka barked again. Owen saw the snow move at the bottom of the hole. He couldn't believe it. Was it possible she was still alive? *Dear God, let it be true.* He began digging frantically until his hands broke through into a hollow inside the snowdrift.

A sheep pushed her head out the hole he had made and bleated loudly. Owen sank back on his heels. Bitter disappointment killed the hope that had risen so quickly in his heart. The pain of it was as sharp as a knife. Why had the Lord given him such hope only to snatch it away? He struggled to draw a breath. Why? Where was Grace's mother? Why couldn't they find her?

Hopelessness yawned like a pit in front of him. All the years of searching for his sister should have prepared him for one more disappointment but it only made this worse. Why couldn't he help the ones he cared about?

Meeka pushed him aside and continued digging. He rolled out of her way until he was sitting in the snow with his back to the drift. The sheep broke free and climbed out. Two more quickly followed. Meeka greeted each of them with a sniff and a wagging tail. Then she lay down a few yards away, panting from her exertion.

"*GOOT* DOG." RUTH put Grace down as she watched Owen seem to fold in on himself. She had seen a fair amount of suffering in her life and she recognized it now.

Grace peered into the hole in the drift. "*Mamm*'s not here."

"*Nee*, darling, Meeka only wanted to show you she had found our lost sheep."

Grace walked over to Meeka and knelt beside her. She stroked the dog's massive head. "That's okay. I'm not mad."

Owen looked up at Ruth. "I saw the snow move and I thought I had found her. I thought by some miracle she was alive."

The despair in his words touched her deeply. Ruth sat down beside him. "I know you did."

"I wanted so badly to find her. I know what Grace is going through." His voice cracked. He wiped at his eyes.

Ruth laid a hand on his arm. "You couldn't find her, Owen, because she was never here."

"It was just a few stupid sheep." The bleakness of his tone worried her.

"I'm sure they are grateful to be free." One of them came back and nosed at his boot, looking for something to eat.

He gave a harsh laugh at the absurdity of the situation and looked at her. "You knew, didn't you?"

She nodded. "I suspected it was our missing ewes by Meeka's reaction. Like you, I was praying for a different outcome."

Grace threw her arms around Meeka and buried her face in her fur. Her little body shook with sobs. "I thought you found *Mamm*, but you didn't."

Owen motioned toward the child. "Take her and go back to the house, Ruth."

"What about you?" This wasn't the flippant fellow who liked to goad her. Owen was deeply affected. She suspected he had been keeping a lot of his emotions about Grace and her missing mother bottled up. This event had served to uncork them.

He drew up his knees and folded his arms across them. "I'll be along in a little while."

"Owen, it isn't your fault."

"Please go."

She wasn't going to trudge off and leave him mired in grief and stewing in an undeserved sense of failure. She stood and offered him her walking stick. "Freezing your backside out here won't solve anything. I thought you were here to help me? I can't herd the sheep back to the corral by myself. Grace isn't going to be any help."

"Isn't that what you have a dog for?" He didn't look up.

"Great Pyrenees are not herding dogs. Meeka is a guard dog. Get up and help me or be on your way. I don't need a slacker making more work for me."

He cast a sidelong glance up at her. "Has anyone ever told you that you are a mean woman?"

"Not to my face. However, I'm sure it has been mentioned a time or two behind my back. First you tell me I'm amazing, then you tell me I'm mean. Make up your mind." She turned away and began limping toward one of the ewes meandering in the wrong direction. Was she right in prodding Owen?

"I'm not sure there's much difference between the two where you are concerned," he called after her. He struggled to his feet. Grace was still sitting with Meeka, but she was watching him. He gestured for her to come on. She jumped up and ran to him. He wiped the tears from her cheeks. "Help us get these silly sheep and their amazing shepherdess back to the barn."

Ruth spun around to look at him. Did he really think she was amazing?

Grace took his hand. He sank to his heels to gaze into her eyes. "I'm sorry we didn't find your mother." His voice cracked, and Ruth's heart ached for him.

"It's okay." Grace seemed to realize he needed re-assurance. "*Gott* is watching over her. She'll come and get me soon. I'm kind of hungry. Can I have something to eat?"

"Once we get home."

"Home?" She looked at him with an eager light in her eyes. "Are we going home?"

"I meant as soon as we get back to Ruth's house."

"Oh." She sighed. "Okay. Can I have a peanut butter and jelly sandwich?"

"I think I can handle that." He stood and walked over to discourage one of the sheep from turning in the wrong direction. The ewes seemed to get the idea and began plodding toward the barn. Ruth came along behind them using her stick as an occasional prod. Together the three of them managed to get the sheep back with the rest of the flock in the corral. Meeka stayed beside Grace the entire way.

As they headed toward the house, Grace suddenly jogged ahead of them. "Don't forget to leave those muddy boots on the porch and wash up," Ruth said as Grace started up the steps.

"Okay."

When Grace went inside Owen turned to Ruth. "I want to apologize for falling apart back there."

"Did you? I didn't notice." Ruth looked him in the eyes. "I want to apologize for being mean."

The corner of his mouth lifted in half a grin. "Now you're being kind again. I appreciate the reminder about why I'm here. And just so you know, I don't think you're mean. I sincerely apologize."

"Apology accepted. I knew you were upset and for some reason you were blaming yourself for things you had no control over. All I did was give you a reason to get up. Sometimes that's all a person needs."

"Blaming myself seemed easier than accepting it is *Gott*'s will. It just seems so unfair."

"We're not promised a fair life on this earth. We endure what we must and cherish that which is *goot* knowing our stay here is but a stepping-stone to eternal happiness. Faith requires that we admit *Gott* is in control and we are not. And now I am preaching, which is not what I meant to do."

"I will take your words to heart. I will also try my best not to make more work for you."

"I believe that." And she did. Until now she had been afraid he would disappear when she needed him the most. Maybe this time would be different. She would give him the benefit of the doubt. "Until Ernest and Faron leave I don't want you to worry about helping me. I think Grace is the one who needs your support the most."

"I wish I could do more for her. I believe the sheriff is doing all he can, but I can't help thinking that somewhere Grace's extended family is wondering what happened to her and to her mother. Somebody must be missing them. Someone has to be looking for them but maybe they don't know where to look."

"This mystery will be the talk of our community for ages. Everyone will be mentioning the story in their letters to their relatives far and wide. Word will spread. We have to hope word spreads to the right people."

She climbed the steps of the porch as she considered how they could spread the word to other Amish communities faster. She stopped with her hand on the doorknob. If she wrote an article about Grace and the Amish newspaper *The Diary* published it, then Amish and *Englisch* people around the country would learn about this lost child and her missing mother in a week or two.

That was exactly what she would do. She'd send a copy to the Amish *Family Life Magazine*, too. She could get it in the morning mail.

Inside the house she found Grace already seated at the table. She held up both palms. "I washed my hands and face."

Ruth grinned at her. "I believe we are going to have peanut butter and jelly sandwiches for a snack. Do you want to help me make them?"

"Sure." Grace started to wiggle off her chair.

Owen held up one hand. "Wait. I said I could manage this. Grace and I will make sandwiches. Ruth, you may take a seat at the table, rest your knee and supervise."

Ruth chuckled, took a seat and folded her arms across her chest, waiting to see how well Owen managed an energetic three-year-old armed with strawberry jelly, peanut butter and a table knife. "Gladly."

"I'll get the bread." Grace hopped off her chair. The loaf was on the counter and within her reach. The bread hadn't been sliced. She frowned at it and then opened the drawer containing Ruth's cooking utensils. She pulled out an enormous knife meant for chopping vegetables, not slicing bread.

Ruth started to caution her, but Owen was quicker. "Oh, that's not the right kind of knife, Grace."

"It's not?" She held it out to him point-first.

"Lay it on the countertop. Be careful. It's very sharp."

She did as he asked and he quickly moved the knife out of her reach. He opened the drawer and withdrew a serrated bread knife. "This is the kind of knife that's best for slicing a loaf of bread." He glanced at Ruth from the corner of his eye. "It's also good for filleting fish and for trimming small tree branches if you don't have a saw."

Ruth couldn't let that go. "*Nee*, it's not. That might be true for someone else's bread knife but not for mine."

He gave her a stern look. "I thought you were supervising only."

"Correcting bad information is supervising."

He chuckled and turned back to Grace. "Now we need a cutting board. Why don't you bring a chair over here so you can reach the countertop?"

"Okay." She grabbed a chair, slid it across the floor and climbed onto it. "Now what?"

"Before we start preparing any meal we need to gather our ingredients. What do we need?"

"The peanut butter and the jelly, silly."

"Right." He withdrew them from the cabinet and set them on the counter. "Don't we need a plate to put them on?"

"Nope. I hold mine in my hand."

"Let's be polite and put Ruth's on a plate."

Grace looked over her shoulder at Ruth. "Do you want your sandwich on a plate?"

"*Ja*, a small plate will be fine."

Grace shrugged. "Okay, but it just makes more dishes to wash."

Ruth chuckled. "I'm supervising. I won't have to wash dishes. I believe Owen volunteered for that task."

"Washing dishes is for women to do," Grace declared.

"Not always," Owen said. "Men can wash dishes, too. A man without a wife washes his own dishes and cooks his own meals."

Grace cocked her head sideways as she looked at him. "Why doesn't he just get a wife?"

He leaned down and tweaked her nose. "Because no woman in her right mind would have him. Are we making lunch or not?"

"We are. Cut the bread for me."

He sliced the loaf and handed her the first two pieces. "Here you go. What's next?"

"I need a knife to spread the peanut butter."

He opened the flatware drawer and handed her a table knife. She stuck it into the jar of peanut butter and pulled out a large glob. She spread it quickly on the bread and then reached for the jelly. She tried to pull out an equally large dollop of jelly but most of it fell off the knife. She looked down at the floor. "Oops. I dropped some."

Ruth covered her mouth to stifle her laughter. The jelly had landed on the toe of Owen's shoe. He didn't seem to notice as he showed Grace how to take a smaller amount and spread it on the bread. When she put the two slices together, he held up both hands. "You did it."

Grace grinned. "I need more bread, please."

The sandwiches were messy, overfilled with jelly but still edible. Grace had jelly on her dress and a smear of peanut butter on her sleeve. Owen wound up with only one glob of jelly on his shoe; the rest of his clothes were unscathed.

He was surprisingly good with the child. Ruth had learned more about him by watching him instruct Grace with gentleness, humor, a healthy dose of self-restraint and praise. She was growing increasingly attached to Owen and to Grace even though she knew both would leave her life before long. How could she guard her heart when she wasn't aware until now that Owen was somehow working his way past the wall she had built to keep him out? She couldn't face another loss.

One answer was to spend less time with him. She rose from the table. "I'd better get going if I'm to join the search parties at Ernest's home."

"Grace and I can drive you over there." He started to get his coat.

"*Nee,*" she said quickly, stopping him in his tracks. "I'd rather go by myself," she finished lamely. She needed to spend less time with him, not more, but she couldn't tell him that.

A look of disappointment flashed across his face. "I understand."

Did he? Had he somehow guessed her feelings toward him had softened? She prayed that wasn't the
case. She wanted to be his friend. Nothing more. She
grabbed her coat and hurried out the door.

CHAPTER TEN

RUTH'S CHILDREN AND Ernest reported another full day of searching had turned up nothing new. Owen had no reason to remain at Ruth's for another night. He and Grace returned to Ernest's farm that evening. Grace sat on the worn sofa, looking forlorn and worried.

Ernest opened the oven door and peered inside. "We are not going to have to worry about cooking for a day or two. The women have left us a couple of casseroles. Do you prefer chicken or tuna?"

Owen sat down beside Grace. "Which do you like better? Chicken or tuna?"

"Tuna," she answered in a tiny voice.

"Tuna it is," Ernest said from the kitchen doorway. "I'll put the other one in the freezer."

Owen tipped his head to better see her face. "What's the matter, Grace?"

"Where is the safe place here?"

"The whole house is a safe place for you. You don't need to hide when you are here."

She looked around. "It's too big. A safe place is small."

He straightened her *kapp*. "We aren't going to

play that game while we are staying with *Onkel* Ernest. Okay?"

She nodded, but she didn't look convinced.

They ate their supper in silence. When they were finished, Owen fixed a cot for her in his bedroom. He stepped out while she changed into a nightgown that Ruth had given her. When Grace called him back, he saw the gown was too big for her.

He had her turn around while he took the pins out of her braids and let her hair down. He found a hairbrush and smoothed out the ripples, then he plaited her hair into a single braid and tied the end with an elastic band Ruth had supplied.

Ernest watch them from the doorway. "Where did you learn to braid hair?"

Owen smiled. "I used to work on a horse farm where the owner's daughter taught me how to braid manes and tails."

"Owen, can Meeka sleep in here?" Grace asked.

"I'm afraid not."

Ernest slipped his hands in his pockets. "Meeka has work to do. She must protect the sheep from the coyotes and other predators. Most of her important work is done at night."

"I'm sure she will be around in the morning because she knows you are here," Owen said to reassure the child.

"I miss my *mamm* an awful lot."

"I know you do. Let's talk to *Gott* about her." He knelt beside Grace as she said her prayers and asked the Lord to bring her *mamm* home soon.

When she was finished, she crawled into bed. "Do you think He heard me?"

"I know He did." Owen tucked her in. "I hope you find sweet dreams waiting for you on the dreamland tree."

He left the room and found his uncle seated in his chair by a small potbellied stove in the living room. While Ernest used propane for his appliances and heating, he claimed he enjoyed using the old-fashioned stove to keep the cold out of his bones without heating the whole house.

"What will you do with the child after I leave? We aren't likely to find her mother alive if we find her at all."

Owen sat on the arm of the sofa. "I know. Grace can stay with me. She seems to need me close at hand unless she is with Meeka. She will stay with Ruth for short periods of time, but I don't think she's ready to stay overnight without me."

"I wonder what it is that makes her so attached to you?"

"Maybe it was because Meeka brought her to me. She seems to be more accepting of you today."

"I knew she would come around. I'm a likable fellow. What will happen to her if we don't locate her mother?"

"I have no idea."

"How are you and Ruth getting along?"

Owen looked at his uncle sharply. The question seemed casual, but his uncle's tone betrayed more than a passing interest.

"Like cats and dogs."

Ernest frowned. "Still? I thought you would be over that by now."

"Why are you giving it any thought at all?"

His uncle shrugged but there was a hint of rising color in his cheeks. "No reason, really. I like you. I like Ruth. I thought you could get along. Why don't you try being nice to her?"

"I'm always nice to Ruth and her family."

"I know that but sometimes women like to be singled out."

"Singled out, how?" Owen had an idea where the conversation was heading but he was going to make his uncle spell it out.

"You know what I mean. Do something special for her or take her to eat at that restaurant over on the highway."

Owen arched one eyebrow. "You want me to ask Ruth out on a date?"

Ernest cleared his throat and shifted in his chair. "I wasn't suggesting that, but it's a good idea."

"That is a fib as big as any of your fish stories. Having me ask Ruth out is exactly what you were suggesting."

"What's so wrong with that? You are single. She's a widow whose children will be leaving home soon."

"Ruth wouldn't go out with me if I was the last man on earth. And I don't blame her. If you think for a minute that I could replace Nathan, you are *narrisch*."

"Is it crazy to think that two people who liked

each other years ago could like each other again? And you both liked each other."

"It's nutty to think that an old bachelor like you is trying to play matchmaker."

Ernest dismissed him with a wave of his hand. "I might be old, but I still believe in love, especially when two people deserve each other."

"If you want to play matchmaker for Ruth you have my blessing, but I'm not going to play the suitor."

Ernest leaned back in his chair. "You wouldn't mind if Ruth found someone new?"

Owen hesitated a moment too long. "Of course not."

"Ha! That's exactly what I thought. Who is telling a fib now?"

Owen ignored his uncle's taunt. He didn't have an answer because he didn't know how he really felt. On one hand, he should be glad if Ruth found happiness with someone else. On the other hand, the idea didn't sit well at all. He tried to imagine her being kissed by some other man and it made him ill. What kind of friend was he turning out to be?

THE SEARCH RESUMED the next day. The sheriff and law enforcement officers met with the volunteers gathered at Ernest's farm to continue sweeping areas that had been inaccessible due to the snow. A few of the young Amish men and women came on horseback. Their *Englisch* counterparts came in four-wheel drive pickups and off-road ATVs. The rapidly warming temperature was turning the pristine white landscape back to its drab winter brown, dotted with shrinking dirty snowdrifts, puddles and running water that filled the gullies and ditches.

Owen, Meeka and a subdued Grace walked to Ruth's house as soon as the volunteers began arriving. It was only a quarter of a mile across the pasture while it was closer to a half mile if they stuck to the roads. Owen wondered if Grace was getting sick. He'd never seen her so sullen. "Don't you feel good, *liebchen*?"

"*Nee*, I don't."

"What troubles you?"

"I don't like it here anymore. Take me home. I want my *mamm*."

"Many people are looking for her. They will find her. And then I'll take you home."

"I don't think they are looking very hard."

"I can go help them look if you will stay with Ruth."

"*Nee*, don't leave me." She wrapped her arms around his leg and wouldn't let go until he promised he would stay at Ruth's farm.

Nothing he nor Ruth said could convince her that he would be back. She was tearful and angry throughout the morning, refusing to help with housework, play with any of the games or toys Ruth provided. At one point she ran to her "safe place" and refused to come out.

By midmorning Owen was ready to tear his hair out. He paced back and forth in the kitchen. "What has come over her? She's so difficult today. She's like a different child. Is it something I've done?"

"I'm surprised we haven't seen this earlier," Ruth said as she prepared a beef roast for supper. They were expecting the King family to join them.

He stopped his pacing. "You expected her to act like this?"

"Children often act out when they are grieving. She's frightened. She can't make sense of what's going on. She doesn't understand why her mother hasn't come back. She isn't old enough to have the faith she needs to face such difficulties the way you and I do."

"I guess you're right. She's such a sweet kid. I never expected she could act differently."

"There have been so many changes for her in the past week that it must all seem terribly confusing. Does she live here now? Does she live with you and Ernest? Children need security. That's part of the reason she clings to you. You are her security."

"You will notice she is not clinging to me at the moment. She's hiding in her safe place. I could be out helping with the search instead of babysitting her."

"Now who is being difficult?" she asked with a tiny smile.

"You're right. Is there anything I can do to help you since I'm confined to the farm? The outside chores are done."

She thought for a moment. "You could wash the buggy so it will be clean for Sunday service and take my letters to the mailbox. I've written an article about Grace for *The Diary* and for *Family Life Magazine*."

"I'll get right on it. If Grace comes looking for me, send her outside and I'll put her to work. Maybe that will help her mood."

Owen came in for lunch and found Grace sitting at the kitchen table. Her eyes were red from crying but she seemed calmer. She ate a little but spent more time pushing the food around on her plate. It wasn't until she heard Meeka barking outside that she perked up.

"Can I go play with Meeka?" she asked hopefully.

Ruth pointed to Grace's plate. "Finish your lunch and then you can."

That was all it took for the child to gobble down the rest of her meal and slide out of her chair.

Owen smiled at Ruth. "It's a good thing Meeka can cheer her up."

"The dog has been amazing with her. It breaks my heart to see her so unhappy sometimes."

"It does mine, too. I know how much she misses her mother. I wish I could do more for her."

Ruth shared a warm knowing look with him. Owen sensed she understood what he was going through.

The searchers returned in the late afternoon. Owen was waiting on the porch. He could tell by their faces that nothing had been found. He was surprised to see the sheriff pull in behind them and get out of his car. It was a subdued group that gathered in the living room. Grace was still playing outside in the backyard with Meeka. Owen stood by the window to keep an eye on her.

"The only place left to search is the bottom of the lake," Faron said. "We have covered every inch of the roads within five miles of this place. The fields and pastures have been searched and still no sign of a car."

"Or of the woman driving it," Ella added.

Sheriff McIntyre turned his hat in his hand without making eye contact with anyone. "It's been five days. I can't expend more resources on a large-scale search." He looked up and met Owen's gaze. "I'm officially calling the search off."

CHAPTER ELEVEN

OWEN DIDN'T LIKE the idea of giving up. "She could still be alive. There are some areas covered with large snowdrifts."

"That's true," Ernest said.

The sheriff sighed deeply. "We can always hope, but according to Grace she didn't have any supplies with her. No extra blankets for warmth and the car wasn't running, so no heater. After five days the odds of survival in weather like we've had goes down quickly. Volunteers can continue searching, but my men and I won't be directly involved the way we have been. That said, I know some of us will be out looking on our own time. It's possible her vehicle will be uncovered when the last of the snow melts. Then the mystery will be solved, but that won't help Grace unless her Amish mother has some kind of identification on her, or we are able to trace the car to the owner. We need to locate Grace's relatives, otherwise she is technically an abandoned child."

"She's not abandoned," Ruth said. "She is being cared for."

Owen felt a chill along the back of his neck. "You're not going to take her away from us, are you?"

"The welfare of the child comes first. The law is clear on that. However, I've spoken to our child protection people and they agree that an Amish child should be with an Amish family. By law the Child Protective Services have a responsibility to see that she is being taken care of properly."

"What does that mean?" Ruth asked.

"It means they will have to monitor her situation. They will make an initial visit to assess her health and well-being and they will make periodic follow-up visits until Grace can be placed in a permanent situation. Hopefully, that will be with her family."

"If we don't know her last name, how are we going to find her family?" Ella asked.

Ruth cleared her throat. "I have done something I hope will help."

The sheriff pinned his gaze on her. "What?"

"I wrote an article about finding Grace and sent it to the Amish newspaper *The Diary* and to our *Family Life Magazine* in the hopes that someone will come forward and identify her."

The sheriff gave a slight shake of his head. "Don't all the Amish in this area already know about her?"

"*The Diary* and *Family Life* are national publications."

He looked taken aback. "I see. I kinda wish you hadn't done that without checking with me first."

Ruth looked surprised. "Why?"

"Because we may find ourselves swamped with people wanting to claim her. I've seen it before. News of an abandoned child brings out the people desperate to have a child or who have deluded themselves into believing the child is theirs."

Ruth looked at Owen. "I'm sorry. I thought I was doing the right thing."

"You did what you thought was best." Ruth often did what she thought was best without consulting others. Hopefully this time it would turn out to be the right thing.

"THE KINGS ARE HERE."

This time it was Ella standing and holding open the front door as she bubbled over with excitement. Ruth didn't have the heart to scold her daughter. Besides, the fresh air drove some of the excess heat out of the kitchen. Ruth pulled her pot roast from the oven and set it on top of the stove. She slipped her pan of biscuits in and dusted her hands on her apron. Ella dashed out to greet her friend Sarah as soon as their tractor stopped. Ruth walked to the door to welcome her guests.

The two young women embraced and immediately began sniffling. Sarah wiped her eyes with her fingers. "I can't believe you're really leaving us, Ella. What will I do without you?"

"We will write each other every week."

"But you were the best volleyball player on our team. Those boys are sure to beat us now."

Ella laughed. "They will, won't they? I pray you will find a husband of your own to make you as happy as I am."

"Not in this Amish community I won't. There

isn't anyone here I would remotely consider marrying."

"Then you shall come and stay in Jamesport with Zack and me. We will find you some suitable fellows to consider."

Sarah glanced to where Joshua King was helping Laura Beth and baby Caleb out of the trailer hitched to the back of his tractor. Sarah leaned toward Ella. "Laura Beth thinks the unsuitable ones are the most interesting."

"I heard that," Joshua said.

His wife patted his cheek. "My little sister is right about that."

Joshua shook his head. "One unsuitable husband in the family is enough."

"You are quite suitable now." Laura Beth winked at him.

Owen came out of the house with Grace standing shyly at his side. Although he had met the family before, Grace hadn't. Ruth introduced her to Laura Beth and Caleb. Grace stood on tiptoe to get a better view of the baby in her arms. Caleb grinned and cooed with happiness at the sight of her.

Grace looked at Owen. "I think he likes me."

"I'm sure he does," Laura Beth said. "Would you keep an eye on him while I help Ruth in the kitchen?"

Her eyes grew wide. "Sure."

Grace followed Laura Beth and Sarah into the house. Ruth smiled at Owen. "We didn't even have to tell her that Laura Beth and Caleb are safe."

"Maybe she's getting over the fear of meeting new people. I hope so."

She glanced at Joshua opening the tailgate on his trailer. He had found acceptance and love in the community when he expected rejection. Before that he had been a wanderer like Owen. Would Owen ever find a place to put down roots and start a family the way Joshua had? Ruth hoped that he would. He deserved to find happiness. It surprised her how much she wanted that for him. If only he could settle down the way Joshua had. But then Joshua had Caleb and Laura Beth to hold him in Cedar Grove. What would it take to hold Owen? A wife? A family?

She realized where her thoughts were taking her and pushed them aside. "I'd better get back to the kitchen before I burn the biscuits."

OWEN WENT DOWN the steps to help as Joshua lifted two heavy baskets out of the trailer.

"*Danki*. My wife brought enough food to feed ten people. I told her Ruth wouldn't let us go away hungry, but she said it was impolite not to bring enough for everyone."

The women were all busy in the kitchen chatting and laughing. Ernest was in the midst of them trying to sample the food they were dishing up. A blue-and-white quilt had been laid on the floor in the corner. Grace lay on her stomach face-to-face with Caleb, who was laughing at the expressions and sounds she was making.

"Where do you want these?" Joshua held out his basket.

"On the table will be fine," Ruth said.

Owen put the basket he carried on the table, too. "Can we do anything to help?"

Sarah and Laura Beth turned startled eyes in his direction. "In the kitchen?" Sarah asked.

"Whatever you need." Owen rubbed his hands together, indicating he was ready to get to work.

"Get Ernest out of our way," Ruth said, giving the older man a gentle push toward the door.

"That gravy needs more salt," he said as Owen took his arm.

"Come along, *Onkel* Ernest, the women can manage without you."

"Did I ever tell you about the time I held a fish fry and did all the cooking, including making cupcakes by myself?"

"Ja," all the women said in unison.

Ernest looked momentarily deflated but quickly brightened. "But did I tell you about the time I made supper for the bishop and accidentally filled the sugar bowl with salt?"

"We have all heard that story a dozen times," Owen said as he steered his uncle out of the room.

"Well, it's a good story." Ernest walked ahead of them into the living room.

Faron was setting up the checkerboard. "How about a game, *Onkel* Ernest?"

"I'd love to. Did I ever tell you about the time

I won fifty checkers games in a row taking on all comers?"

Owen and Faron looked at each other and laughed. "You did tell us that story and how it was Granny Weaver who bested you in game fifty-one," Faron said.

"She's as sharp as a tack. Don't let her age fool you. She's a cutthroat checkers player. Speaking of cutthroats, did I tell you about the time I went fly-fishing for cutthroat trout out in Colorado?"

Faron's brow wrinkled. "I don't think I've heard that one."

Grinning, Ernest sat down across from Faron and began his story. Joshua looked at Owen. "I've heard this one. I'd like a chance to see the Icelandic sheep Ruth has been talking about."

"Sure, come on." Owen nodded toward the back door.

Ernest looked over his shoulder. A wide grin split his face. "If you want to hear a good fishing story, Owen, ask Joshua about the time he used his car for bait."

"I know I haven't heard that one," Owen said as he and Joshua walked out. The sheepish expression on Joshua's face told Owen it was quite a tale.

"Ernest is talking about the night I arrived in this community. I wasn't Amish back then. I took a wrong turn during a thunderstorm and accidentally drove into some floodwaters below Laura Beth's place. My car was swept away but not before Laura Beth managed to save me and my son. I had a lot of important things in the car. Money, cell phone, my release papers from jail, my tools, all things I was going to need at my new job once I had dropped Caleb off with his grandparents. It was my estranged wife's last wish before she died. She wanted Caleb to be raised by her Amish parents. I was ex-Amish. I didn't like the idea, but I was a single father. I worked as an oil rig mechanic in some out-of-the-way places. I couldn't raise the kid."

Owen opened the gate to the pasture and let Joshua walk through before closing it behind them. "I can see your dilemma."

"I was stranded at Laura Beth's place for several days. She fell head over heels in love with my son before I fell for her. Talk about a mismatched couple. She was a childless widow planning to move to Ohio to find a new husband. I was a drifter looking to stay out of jail and land a new job. I met Ernest while I was searching for my car downstream. He was fishing. He has been telling endless tall tales about seeing big fish driving my car around the lake ever since."

"It appears things worked out for you and Laura Beth."

He grinned. "It did. I give all the credit to *Gott*. It took me a while to see what I really wanted and that was to come back to the Amish. From there marrying Laura Beth was easy and the best thing I ever did. I hear you are something of a drifter."

"I've seen a lot of the country. My sister and I were separated after our parents and the rest of our brothers and sister died in a buggy-and-car crash. I was thirteen, she was three. As soon as I was able, I went looking for her. The maiden aunt who took her in was afraid I would take her away, so she moved around a lot. I followed one lead after another for years."

"Did you ever find her?"

"I did. A few months ago. She didn't remember me or our family."

"That must've been tough."

"It was." Mindful of his sister's letter, Owen didn't share more information about her. He pointed ahead of them. "There's one of Ruth's Icelandic sheep."

Joshua stopped and propped his hands on his hips. "Are you kidding me? That walking brown mop is a registered sheep breed? That must be a ram with the horns."

"Nope. Even the females have horns. There is a polled or hornless type, but Ruth prefers the ones with horns. She says it makes them easier to control. They are remarkably tame. She can take one by the horn and lead it anywhere."

"Does that double coat make it harder to shear them?"

"I'm gonna find out any day now. I'll let you know. Care to join us?"

"I'll leave the sheep wrestling to those who are so inclined. We grow lavender. Smells a lot better and doesn't put up a fight when you cut off the blooms."

Owen laughed. "I'm not sure I could interest Ruth

in doing something easier than raising sheep. She's hardheaded and she likes to do things her way."

"It must be something in the water out here. My wife and her sister can be very stubborn women."

"Supper is ready!" Laura Beth yelled from the back door.

Joshua's soft smile as he waved to let her know they had heard her told Owen how much he loved his wife. "She might be set in her ways but she's a really *goot* cook."

The men started back toward the house. "If you get tired of roaming, Owen, you could do worse than settling here. The people and the place grow on you quickly if you give them half a chance."

Owen didn't reply. He was already feeling the tug of a connection, but it was Ruth making him feel that way. When Faron left, would she continue to blame him, or would she accept his presence for a few weeks without dredging up hard feelings from the past? They had decided they could be friends, but he was starting to worry that friendship wouldn't be enough for him.

AFTER A DELICIOUS MEAL, the men went into the living room to continue visiting while the women stayed to clean up in the kitchen. Ruth was washing the dishes while Laura Beth rinsed them and handed them to Ella and Sarah to dry and put away. Ruth didn't realize she had been ignoring the conversation around her until Laura Beth nudged her with her hip. "What's your opinion?"

Ruth felt the heat rising in her cheeks. "I'm sorry. I wasn't listening."

"We were talking about Grace's mother," Sarah said, putting a plate into the cabinet beside her.

Ruth looked around, but Grace was out of sight. Ruth hoped she was out of earshot, too. "I think she raised an adorable child, but something wasn't right in their house."

Laura Beth accepted a sudsy plate from Ruth. "Why do you think that?"

"Because Grace has been taught to hide whenever her mother tells her to go to a safe place. Here, the safe place is under the sink in the bathroom."

"Why would anyone teach a child to do that?" Sarah asked.

Ruth shrugged. "We don't know."

Sarah passed the dried dish to Ella. "I don't want to believe that she drove off and left her child, but I think it is possible, otherwise we would have found the car by now."

"Faron says the only place left to search is the bottom of the lake," Ella added.

Laura Beth stopped rinsing the glasses. "What will happen if her family is never located?"

"I assume that the bishop will have her placed for adoption."

"Will you take her?" Laura Beth asked.

Ruth stared at the suds in the sink. She had given a lot of thought to the question and she still didn't know the answer. "I'm very fond of the child, but I'm not sure what the right thing is for her. My children are grown. Perhaps a younger family would be better."

Laura Beth laid a hand on Ruth's arm. "Just so you know, Joshua and I would be thrilled to take her."

Ruth smiled at her. "You would make wonderful parents for Grace, but the decision isn't going to be mine to make."

Parting with the child would be hard for her. She suspected it was going to be much harder for Owen.

RUTH TRIED TO prepare herself, but she wasn't ready to say goodbye to her children when Ernest arrived on his tractor early the next morning. She had given up trying to talk Faron out of going. Was Owen right? If she forbade Faron to leave would he take off on his own? She couldn't take that chance. She didn't like it, but he would be better off traveling with some of his family to look out for him. Knowing that didn't stop the tears that welled up in her eyes. She blinked rapidly to keep them from sliding down her cheeks.

Ernest's mother occupied one of the several chairs he had placed in his homemade trailer. Like many of the Amish in the community, Ernest had taken the bed from an old pickup and fashioned it into the trailer to be pulled behind his tractor. Unlike many other people, Ernest had painted his trailer to match his red tractor. Some people considered it too fancy, but Ernest claimed it would soon be scuffed enough to match the unpainted and rusty ones on the road so the bishop didn't object.

Ernest got down from the tractor and walked to Ruth's side. "Cheer up. You are going to be just fine until Faron and I come back. Owen will take good care of you and the farms."

Zack and Owen walked past him and put down the tailgate at the back of the trailer. Faron climbed up over the wheel and took the suitcases Owen passed to him. Faron was the only one with a big smile on his face. Grace watched everything from the porch with Meeka sitting beside her.

Ruth drew Ella into a hug. "Write as soon as you can. Keep a close eye on your brother. Don't let him get into trouble. Lock him in his room if you have to."

"I'm not going to get into trouble," Faron replied in a long-suffering tone.

Ruth sent him a stern look. "That's what you said the first time your father let you drive the buggy. Who took the corner too fast and upset the buggy in the ditch?"

Faron shook his head and glanced at Ernest. "She's never going to let me forget that. Thanks for squealing on me that day."

Ernest laughed and slapped his knee. "Aw, the look on your face was too funny not to share. You were standing in the road pulling your hat down over your head with both hands saying, 'My *daed*'s going to kill me. My *daed*'s going to kill me.' And that was before you even saw me in the field coming to help you. I never did figure out if you were praying out loud or just talking to the horse."

Ernest's mother, Lavinia, grinned. "I remember that day. That was a good story, *sohn*. You had us all laughing the way you told it. Owen, come and give your *grossmammi* a hug. You had better visit me before you leave again."

He hopped in the back, gave her a hug and a kiss on the cheek. "I promise to come over when you've recovered from this trip."

"At my age you don't recover from things, you just accept that you can't do what you did before."

Faron glared at his great-uncle. "I don't mind that you found the situation funny, but you could have helped me get the buggy upright without telling my folks and everyone else what happened. I could have fixed the scratches on the side and no one would have been the wiser."

"Faron." Ruth stared at her son in disbelief.

Faron's gaze snapped to his mother's face. "I didn't mean I intended to deceive you. I was going to tell you and *Daed* what happened. It's just, well, I wanted to fix what I had done before telling you," he finished in a rush.

Ernest started laughing again. "See if you can get your other foot in your mouth. You surely do have a knack for it."

Ruth took Ella by both shoulders. "As I was saying, keep a very good eye on your brother and try to keep him out of trouble."

Faron flopped down on one of the chairs. "Everyone treats me like I'm a little kid. No one wants to admit I'm an adult."

Owen helped Ella into the trailer. She patted the top of her brother's black hat. "It would help if you stopped talking sooner."

He ducked his head away from her. "What do you know? You're a girl. A fellow wants a chance to fix his own mistakes before everyone learns about them. You understand, don't you, Zack?"

"I understand that my wife is right. My wife is almost always right. If she isn't, I keep my mouth shut. You should do the same."

Owen closed the tailgate and climbed up to stand behind Ernest. He would bring the tractor and trailer back to the farm after the family boarded the bus in town. Ernest climbed up to the tractor seat. "This is going to be a fun trip. Ruth, I wish you were going with us."

She wouldn't admit it aloud, but she was sorry to miss the adventure, too. Not because she wanted to travel but because she had never been separated from her children for so long. "Take good care of them, Ernest. *Gott* go with you."

He raised his hat in a brief salute and drove out of the yard and down the lane. Ruth climbed the steps to the porch and stood with her hand resting on Grace's shoulder until the tractor turned onto the highway and was soon out of sight.

Ruth's throat grew tight and tears blurred her vision. Grace leaned against Ruth's side. "Don't be sad. They'll come back. Owen said so."

Ruth sniffled and wiped her eyes. "I know they'll be back, but I miss them already."

Grace pressed against Ruth's skirt. "Me, too."

Ruth drew comfort from the child's touch. "Let's go make a pie for supper. That will cheer us up."

Grace tipped her head to the side as she gazed at Ruth. "Will it?"

Ruth nodded vigorously. "Baking always makes me feel better. When I make it, *and* when I eat it. What kind of pie shall we make?"

"I like all kinds of pie."

"Then I think I will make an apple pie if you can peel the apples for me."

"I don't think I know how to peel an apple."

"It's easy. I will put the apples on the peeler for you and all you have to do is turn the crank." Ruth glanced over her shoulder as the tractor reached the highway. Zack and Ella would be back to visit at Christmas. Ernest and Faron would be back in a month. Owen would be back in an hour. Then he would spend weeks working the farm with her. The two of them alone except for Grace, and there was no telling how long the child would remain with them.

Could she count on him? Ruth wanted to believe she could, but trust was something easily broken and hard to repair. Was he willing to put in the effort it took to show he had changed, or would he disappoint her once again?

She desperately wanted to believe he would stay, because she was beginning to like Owen Mast more than she should.

CHAPTER TWELVE

Owen dropped the family off at the bus station and after a short goodbye he drove back to Ruth's as quickly as he could. Grace hadn't objected to his leaving, but he wasn't sure how long that frame of mind would last. He didn't want Ruth to deal with a frantic child on top of sending her own children off. Not that she couldn't handle it, but he couldn't relax until he knew they were both okay.

To his relief Ruth and Grace were both in the kitchen eating fresh apple pie with a scoop of ice cream on top. The whole house smelled like baked apples and cinnamon. His mouth started to water the moment he came through the door.

Grace caught sight of him. "Look, Owen, we made pie."

Ruth glanced at him but quickly looked away. "Would you like some?"

Did she still blame him for Faron's departure? It was more likely she was sad and trying to hide it. "I thought you would never ask. Don't get up. I'll get my own."

He got a dish out of the cupboard and cut a large wedge from the pie. It was still warm. He opened the freezer compartment and brought out the ice cream. He added a scoop to his slice. "Does anyone want more ice cream before I put it back?"

"Me. I do." Grace held out her bowl.

Owen looked to Ruth for permission before giving the child more.

She nodded her consent. He gave Grace another half scoop and sat down at the table to eat his. The first bite was every bit as delicious as the aroma had been. "*Goot* pie," he muttered around his mouthful.

Grace tipped her head. "*Danki*. Ruth helped me."

He glanced at Ruth, but she still wouldn't meet his gaze. "It's always best to give credit where credit is due," he said in a firm tone.

Grace's mouth turned down in a pout. "Maybe I helped Ruth some."

He smiled and patted her head. "That's what I like. An honest answer."

It bothered him that Ruth didn't smile and wouldn't look his way. Was she uncomfortable having him in the house now that her children were gone? The last thing he wanted to do was cause her discomfort.

"Hurry up and finish, Grace. We need to get back to the house and do our chores."

"Okay." She dug into her treat with renewed relish.

Ruth looked up with a small frown etched into her forehead. "Aren't you going to stay for supper?"

"We have plenty to eat at *Onkel*'s farm. We don't want to be any trouble to you."

"I see." She looked away again.

Had he given her the wrong answer? Should he tell her he would love to stay, or would that be too forward now that he had already turned down her invitation? He decided on a different course of action. He leaned back in his chair. "I know it will probably seem lonely without Faron, Ella and Zack here. If you would like Grace to stay with you tonight, I understand."

Ruth looked up with a small smile. "It does seem lonely without them. That must seem silly because they were gone much of the time recently. If Grace wants to stay with me she's more than welcome, and *danki*."

"What do you say, Grace? Do you want to spend the night with Ruth?"

"Sure."

"Even though I won't be staying with you?"

Grace stopped eating and scowled at him. "Why won't you stay?"

"Because it wouldn't be proper, and I'm not going to discuss that any further. Will you stay here without me?"

"Okay. I like this house better." She went back to eating her pie.

Owen glanced at Ruth. She looked every bit as shocked as he was. This was the child who, four days ago, had screamed whenever he stepped out of her sight?

"*Goot*. I reckon I'll see you both in the morning, then."

"Stay and finish your pie," Ruth said.

"I wasn't going to leave it on my plate. Who knows when I'll get a piece of hot apple pie again?"

Grace grinned at him. "Silly. You can always ask Ruth to make you another one."

He wasn't going to be around to ask her anything after Ernest came back. The thought left him feeling hollow. It was difficult to keep his smile in place. "I'll remember that."

He finished his pie, pushed back from the table and went out into the cold evening.

He drove the tractor to Ernest's farm and finished the evening chores, making sure the cattle and horses had plenty of feed and fresh water. The daytime temperatures had been staying above freezing, but once the sun started going down, the temperature dropped rapidly into the twenties. Because of that, the ice never fully melted off the large stock tanks. Keeping them open was a twice-a-day job.

When he was finished, he stood by the barn door, looking out over the countryside. The drab brown-and-gray landscape was only broken where the winter wheat fields hung on to their green color and where the deep snow hadn't yet melted away.

Grace's mother was out there somewhere. The muddy fields near the farmhouse were crisscrossed with the footprints of searchers and the tracks of four-wheelers. He didn't know where to look that someone hadn't already explored ahead of him.

It was a sad reminder of all his fruitless searches for Rebecca. The most painful part had been learning she didn't remember him when he'd finally found her. At least she was willing to see him again.

If they couldn't locate Grace's mother, Grace would lose her memory of the woman who gave birth to her. Maybe that was a good thing. Maybe it was better not to remember the things she had lost.

The loss of his parents, his brothers and his older sister stayed with him every day. He knew they were happy with God in heaven, though he still didn't understand why he had been left behind.

Meeka got up off the porch and came to his side. He patted her large white head. "I wish you could speak and tell me where you found her."

Meeka yawned and trotted off toward the sheep pasture. Her job was to protect the sheep, not to answer foolish humans. He went into the house and came out with a flashlight. It would be dark soon, but this was the first chance he'd had to look for Grace's mother. He wasn't going to waste it.

Hours later, muddy and exhausted from climbing down into gullies, probing snowdrifts and hiking along the edge of the lake, Owen returned home, discouraged and depressed. Like the searchers before him, he hadn't found a single trace of Grace's mother or her car.

THE FOLLOWING MORNING Owen hurried through his chores and drove the tractor to Ruth's place, eager to see how she had fared with Grace. Or maybe he was just eager to see Ruth. She and Grace were already out feeding the chickens and ducks. Grace came running up to him. "I gathered the eggs already. Have you seen my mother?"

He shook his head. "I didn't see her."

Grace's expression grew sad. He wanted to cheer her up. "I'm happy you are helping Ruth with the chores. How many eggs did you find?"

"Lots and lots. One hen tried to peck my hand when I took the egg out from under her."

"That happens to me all the time. I don't think chickens like me."

Ruth came over to stand behind Grace. "I had no idea that chickens were so perceptive."

He grinned. "So it's gonna be like that, is it? Tit for tat? Insult for insult?"

She tried to look prim but couldn't carry it off. "You left yourself wide-open, admit it."

"Maybe I did. I'll be more careful in the future. How did the night go?"

She smiled at Grace. "Not too bad. One squawk out of our chick at three this morning."

Grace looked up at her. "What chick?"

"You."

"I'm not a chick. I'm a girl."

Owen nodded. "That's right. She's a girl. I'm sorry for your interrupted sleep."

"It's okay. I knew the words to your song, so I stood in for you until she went back to sleep. Would you like some coffee? Have you had breakfast?"

"*Ja*, coffee sounds *goot* and I haven't eaten. I was hoping for another piece of pie."

"Pie for breakfast?" Grace shook her head. "That's just silly."

"What? It's fruit and pastry."

"Breakfast is oatmeal and eggs," Ruth said to end the discussion.

He nodded. "That will work, too."

"When do you plan to shear your sheep?" Owen remained at the table when the meal was finished, sipping on a cup of black coffee.

Ruth sat across from Owen, looking prettier than she should have, considering the night she'd had. She leaned back in her chair and met his gaze. "We need to start Monday. The ewes should begin lambing in two weeks."

"That's a tight schedule."

"I had hoped to get the shearing done before Ernest left, but something slowed us down."

He knew she was referring to the search. Everyone who had come to help had left their own work undone in the hopes of locating the woman. "Let's pray the weather cooperates from now on out. The newspaper said we can expect warming temperatures and sunshine for the next two weeks."

"The rain won't stop our lambs from being born."

"Being cold and wet might affect the number of your lambs that survive."

"True. We'll have to deal with that when the time comes. Ernest said you had experience on sheep farms."

"I know how to use a pair of shears if that's what you're asking."

She looked relieved. "That's exactly what I'm asking. With eighty head to be shorn I was afraid I might have to hire someone this year."

"Are you thinking that you and I can do this ourselves?" It seemed mighty optimistic to him.

"I can handle my share of the work. My knee barely hurts anymore."

"Maybe, but I would feel better with one more fellow to give us a hand."

"If it looks like we can't manage I'll hire someone."

He took another sip from his mug. "Are your catch pens ready or do I need to check them?"

"They should be in good shape. Faron was to see to it before he left, but it wouldn't hurt to make sure all the holes are plugged. You know how sheep are. If one gets out all the rest will try. There are additional fencing panels stored in Faron's workshop."

"I'll take care of it and set up the shearing station. Do you have electric clippers?"

"We use hand shears. It leaves a longer coat on them than electric clippers. With our unpredictable weather it's better that they don't get shorn too short."

"I know the sheep need to spend at least a night inside the barn to make sure the wool is dry and won't rot in storage. What about your Icelandic sheep? Do they need to be dry longer?"

"Their long outer coat sheds water very well. If the weather stays dry, we won't have any trouble with them. We should move them all into the closest pen today."

He rose to his feet. "Okay. Thanks for breakfast. Grace, do you want to help me in the barn or help Ruth here in the house?"

"I want to go with you. Do I have to stay here tonight?"

"*Nee*, you can come home with me. I thought you wanted to stay with Ruth."

"I got scared without you."

Ruth smiled at her. "You can stay with me anytime you like. I will finish my housework and then we can both help Owen with the sheep. How does that sound?"

"*Goot*," Grace replied with a grin.

For the rest of the day Owen and Ruth worked to herd most of the sheep in from the large pasture to the smaller one. He knew they could collect any strays in a day or two. Together they worked to make the catch pen secure. Faron had been lax in his efforts to make it escape-proof. By the end of the day they were satisfied with their results. After a light supper Owen rose and said, "We should be getting home."

Ruth laid her dish by the sink. "I'll walk with you part of the way. It's a nice night out and I'm not feeling sleepy."

"Don't expect me to object. I enjoy your company." He had no objections, but he was surprised, to say the least. He thought he detected a blush in her cheeks, but he could have been mistaken. The lamplight's soft glow was flattering to her complexion.

He tore his gaze away. He needed to practice ignoring such thoughts because she had accepted him as a friend. Noticing the attractive curve of her cheeks, her slender neck and the fullness of her lips were not observations that a friend would make.

"You're staring at me. Do I have something on my face?" She brushed her mouth and chin.

He tightened his lips. "You did, but you got it." He turned away, hoping she didn't ask for more of an explanation. "Grace, are you ready to go back to our place?"

"I guess so."

"Let's clear the table for Ruth so she doesn't have to come back to a mess after our walk." He carried his dish and tableware to the sink and began rinsing them.

"Okay." Grace got down and began carrying plates and glasses to the counter beside the sink.

"*Danki*, both of you," Ruth said. "I miss having my daughter help me with my chores. We were always laughing about something."

"I'll make you laugh." Grace stuck out her tongue and pulled her cheeks down away from her eyes, making an ugly face. Then she began to spin in a circle. She quickly made herself dizzy and staggered to the side. Both Owen and Ruth reached for her. It was Ruth who caught her before she fell.

Owen made eye contact with Ruth and rolled his eyes. "Hilarious."

Ruth giggled. "It was pretty funny."

Grace grinned at her success. Owen took her hand and led her to the entryway, where he helped her put on her coat. He fastened it and then slipped on his own jacket. The worst of winter seemed to be over, but there was still a chill in the evenings.

Ruth wrapped a dark maroon shawl over her shoulders. Owen held open the door and ushered his ladies outside.

A three-quarter moon was just rising. It gave plenty of light to see by once Owen's eyes adjusted. The white sheep stood out sharply against the grass that looked dark gray in the moonlight. There was only a slight breeze and it was warmer than he had expected. "Spring is definitely on its way," he said as he buttoned his jacket.

"But it's not here yet. I'm waiting for the smell of it. Then it will be here."

He knew exactly what she meant. The loamy scent of warming earth mixed with the freshest new growing grass and early flowers was what he was looking for, too.

They began walking down Ruth's lane with Grace between them. They hadn't gone far when she reached up and took each of their hands. "Swing me."

Owen groaned. "My bones are too old and too tired to swing a big girl like you."

"I'm not a big girl. Ruth is a big girl."

He chuckled. Ruth sent him a stern look. "If you make any remark, you will be doing your own cooking until Ernest returns."

"You wound me. I wasn't going to say anything."

"Ha. Like I believe that."

"Owen, swing me, please?" Grace asked again.

He looked at Ruth. "Ready?"

She nodded. Together they lifted Grace off her feet and swung her between them. She squealed with delight. They ended up repeating the fun a dozen or so times until they reached the county road. They stopped and Grace skipped along the edge of the blacktop toward Ernest's farm. Owen found himself at a loss for words as he stood in the moonlight with Ruth beside him. She crossed her arms but didn't seem in a hurry to leave. He pushed his hands deep in his pockets. A strange connection seemed to stretch between them pulling him closer. He took a single step.

She didn't retreat but she hitched her shawl higher and stared at the ground. "The dishes won't do themselves. I should go."

She really should or he was going to kiss her and that would be a bigger mistake than anything he had done so far. Jeopardizing their fragile friendship was the last thing he intended to do. "We will see you in the morning. Good night."

"*Guten nacht*, Owen."

Grace held up her arms. Ruth bent down. Grace kissed her cheek and patted Ruth's face. "You have sweet dreams from the dreamland tree."

"*Danki*, and the same to you."

"And to Owen," Grace said.

Ruth straightened and glanced shyly at him. "And to Owen."

She turned and walked toward home. Owen stood watching her until her figure was lost in the darkness.

RUTH WASHED HER face the next morning, patted her skin dry and stared at her reflection in the bathroom mirror. Grace's wish for her had come true. She had dreamed of Owen, of walking hand in hand with him down a long and winding road. A sweet dream that had ended abruptly as he was about to kiss her. The ring of her battery-powered alarm clock had jolted her awake. It had taken a moment to realize it was only a dream. She'd sprung out of bed determined to forget the whole thing.

She stared at the woman in the mirror. "You will not fall for Owen Mast. Not even in a silly dream. He's leaving, and you are staying here, where you belong. Is that understood?"

Her reflection nodded once, but her eyes held doubts. Ruth sighed. It wasn't too late to take her own advice, but it was becoming increasingly difficult. There was so much depth to Owen, something she had never expected. Every time she discovered something new about him, it only made her want to know more.

He had been a serious teen, older than his years back when they were going out. She had known that he suffered deeply from the loss of his family. Ruth realized she had been drawn to him because of it. She had wanted to ease his pain, but Owen had excelled at keeping people at arm's length. Even the girl who thought she was in love with him never knew him well.

"At least I'll be too busy to give him a second thought for the next two weeks."

With that thought firmly in mind, she went down to prepare a breakfast of hot oatmeal sprinkled with cinnamon and loaded with raisins. She reached for the egg basket and then remembered Grace wanted to gather the eggs for her that morning. By the time she set the table and had the coffee brewing, the outside door opened and in walked Owen. She waited but Grace didn't follow.

"Did you leave her at home?" Ruth turned back to stir the oatmeal.

"We may wish I had before the day is over. She has gone to gather the eggs for you. She insisted on bringing her own egg basket in case you didn't have one. She also wants to fix lunch for us again and brought the marshmallow creme to make church spread."

"At least she likes to be prepared. Any word from the sheriff?"

"Nothing. If he must declare her an abandoned child, the *Englisch* court system will decide her fate."

"Surely Bishop Weaver won't allow that. The child is Amish. The bishop should be the one who decides what happens to her."

"The sheriff doesn't want to open a custody can of worms. He is ready to say her mother left her. I'm not ready to agree with him."

"But there has been no sign of her or the car. Even the biggest snowdrifts are nearly melted except those in the heavy shade."

Grace came in the door carefully carrying a wicker basket filled above the brim with eggs. Ruth hurried to take them from her before they rolled out.

Grace blew out a sigh of relief. "Whew, you have a lot of chickens."

Ruth caught Owen's eye. He was trying not to laugh. She set the basket on the counter. "I do. Tomorrow you should use my basket. It's bigger."

"Maybe we should have fried chicken for a few days," Owen suggested. Both Grace and Ruth scowled at him. He held up both hands. "Just a suggestion."

Grace shook her head. "Not a very *goot* one."

Ruth scrambled the eggs, adding crumbled sausage, cheese and minced onions to the mixture. She dished everything up and took a seat at the table. Everyone bowed their heads to say a silent blessing. Grace peeked with one eye to see if Owen was finished. Ruth tried not to laugh. Owen remained still and quiet in silent prayer. When Grace peeked at him a second time, Ruth couldn't hold back a giggle. She pressed a hand to her lips, hoping he hadn't heard. Her hope was in vain.

He raised his head and fixed his gaze on her. He arched one eyebrow in a silent question.

Grace began loading her plate with eggs. "That was a really long prayer, Owen. You should learn a shorter one."

Ruth began laughing, and he quickly joined her. Their eyes met across the table. Her laughter died away as did his. The intensity of his gaze stirred the memory of her dream and brought to mind their kiss so many years ago. What would it be like if he kissed her now?

CHAPTER THIRTEEN

ON SUNDAY MORNING Ruth slowly sliced her fresh loaves of bread. She would pack them in her basket along with a jar of church spread, two pint jars of beets and a plate of brownies. For the first time in her life, she wasn't looking forward to attending church services. She knew speculation about Grace would be the primary focus of the visiting after the service. She also knew her association with Owen was going to be scrutinized by the people of her church. The problem was she didn't have a clear understanding in her own mind about her relationship with Owen.

She had agreed to a friendship. That was all she wanted but it didn't seem to be working out that way. There were times when he seemed lonely and in need of comfort and then there were times when he seemed like a jovial fellow who didn't need anyone. Which man was he? Or was he both? Sometimes when she caught him looking at her, she thought she saw more than friendship in the depths of his eyes.

Did it really matter when he was going to be leaving in a few weeks?

In truth it didn't, but she wasn't sure how the church community was going to accept their situation. Owen wasn't any relation to her. He was her deceased husband's cousin. While Ernest had made it clear that Owen was looking after his farm, the majority of people knew Owen would be coming to her place every day, too. She was thankful for Grace's presence, in that it would stem some of the gossip. Her reputation in the community would surely keep speculation about them to a minimum, but there were always a few people who liked to stir the pot and see what bubbled to the top.

Was Owen prepared for some subtle interrogation about their relationship? How could she broach the subject with him without causing them both undue embarrassment? Was it best to say nothing and hope he took it in stride? Or should she warn him and offer suggestions?

She was sure that she could count on Bishop Weaver's support. He knew all there was to know about Grace and her situation. She hoped he would call on her if others found the situation objectionable. It wasn't like Owen was living in her house now that her children were gone.

Finishing one loaf, she slipped it into a plastic bag and closed it tightly. She tipped another loaf from the pan but stood contemplating her dilemma instead of slicing the bread.

"You're deep in thought."

Startled, Ruth spun around. The knife slipped from her hand and stuck in the floor a few inches from his left foot. He tipped his head slightly as he stared at the utensil. "What is it with you gals and knives? I'm glad I have on a good pair of boots. That might have cost me a toe."

She reached down and retrieved her knife. "You scared me."

"I'll try not to do that again. At least not when you're armed."

"Did you want something?"

"I was wondering if I could drive you to church this morning? Grace is outside in Ernest's buggy. We'll wait if you aren't quite ready."

"Don't you think that would lead to speculation about us?"

He frowned. "Speculation? I'm not sure I know what you mean."

"I mean, don't you think driving me to church will give people the wrong idea about us?"

"Maybe. What would be the right idea about us?"

"That we're not in a romantic relationship."

"Oh. And driving you to church will cause people to think we are involved with each other beyond the farmwork? It seems to me that driving you to church is a kindness that my uncle often extended to you and I'm here taking his place."

"I understand. I'm just saying not everyone will."

"So just to be clear, you don't want me to take you to church?"

She turned around and began slicing her bread again. "I didn't say that."

"You do want me to take you?"

"It would be very kind of you. I suppose we can ignore any gossip that your kindness stirs up."

"What if I promise to start a public argument with you? Do you think that would do the trick?"

She rolled her eyes at him. "That would be deceitful."

He shook his head. "I'm not sure about that."

"What is that supposed to mean?"

"It means you are a woman who likes to argue over the silliest things. And gossip that hasn't happened yet certainly qualifies. Grace and I are on our way to church. If you don't come with us, what will the gossips say about that since you obviously seem to know what other people are thinking?"

"They may think we don't get along."

"Or they might think badly of me for not offering to take you since I had to come right by your farm."

"This is ridiculous."

"My point exactly. Grace and I will be waiting outside."

Ruth fumed as he walked out the door, but she quickly reminded herself that wasn't the frame of mind she should be in while attending the prayer service. She drew a deep breath and finished packing her basket. She brushed the crumbs off her Sunday dress and apron, straightened her freshly washed and ironed *kapp*, donned her maroon cloak and best black bonnet and carried her basket out the door. No matter what anyone said, she would present a calm and unruffled front.

Owen was staring straight ahead over the horse's back. Grace smiled and waved. "We're going to church. I'm going to meet lots of other children, and I might even get to hold Caleb again. Come sit beside me."

She couldn't help but smile at the giddy child. It was amazing how quickly Grace had come out of her shell. "I'm delighted that you stopped to offer me a ride. I would've been late by the time I hitched up Licorice."

She hoped that Owen accepted her offhand apology and realized that she was grateful.

He glanced her way. "Happy to be of service."

They weren't late, but they were some of the last to arrive at the home of Thomas and Abigail Troyer. The couple's short lane was already lined with the black buggies of the people who had reached the farm ahead of them. There wasn't a single tractor in sight. Transportation to church could only be on foot or by buggy. Although they farmed with modern equipment, the "wheeled Amish," as they were often called, had to attend services as their parents and grandparents had done.

Thomas farmed and ran an engine repair business on the side. The services were to be held in the hayloft of his spacious new barn. An earthen ramp led to the loft at the rear of the barn so no one had to climb a ladder. The gray boxlike bench wagon sat at the top of the ramp, where men were unloading it and setting the seats in rows with an aisle between them. When they finished, Thomas's son Peter turned the horses around and drove them down the ramp and parked beside the house.

Owen stopped at the buggy behind it. Ruth got

out with Grace. Owen handed her a smaller basket. "What's this?" she asked.

"My contribution to the lunch after the service. It's one of the casseroles the ladies made for Ernest and me. I didn't want to come empty-handed." He slapped the reins on the horse's back and drove to the end of the buggy line. Thomas's second son, Andy, helped him unhitch the animal and lead it to the corral, where a long row of horses still wearing their harnesses were munching hay.

Ruth went in the house and into the kitchen, where Abigail Troyer was directing other women setting out the dishes they had brought. Abigail hurried over to Ruth. She smiled at Grace. "You must be the little girl we've heard so much about. Welcome. Glad you could join us today. If you would like to go down to the basement, where the other children are playing, I can show you the way. My son Melvin is down there."

Grace wore a worried frown as she looked up at Ruth. "Is it safe?"

Ruth nodded. "It's very safe, and I see Laura Beth is here so that must mean Caleb is downstairs, too."

That convinced Grace. She followed Abigail to the basement steps and went down to join the other noisy preschoolers being watched over by two of the young women from the district.

Abigail shook her head as Grace went down the stairs. "The poor child. Is there still no sign of her mother?"

"Nothing as far as I know. We're grateful for all

the hours Thomas and the others have put in searching for her."

"They will continue to look until the last snowbank has melted. No one is holding out much hope of finding her alive, but I still pray for that."

"So do I."

Ruth answered dozens of questions about Grace. To her surprise, no one mentioned Owen. Once the food was readied, the children were called from the basement and the women filed out of the house to the barn. The men were already seated. The married women, including Ruth, took their places on the front benches while the unmarried girls and women took their places behind them. Grace, because she was considered too young to sit by herself, had a place beside Ruth.

The song leader announced the first hymn and the rustle of pages filled the air as everyone picked up their songbooks, the *Ausbund*, and thumbed through them. One of the men started the song and everyone joined in. There was no music and no musical notation in the *Ausbund*. The hymns were sung from memory, having been passed down through generations of Amish worshippers. Ruth held the book so Grace could see the words. She was too young to read the German language, but not too young to begin learning the songs themselves.

The bishop and his minister came in and began the service that would last approximately four hours. There were no notes. No typed-up sermon. The men had decided on the topic prior to entering and spoke from the heart as God moved them.

Ruth knew Owen would be seated toward the back of the men. She was tempted to look back but knew it would only draw attention to her. She tried to keep her mind focused on the words of the sermon. Had anyone asked him about her?

When the service was finally over, Ruth turned Grace over to the two young, unmarried girls who were in charge of the babies and toddlers after assuring her they were also safe people. She went in the house to begin serving the meal. The men stacked some of the benches into tables and the congregation began eating in shifts.

When everyone was finished eating, the dishes were cleared, the benches loaded back into the bench wagon and people formed up in family groups or groups of friends to visit. The youngsters began a game of volleyball. Ruth was sitting beside Abigail and Laura Beth and a group of several other women when Granny Weaver approached her.

"How is your knee?"

"Much better." She extended her foot and moved it up and down. "It aches at night some."

"I'm glad it wasn't more serious. How is Owen Mast working out as your hired man?"

At least Granny seemed to understand the situation. "Fine. He seems to know his way around sheep. Of course, everyone has been too busy with the search parties to get much work done."

Granny Weaver nodded slowly. "And the child? How is she? Have we learned who she is?"

"Still nothing more than her first name and her age."

"Very strange business. I heard she is greatly attached to Owen. I can't blame her. He is a nice-looking fellow with a sweet disposition, don't you think?" Granny Weaver tipped her head slightly as she waited for Ruth to answer.

Ruth could feel the heat of a blush rising up her neck. She wasn't prepared for such a pointed question. "He's well-enough-looking. As for his disposition, I don't think my sheep really care."

Granny Weaver threw back her head and laughed. "Well said. I must come out and visit little Grace one of these days."

"You are always welcome in my home."

When Granny walked away, Abigail leaned closer. "I don't think you convinced her."

"Convinced her of what?"

"That you don't like Owen."

"I never said I didn't like him. I said my sheep don't care about his disposition."

"Which means you do care," Laura Beth said. "There's nothing wrong with considering taking another husband. You've been a widow for four years. Many of us thought you would marry before now."

Ruth couldn't believe what she was hearing. "I'm only going to say this once. I am not looking for another husband. And if I was, I certainly wouldn't consider Owen Mast a potential spouse. And I don't want to hear anything like this again. Especially not from my friends."

She surged to her feet and spun around. Owen was standing a few yards away with Joshua and Thomas. The hurt in his eyes pierced her heart. She wanted to sink into the ground.

He raised his hands and clapped softly. "Much more effective than a public argument."

He turned and walked away. Ruth reached out her hand but then let it fall to her side. She wouldn't have to worry that their friendship was turning into something deeper. It was unlikely he would consider her his friend after this.

OWEN WALKED AWAY from the farmhouse with long strides. He didn't care where he was going, he just wanted to get away. He heard what he had expected to hear. He just wasn't expecting it to hurt so much. What a fool he was to cherish the secret hope that she could care for him. He might've been denying it to himself, but he faced the facts squarely now. He was already half in love with Ruth and he didn't know how to undo those feelings. At least he hadn't said anything to her. It was some consolation after hearing her insist that she would never consider him for a spouse. He couldn't replace Nathan in her mind or in her heart.

At the moment he could cheerfully buy a ticket on the first bus leaving town and not even ask where it was going.

And that would leave Ruth in a bind and no one

to take care of his uncle's farm. He couldn't run out on her. Not again.

He was stuck in Cedar Grove for another month. How was he going to endure working with her every day knowing how she felt about him? He kicked a pebble with the toe of his boot.

"Owen, I'm sorry you heard that." She spoke from behind him.

He didn't turn around. "You should never be sorry for telling the truth."

"It wasn't actually the truth." She took a step closer.

He stared off into the distance. Did he dare believe her? "Which part wasn't true? That you're not looking for a husband or that you'd never consider me in that role?"

"It was an awful thing to say and I'm sorry. I wasn't ready to talk about something so personal."

He turned to look at her. "You could've told them that we're just friends."

"I wish I had said that. I don't know why I blew up at everyone."

He shoved his hands in his pockets. "I like you, Ruth. I've always liked you."

"I've always liked you, too, although sometimes it is hard to remember that."

That made him smile. "It seems we have spent a lot of time hurting each other to disguise that fact."

"I'm willing to put it all behind me if you can."

"Where would that leave us?" he asked.

"Maybe we could work on becoming the friends that Nathan wanted us to be. I know you're not going to be around for long, but I want you to feel free to come back as often as you'd like."

"You just don't want to lose a free sheep shearer."

Her lips lifted in a half grin. "There is that."

He gestured toward the house with his chin. "What are we going to tell people?"

She gave a dismissive wave of her hand. "We will leave them guessing."

"All right. We, you and I, are two people who will try to be friends." He started walking back toward the house and she fell into step beside him. He glanced at her pensive face, but he couldn't tell what she was thinking. How much of her apology was because it was expected of her and how much of it did she really mean?

CHAPTER FOURTEEN

AFTER CHURCH OWEN and Grace spent a quiet day at his uncle's farm. They read a couple of stories he had borrowed from Ruth and he helped Grace learn to read some new words. She was an attentive and eager learner and Owen found the teaching to be a pleasant distraction. He wasn't up to facing Ruth and chose to have warmed up chicken casserole for supper instead of going to her home to eat. He forgave her, but he didn't know if their friendship could recover. He thought she had been making progress in trusting him, but he wasn't sure of her real feelings.

He spent most of the night wrestling with his own emotions. He cared deeply for Ruth, but his feelings weren't returned and never would be. She had apologized for the things she'd said and the way she'd said them, but he knew underneath her apology that she had spoken the truth. She wasn't looking to marry again, and he wasn't someone she would consider, but at least she still wanted to be friends.

Friendship was the only solution open to him. Maybe becoming Ruth's friend was God's plan for him all along.

He could be a good friend. Someone who could

put his own feelings aside and do what needed to be done for her until his uncle and her son returned. Then he would go back to Shipshewana with a clear conscience, knowing he had proved she could depend on him. After that he would focus on helping Rebecca, get to know his sister, and maybe he could finally find the sense of peace and belonging that had eluded him for years.

On Monday morning he tried to race through his chores at Ernest's place while Grace was still asleep, but he discovered some of the cattle had gotten out of the corral. It took him a good half hour to find them, round them up and repair the fence they had pushed down. After that he started the tractor and let it warm up before getting Grace dressed for the day.

On the way to Ruth's home he wondered how he should act. Would things be stilted and uncomfortable between them? Or could they truly put the past behind them and work on becoming friends?

Once he reached her house and went inside with Grace leading the way, he immediately sensed the tension in the air. Ruth's smile appeared forced and she had trouble meeting his eyes. "Good morning, I hope you are ready for breakfast."

"Yep, I'm hungry." Grace climbed onto a chair at the table.

"Just coffee for me," he said, moving to get it himself.

After a silent prayer Grace dug into her oatmeal. Ruth pushed her eggs around on her plate but didn't eat much. He sipped his coffee, trying not to stare at her. It was going to be a long month if this was how it was going to play out.

"Grace, are you ready to help shear the sheep today?" he asked.

She nodded vigorously. "Yep. What does that mean?"

Ruth smiled at the child. "It means we take off their heavy winter coats."

Grace tipped her head to the side. "Where are the buttons?"

Ruth chuckled. "They don't have buttons. We have to cut their fleece off with clippers, collect the wool. And then I sell it."

"Buttons would be easier," Owen said, fighting back a smile.

"Zippers would be easier yet." Ruth grinned at him and his heavy heart grew lighter.

"No zippers," Grace said seriously. "Not for Amish sheep."

She looked bemused as both Ruth and Owen laughed. He thanked God for the child who could smooth rough waters without even trying.

Ruth folded her arms across her chest. "I hope you have forgiven me for my unkind words yesterday."

He looked at her from the corner of his eye. "That depends."

"On what?"

"On when I get another apple pie."

She chuckled. "If we get through shearing and lambing without tearing each other's hair out, I will make you a dozen apple pies."

"Then you are forgiven, and we can be friends."

He grinned but he already knew he would have trouble living up to his end of the bargain. The longer he stayed, the harder it was going to be to keep his true feelings for her hidden.

RUTH WAS ABLE to relax and finish her breakfast. Owen disrupted her peace of mind, but once Ernest and Faron returned, Owen would leave and her life would get back to normal. Until then she would make an effort to foster the friendship between them for Grace's sake. Upsetting the child was the last thing either of them wanted.

She glanced covertly at him as he teased Grace about getting more oatmeal on her napkin than in her mouth. His obvious affection for Grace cast him in a different light than she was used to seeing. His eyes twinkled with humor. His smile deepened the creases in his lean cheeks. He had a habit of brushing his hair off his forehead by smoothing it back with one hand, but the stubborn curls would quickly drop into place again. He needed a haircut, but she didn't offer. She liked the way his curls softened his otherwise-solid features. When he caught her staring, his smile widened, and she smiled back.

After breakfast they went out to the barn. Ruth had penned up the sheep the night before being careful to keep the Icelandic sheep together to be shorn last. They were still in the open pen. They would spend tomorrow night in the barn.

Two hours later she and Owen had portable fence

sections in place to form an alleyway and the catch pen. Ruth moved the first twenty animals out of the barn and into the pen. Owen looked at Grace. "Your job today is to keep the floor clean around where I'm working. Brush away any straw or dirt so it doesn't get into the wool." He handed her a broom. She began to sweep the wooden floor.

When she was finished, she looked up at him. "Is that good enough?"

He nodded. "Pretty much perfect. Ruth, are you ready?"

"I am."

"Bring in the first one."

Ruth separated one sheep from the bunch. Placing her hand under the jaw and around the nose, she lifted the ewe's head and placed her other hand on the animal's hindquarters. Pushing against the sheep with her thigh, she backed the animal to the shearing platform. Owen grabbed the animal, lifted it and laid it down on its side, gripping its neck with his knees. While he was cutting the fleece off, Ruth made a note of the animal's ear tag number in her logbook along with notations about the animal's overall health. She would enter the number of lambs the females delivered in the spring and eventually sell animals that had poor wool quality or were getting old.

Owen's first attempt at shearing resulted in the fleece coming off in several sections instead of one neat piece. "You have done this before, right?" Ruth asked, making sure he noticed the twinkle in her eye.

He did, and he grinned in return. "I need a little practice, that's all."

"A little practice. Does that mean you want a smaller sheep next time?"

"Are you forgetting something? Aren't you in charge of deworming?"

"Oh, I am." She jumped toward the medications lined up on the counter and drew up the correct amount in a syringe and squirted it into the animal's mouth.

Owen released the naked-looking ewe, and she galloped toward the outer door. He rolled up the fleece and tossed it into a bin, then stood up straight. "One down, seventy-nine to go. Grace, sweep the floor for me."

She hopped up to do her job. Ruth smiled at her eagerness. She was determined to be as much help as she could. Grace patted the pile of fleece. "Why are we taking their coats off?"

Ruth stepped back into the catch pen. "It is important to shear the ewes before their babies are born. If the weather turns cold or rainy during the lambing season, most of the ewes will seek shelter in the barn rather than have their lambs out in the open, where the wet and cold could kill the newborns."

"Having healthy lambs is important to Ruth. She will earn money when she sells them, so we want all of them to survive," Owen said, adjusting the shears on his hand. "Let me have the next one."

Ruth noticed the vigor in the way Grace tackled her job. She was going to wear herself out if she kept trying so hard. "Pace yourself, Grace. We have a lot more to do."

When Grace had the floors cleared, Owen gestured to Ruth. "Bring me another one."

"As soon as I finish this note." She flipped through the pages of her record book and quickly made a comment.

"Never mind. I'll get one." By the time she finished writing, he had the fleece off and allowed the ewe to regain her feet. He was getting faster. Bleating loudly, the ewe scampered down the runway and out into the corral beyond.

"I'm ready. Bring me the next one."

"Aren't you going to roll up the fleece?" Ruth asked.

"I'll wait till we have a few piled up. Then we will clean and bag them."

"Grace can clean them."

"Yeah, I want to help," Grace replied, nearly bouncing in her eagerness.

"Come here and I'll show you what to do." Ruth couldn't help smiling at the child's enthusiasm. Ruth knelt by the shorn fleece and began removing twigs, straw and any mud balls from the wool.

Grace nodded and began work on the fleece while Ruth grabbed the next one and moved it within Owen's reach. He pulled it from the pen and proceeded to shear it. They went through the morning without difficulty. Sometimes, Ruth managed to have one ready for him, sometimes he had to step in and help her.

At noon, Ruth wiped the sweat from her brow. She was breathing hard but pleased with their accomplishments so far. "That was the last one in this first bunch. Are you ready for a break?"

He laid the shears on a nearby table. "My stomach is complaining that I skipped breakfast."

"You should have said something. We could have stopped earlier."

"I wanted to get the first bunch done. You two go on up to the house. I'll sharpen my shears, sweep off the platform and we'll be ready to start again when we come back."

Grace grimaced as she rubbed her hands together. "My fingers feel icky."

"It's lanolin from the wool. It gives you soft skin," Ruth said. She held out her hand. Owen drew his finger across her palm. Ruth's mouth went dry. She inhaled sharply as her heart beat faster. Owen looked into her eyes and her gaze locked with his. The noise of the sheep and Grace's chatter seemed to fade away until she and Owen were alone. He took a step closer. She leaned toward him and closed her eyes.

She wanted more than the brief touch of his fingers. She wanted him to hold her hand, to pull her close. She wanted to lean into his strength, to be held in his arms, to know the gentleness of his lips against hers. The intensity of her feelings shocked her. Her eyes flew open. She took a quick step back. "I'd better get lunch ready. Go wash up, Grace."

She rushed toward the house as if she could outrun her troubling thoughts. Had he noticed how she had practically fallen into his arms? What must he think of her behavior after her comments yesterday?

OWEN RAKED HIS fingers through his hair. For a second there, he thought he was going to throw caution to the wind and kiss Ruth. When she closed her eyes, he mistakenly thought it was an invitation. It was a good thing he hesitated because she had bolted like a frightened deer when she realized how close she was to him.

He took his time sharpening his shears and sweeping the shearing area before he went up to the house. It gave him enough time to decide how he was going to act around her from now on. He would pretend there was nothing but friendship on his mind.

No, it couldn't be a pretense. He wanted to earn her trust. He needed her to believe she could rely on him.

At the house he found her setting the table. The delicious aroma of beef stew filled the air. It had been simmering on the stove while they were working. She turned to the stove and lifted the lid from the pot. She cried out and jerked away when the hot steam burned her wrist. He immediately pulled her to the sink and turned on the cold water to soothe her arm. Tears gathered in her eyes. One slipped down her cheek. He used his hand to gently wipe it away.

She closed her eyes and tipped her head to rest her cheek against his palm. She was so delicate and soft. He wanted to wrap her in fleece and keep her safe from every harm.

"That was such a foolish thing to do," she said softly.

"Is it a bad burn?"

"I don't think so." She pulled her wrist out from under the water and hissed when the air struck it. She quickly stuck her wrist under the water again. "It's going to be sore for a day or two."

"No more sheep wrestling for you."

She kept her gaze down. "It will be fine. I'll be careful."

Grace came bounding into the room. "My hands are clean. See." She held them up for inspection.

Owen stepped away from Ruth. "See if you can find some crackers to go with our stew. Ruth, where do you keep your bandages?"

"In the cabinet over my head."

Grace immediately rushed to Ruth's side. "Did you get hurt?"

"I burned my arm on the hot pan. It isn't bad."

"Do you want me to kiss it for you?"

Ruth smiled gently at the child. "That's kind of you to offer."

Owen opened the cabinet and pulled down the adhesive bandages and some antibiotic ointment. He wanted to defuse the tension between them. He tipped his head and looked back at her. "I'd be happy to kiss it for you, too." He wagged his eyebrows.

She rolled her eyes. "That won't be necessary."

"It's no bother. I'd be happy to do it." He kept a wide silly grin on his face.

She seemed to relax. "I said that won't be necessary."

"Okay." He opened the drawer and pulled out a clean kitchen towel. "Dry your arm good with this so the dressing stays on."

After opening the bandage, he applied the ointment and examined her arm. The burn was red and angry-looking with several small blisters. He gently covered the injury, then wrapped some gauze around her wrist and taped it in place. "You'll need to keep this out of water for a while. Grace, that means you and I will do the dishes all week."

"Okay."

Ruth patted Grace's head. "You are a *goot* child. Always willing to help."

Owen used a hot pad to move the pan off the heat and began ladling the stew into bowls on the counter. He carried them gingerly to the table. Ruth and Grace sat down. "Careful, it's hot."

"Are you making fun of me?" Ruth demanded.

"I was warning Grace. I know you already figured that out the hard way." He took his place at the table.

Grace leaned forward to blow on her bowl. "How many more sheeps do we have to shear?"

"Sixty head," Owen answered.

Grace looked at Ruth. "Is that a lot?"

Ruth nodded. "It's a lot. It may take us two or three more days to finish."

Owen propped his elbows on the table. "I once worked on a sheep ranch in Montana where we sheared two thousand head. That was a long week.

There were three of us working with electric clippers. One guy was so fast he could shear a sheep in under a minute. I think he was the state champion."

"Maybe we should see if he is available," Ruth quipped.

Owen was happy to see her good humor returning. "I lost his number. You're stuck with me."

"It will make Faron feel bad to hear it, but you are quicker than he is with the shears."

He pressed a hand to his heart. "I will take that as a compliment, Ruth."

She smiled and bowed her head toward him. "It was meant as one. Treasure it. It may be the only one you ever hear from me."

He laughed and began to eat with a renewed sense of satisfaction. They were back to being friends and he would do his best to keep it that way.

After lunch he and Grace cleared the table and washed the dishes over Ruth's protest. It didn't take long, and they were soon back shearing sheep in the barn.

He kept an eye on Ruth but didn't notice Grace had wandered off until he needed the shearing platform swept again. He stood up and looked around. "Where is that girl?"

She had climbed on the fence and was petting a black-and-white Icelandic ewe who seemed curious about the little girl. "Be careful, Grace," he warned.

Ruth dismissed his concern. "That is Polkadot. She is as tame as the pony."

Grace came running back. "Can I ride her? *Mamm* let me ride our pony sometimes."

"I wouldn't be surprised if you could. Get your broom and clean off the platform."

She quickly swept the area and raced back to her new friend.

Owen finished shearing the sheep he had and noticed that Ruth was having trouble controlling one frisky ewe. The animal bumped her sore arm. A fleeting expression of pain crossed Ruth's face. Owen stepped into the holding pen to give her a hand.

"I can get her."

"I can get her faster." He grabbed the animal's snout and began backing her up. A high-pitched yell made him look for Grace. She was astride the black-and-white sheep, holding on for dear life as the animal streaked around the pen. He and Ruth raced to the fence as Grace flew past.

"Don't worry, sweetie, hang on." Owen jumped over the fence, ready to snatch Grace off the runaway animal.

"Hurry, Owen. Before she falls." The panic in Ruth's voice raised his own level of fear. The sheep was making a second lap with Grace crouched low over her neck. Her hands were wrapped in the sheep's long corded wool. The rest of the flock were milling around the center of the pen.

"Sit up, Grace. I will catch you."

"*Nee*, this is fun!" the girl shouted and crouched

lower. He missed Grace by an inch as the sheep streaked past him.

He looked at Ruth in disbelief. "She's enjoying it."

"I don't think Polkadot is. If she tries to jump the fence, Grace will fall for sure." Ruth dashed into the barn and returned with a bucket in her hand. She climbed the fence and began calling, "Here, sheep, sheep, sheep."

The rest of the flock began moving toward her. She poured a line of grain on the ground. Polkadot immediately slowed as the others lined up for their treat in front of her. Ruth held the bucket out to Polkadot. She moseyed over and stuck her head in it. Ruth lifted Grace off her back and carried her to the fence. She sat the child on the top board. "You frightened me half to death."

"But you said I could ride her."

"I said I thought she would let you, but I didn't mean for you to go and try."

"I'm sorry. Can I do it again sometime?"

"Maybe," Owen said before Ruth could say no. "But she will have to have a halter on, and I will be holding her so she can't take off with you."

Grace grinned from ear to ear. "Okay. Can we teach her to pull a cart?"

"Ask the sheep expert." He nodded toward Ruth.

Ruth crossed her arms over her chest. "Sheep can be trained to pull a cart, but I'm not going to do the training."

Grace put her hands together. "Please, Owen, will you train her?"

"We'll see."

"That means you will. *Mamm* will be so surprised to see me driving a sheep. I wish she could hurry up and get here."

Owen and Ruth exchanged knowing glances. Although many of the people in the area were still searching for her mother, none had found any trace of her. It didn't seem that she would be coming back for her child. When did he tell Grace?

CHAPTER FIFTEEN

"*THE DIARY* CAME in the mail today." Owen stood in her entryway, holding out a newspaper.

Ruth was standing at the sink, peeling potatoes. She put down her knife and wiped her hands on her apron. "Does it have my story in it about Grace?"

"I haven't looked."

She snatched it from his hand. "How could you not look?"

"Because I knew you would want to see it first."

"You are right. This is so exciting." She sat down at the table and opened the paper. She kept reading until she found what she was looking for. She stabbed the page with her finger. "Here it is." She began reading aloud.

"A mystery in Cedar Grove, Kansas. A three-year-old Amish girl named Grace was found during a snowstorm on February 28. She was unable to supply a last name or her father's name. She stated that she was traveling by car with her mother. A search was immediately started for the woman. Neither she nor her car has been found. The child is a brunette with curly hair and brown eyes. She speaks English as well as Pennsylvania Dutch. If anyone has information about a missing mother and child, please contact Owen Mast, Bishop Weaver or Sheriff McIntyre.

"From a concerned scribe in Cedar Grove, Kansas.

"Then I go on to list the addresses and contact information, including the number of our phone shack. What do you think?"

"I think it's enough information for someone who knows Grace to get in touch with us. I pray this brings answers about her."

"The same article will run in *Family Life Magazine*. I could also send it to *The Budget*. That newspaper has a lot of Amish readers." She closed the paper and stared into space.

"What are you thinking?"

She gave him a sad smile. "I was thinking how much I will miss her if we find her family."

"I had thought of that, too. It's selfish, but I wonder if no one claims her maybe she could stay with me."

"Do you have room in your life for a child?"

He sat down to the table. "Two weeks ago I would've said absolutely not. Now I've started to wonder why not? It would mean staying in one place."

"Could you do that?"

"If I had a reason."

Ruth folded her hands on the newspaper. "Do

you mean that you would stay in Cedar Grove?" Her heart started pounding. What if he said yes?

"I have to head back to Shipshewana to meet with my sister as soon as Ernest returns. I'm not sure what's next after that. Cedar Grove wouldn't be a bad place to settle down eventually. You could see Grace as often as you wanted."

"That sounds wonderful." She smiled and looked away. Could she trust him to return as he said, or would she be waiting for something that would never happen?

"That would be only if no one claimed her. The rest of her family must be frantic not knowing where she is or what has happened to her. As much as I want to keep her, they must want her back ten times more."

Reality sank in as Ruth folded the paper. There was too much uncertainty with Owen. Maybe no one would come for Grace. Maybe he would keep her. Maybe he could settle here. She needed certainty before she could risk becoming more involved with him, but her heart acted as if it had a mind of its own. She was growing fond of Owen even as she tried not to.

"I hope you find a reason to settle down one day even if Grace isn't that reason."

"I have a lot of things to explain to you. Reasons for the way I acted in the past."

"You don't have to explain anything." She didn't want to hear his excuses or reasons. She didn't want to dredge up those heartaches. "The past is in the past and it should stay there." She got up and went back to the sink to finish her potatoes. "What we do now is all that matters."

He followed her and stood close behind her. She could feel his breath on her neck. "I'm happy you feel that way, but I am sorry for the times I let you down, Ruth. You didn't deserve that. I know that no man can replace Nathan in your life, but you deserve to be loved for the wonderful woman that you are."

"That will not happen." To open her heart again, to risk the deep pain of loss because he left her willingly or because God took him from her. She wasn't ready to face that.

"Why not?"

She turned to face him. "Because I'm not brave enough. I can't face another loss. I couldn't go through that again. I was a broken woman when *Gott* took Nathan away. If it weren't for my children, I think I would've lain down on his grave and let the grass grow over me until I was part of the earth that held him. I learned to go through the motions of living until those motions became natural again. It took a long time. I'm sorry but I'm not as wonderful as you think."

"Don't be sorry. I'm honored you chose to confide in me."

"*Danki.* We are friends now, aren't we? Like Nathan wanted?"

He gave her a halfhearted smile and then squared his shoulders. "We are."

She laid a hand on his chest. "I'm very glad." She

meant it, and she would do her best to be a friend to him when he needed one.

"Well, I reckon the sheep won't finish shearing themselves."

She drew a deep breath. "I only wish they could. Where is Grace?"

"She went to the barn to visit Polkadot."

Ruth frowned. "She's not going to try to ride her again, is she?"

"*Nee*, we talked about that on the way over here. Polkadot needs a lot of attention. I said she needs to get used to having a little girl around her. First become her friend and then we'll see about getting her used to a halter. How is your arm?"

She held it up so he could see she hadn't gotten it wet. "It stings but it's better. At least I don't notice my knee hurting now. You go on to the barn. I'll get this casserole in the oven and then I'll join you."

A wry smile curled his lip. "It won't hurt me to miss a meal."

She smiled, too. "You might wanna wait until the lambing season is over before you make that prediction."

"I can hardly wait."

He went out the door and Ruth covered her face with her hands. Had she done the right thing? Could she maintain a friendship when every day she spent with Owen made it harder to hide her growing feelings for him? She was a frightened woman, afraid of loving again. She prayed God would show her the path she needed to take.

OWEN STOPPED OUTSIDE at the bottom of the porch steps and raised his face to the sky. There wasn't a cloud in the bright blue vault overhead. There should be low gray clouds to match his mood. Ruth was still suffering from the loss of Nathan, and he couldn't do anything to help except listen to her.

He started toward the barn but the sight of a tractor coming up the lane made him wait where he was. It rolled to a stop in front of him. Joshua King was driving, and Thomas Troyer was riding behind him.

Owen waved. "Good morning. What brings you out this way?"

Thomas stepped down from the tractor. "We heard you might be shearing sheep and we came to give you a hand."

"Could you use some help?" Joshua asked.

"I sure could. Yesterday Ruth burned her arm and Grace decided to go for a ride on one of the sheep so we are falling behind schedule."

Grace came running out of the barn. "Did you bring Caleb to play with me? I want to show him my new friend. She's the sheep, and her name is Polkadot."

Joshua shook his head. "I didn't bring Caleb with me this morning, but my wife is going to bring him by this afternoon."

"And my wife is bringing our young'uns, too. You'll have lots of new friends to play with. I'm sure my boys will be jealous of your friend the sheep. Melvin has a pet pig named Goody. I reckon he'll tell you all about it."

Ruth came to the front door. "I see I'm going to have to make another casserole."

Joshua waved aside her suggestion. "Don't bother. The women are bringing enough for all of us. Owen, show us how to shear a sheep. I know engines inside and out, but I've never worked with woolly creatures."

Owen was grateful for their offer of help, and it also meant he wouldn't have to work directly with Ruth all day. He led the way to the barn. Grace tagged along beside him. "My job is to sweep the shearing platform."

"Is it?" Thomas asked. "I don't even know what a shearing platform is. Guess you can show me."

"Sure. It's the place that Owen makes the sheep sit while he takes off their winter coats. They don't have buttons or zippers, you know, so he has to use clippers."

Joshua grinned at Owen. "I believe we're going to learn a lot today."

Grace was more animated than Owen had seen her before. She didn't seem at all frightened of the men she'd only met briefly and chatted away as they got down to work.

Joshua became the catcher. He had a lot less trouble moving the sometimes-stubborn sheep than Ruth had yesterday. Thomas herded the shorn animal out to the next pen, kept the platform swept between each animal and helped Grace clean the fleece before rolling it up. It left Owen free to shear another ewe and the process went much more quickly.

"I forgot how bad they smell," Thomas said as he rolled up the last fleece from the morning's work.

"You get used to it," Owen said. The men walked out of the barn in time to see a buggy drive up. Laura Beth, Sarah and Abigail were in the front seat. Abigail was driving. The back door opened, and the Troyer boys piled out. The oldest two were twins. Owen hadn't yet learned to tell the two blond and gangly boys apart. The younger boy, about five or six was called Melvin. One of the twins held a baby girl of about two that he passed to his mother when she got out. Laura Beth had Caleb in her arms. Grace shot over to talk to him. He grinned and babbled at her.

"Boys, take all the food inside before you go exploring," Abigail said. "Don't go far because we're going to eat in a little while."

They quickly carried in several cardboard boxes filled with plastic food containers. A few seconds later they piled out of the house and came to stand before Owen. "Is there anything we can do to help?"

Owen cupped his chin as he thought and then nodded. "There is. There are a few stray sheep in the big pasture that we didn't get penned. Why don't you see if you can find them and round them up?"

They started to walk off with Melvin tagging along behind them. The twins stopped and turned to the younger boy. One said, "You should stay here."

Melvin crossed his arms and scowled at them. "But I want to come along."

"You can't keep up with us if we have to run.

You stay here." The twins jogged away, and Melvin came back to stand beside his dad. "They never let me have any fun."

Owen laughed. "I don't think they're going to have much fun getting those sheep out of their hiding spots. The ones who are missing are the young rams. They are not as biddable as the ewes."

Thomas laughed and clapped Melvin on the shoulder. "Looks like they did you a favor. Go talk to Grace. She has a pet sheep she wants you to meet and she wants to hear all about Goody."

"She does?" He brightened and went up the steps and into the house.

Owen shook his head. "I'm not sure Grace will be interested in hearing about his pig."

"She will. Melvin spins a story every bit as good as the ones Ernest tells. Have you heard from him?"

"One letter telling me that they arrived safe and sound in Missouri."

Ruth came out of the house smiling. "I've been run out of my own kitchen."

Thomas chuckled. "I imagine Abigail was behind that move. She likes space when she works."

Joshua crossed his arms. "I read about Grace in *The Diary* this morning."

Ruth's smile faded. "I thought her story would reach more people that way. The sheriff wasn't too happy that I had done it. He said it would bring out the folks without any claim to her."

"Do you think someone would try to say she is theirs if she wasn't their relation?" Thomas asked.

Ruth held her hands wide. "I don't see how. She knows who her mother is. She's not going to accept another woman claiming to be the mother."

"You're right about that," Owen said. "But what if someone claims to be her aunt or uncle and she doesn't know them? Was it because her mother didn't visit them? Or was it because they're no relation? I'm not sending her away with anyone unless I'm sure they are family."

"The bishop will know how to handle this," Thomas said.

Joshua shook his head. "I'm not so sure. I lived in the outside world for a lot of years. You would be shocked at some of the things that go on when it comes to the custody of a child. The only way to make sure she is related to someone is to have them take a DNA test."

"I've heard of it, but I have no idea how it works."

"I do," Joshua said. "They take the cotton swab and run it around inside your cheek. That gives them the cells they need to compare to another person's cells. That's all there is to it."

"You had this done?" Owen asked.

"I have. Pretty much everyone who gets arrested these days has to have it done so they can see if you've committed other crimes. Skin cells, hair, blood, it all contains DNA. If I had wanted to, I could have had Caleb DNA tested to make sure that he was my son. He was four months old the first time I saw him."

Ruth smiled at him. "But you didn't. He was already the child of your heart, wasn't he?"

Joshua grinned. "He is now, that's for sure. Laura Beth says there's no doubt about it. He has my stubborn nature."

"You men should go wash up. The women are about ready to serve the meal."

Joshua and Thomas went into the house. Owen stayed with Ruth. She looked worried. "What are you thinking?"

"I was wondering if the bishop would allow this kind of testing for Grace."

"She is not yet a baptized member of the Amish. I don't think he will object. We are allowed to use modern medicine. I don't see how this is different."

"You're probably right. Bishop Weaver is a wise man. He will do what is right for Grace."

"To worry is to doubt *Gott*'s mercy. I need to go wash up, too. I smell like Polkadot."

"Like a shaggy sheep?" she asked with a touch of humor in her voice.

"I like that."

Her eyes narrowed. "You like smelling like a shaggy sheep?"

"*Nee*, I like that you can tease me and not feel awkward about it."

"Well, I do feel a little awkward, but you make such an easy target."

He threw back his head and laughed. "I hope I continue to give you a good chuckle for as long as I'm here. As your friend it's the least I can do." He gave a slight bow and swept his hand toward the door. "After you."

"I'm going to walk down to the phone shack and check the message machine. Maybe someone has tried to call us already."

His humor drained away, leaving him sick to his stomach. Grace's family could already be on their way to collect her. He hadn't realized how soon he might have to give her up.

Ruth gave him an odd look. "Are you okay?"

"I'm fine. Do you want me to walk to the phone booth with you?"

"*Nee.* Go in and enjoy the company of men. I'm sure you must have been missing that in your days with only Grace and me. I'll hurry back. It's not far. I'm anxious to see if my idea has produced results."

She took off down the lane with a barely noticeable limp. The white ribbons of her bonnet streamed behind her in the brisk wind. He pulled his collar tight around his neck. Even with the sunshine the day wasn't warm. Winter seemed determined to hang on. He went in the house, washed up and joined the others in the kitchen. The women were setting bowls of fruit salad, black beans and rice, and enchiladas on the table.

Laura Beth was filling glasses with lemonade. "I thought Mexican food would be a nice change for everyone and I've been wanting to try this enchilada recipe. I hope you don't mind."

Owen took a seat at the head of the table. "I don't mind as long as I don't have to cook."

"Good answer." She grinned at him. "Where did Ruth go?"

"She went to the phone booth to check if anyone has left a message about Grace."

Grace, sitting beside Abigail, gave Owen a curious look. "Why would someone leave a message about me? I haven't done anything bad."

"Of course you haven't," he said. "We're hoping that your mother would call so we could tell her that you're ready to go home."

"Not before we teach Polkadot to pull a cart. I want to show her that."

"Then we had better get busy training her."

She sat up with bright eyes. "Today?"

He shook his head. "We have more shearing to be done today. Maybe tomorrow."

Melvin sat across from her. He frowned. "My Goody won't pull a cart. He might ride in one."

"Yeah. I can drive my sheep to your house, and we can take your pig for a ride in my cart."

Joshua leaned toward Owen. "I think I'd like to see that. Are you gonna charge admission?"

The twins came in looking mud spattered and out of breath. One said, "We got three of them. One more got away. They sure don't like to go the way you try to herd them."

"Thanks for your efforts, boys."

They started toward the table, but Abigail pointed toward the bathroom. "Leave those muddy shoes on the porch and wash those dirty hands before you sit down at Ruth's table."

They nodded and did as she asked. When they came out of the bathroom, Ruth came in through the front door. Owen could see something was wrong. "Ruth, what's the matter. Was there a message about Grace?"

Ruth nodded. "Owen, there are six messages from people who think Grace may belong to their family. What do we do?"

CHAPTER SIXTEEN

BY THE NEXT day there were three more messages on the answering machine at the phone shack. Ruth carefully wrote down their names and contact information. Owen, with the help of Joshua and Thomas, finished the shearing by the end of the third day. He came in to collect Grace, but he didn't stay for supper. Instead he went home and left Ruth to wonder how he was feeling about so many claims on the little girl he cherished.

Ruth realized she hadn't done him a favor by posting the articles but at least now they had something to work on. It was almost dark when Sheriff McIntyre drove into her yard and got out of his SUV. She stepped out on the porch to speak to him. "Good evening, Sheriff."

"Good evening, Mrs. Mast. I thought you would like to know that I am interviewing several people who claim that Grace belongs to them."

"I have received nine messages on the machine at the phone shack. I left them on the machine if you want to listen to them. I wrote down their names and phone numbers in case someone else erases the message. There are four Amish families that share this phone. Sometimes the children are sent to listen and they accidentally erase information."

"Is Owen around?"

"He has gone home this evening. Grace is with him."

"I'll stop in and see him on my way back to town."

"I can give him a message."

"I'll let you do that. I wanted you both to know that I'm bringing out a caseworker for Child Protective Services tomorrow to interview both of you and Grace."

"Is this something I should be concerned about?" She grasped her lower lip between her teeth.

"Not at all. This is about getting to know you and Owen and Grace, and to make a determination about what kind of care she needs."

"I will let Owen know if you don't want to go out of your way."

He tipped his hat. "That'll be fine. I'd like to make it home in time for supper one night this week. I think my wife is beginning to wonder who she married."

"You should bring your daughter out and let her play with some of our lambs when they are born. Children always love them."

"I may do that. Thanks for the offer."

The sheriff started to get into his car, but Ruth had another question. "Is there a chance that Child Protective Services would take Grace away from Owen?" She held her breath waiting for his answer.

"They have guidelines they have to go by. I don't think there will be a problem. They may have some concern about Grace living with an unmarried man who isn't related to her. I think we can explain the situation to their satisfaction."

"Danki."

"We will be by about one o'clock tomorrow afternoon. Do you have any other questions?"

"I would like Bishop Weaver to be here."

"I'll bring him with us if he is available."

"Will you need DNA from Grace?"

His eyebrows shot up in surprise. "As a matter of fact, we will. I'm a little surprised to hear an Amish person ask about it."

She smiled. "Joshua King was kind enough to tell us about it."

"Ah, that explains it. Joshua's DNA is on file because he was convicted of a crime. That means he better stay on the straight and narrow. You can tell him I said that."

"I will, but I don't think you need to worry. Joshua seems very happy to be back among us."

"He gives the credit to *Gott*, but I give a lot of credit to Laura Beth. She's been really good for him." He touched the brim of his hat, got back in his vehicle and drove away.

Ruth shivered. The sun was going down. The temperature was falling below freezing according to the thermometer on the side of her porch. She went inside, pulled on her heavy coat and covered her *kapp* with a knit gray scarf, then she set off across the pasture to tell Owen what would transpire tomorrow.

She had only gone a little way when Meeka appeared and fell into step beside her. She patted the big dog's head. "I hope you're keeping a good eye on all our mothers-to-be. It won't be long before you have twice as many lambs to look out for. I might have to consider getting another guard dog or perhaps the guard donkey since my flock is growing so well. What would you like? Another dog? Or a long-eared donkey?"

Meeka woofed once. Ruth giggled. "I accept one woof to mean you prefer a dog. I will take up the discussion with Ernest when he returns. He was right to bring you home. And if I haven't said thank you, I mean that from the bottom of my heart. For guarding my sheep and for rescuing Grace."

Meeka stopped and lifted her face into the wind. She gave a low growl and went trotting away. Ruth hurried on toward Ernest's farmhouse. She opened the gate that led from her pasture into his corral and hurried up to the house. It was nearly dark.

She started to knock on the door, but it opened. Owen frowned at her. "Is something wrong?"

"Nee," she assured him quickly. "I came with a message from the sheriff."

"Come in. You must be freezing."

She nodded. "It was a brisk walk."

He gestured toward the kitchen. It was smaller than hers and cluttered with unwashed dishes in the sink and on the cabinet. Everything else gleamed because she and the other women had cleaned the house from top to bottom while they cooked and waited for the searchers to come in.

She sat down at the table and took her scarf off. Owen gestured toward the stove. "Would you like some coffee or hot cocoa?"

"I'm fine. The sheriff stopped by to tell me a social worker from Child Protective Services will be out at one o'clock tomorrow. I asked him to bring Bishop Weaver with him. He said he would if the bishop was available."

"We were expecting this. Once we involve the *Englisch* law we must abide by what they say." He stood leaning against the counter with his arms crossed.

She clasped her hands together on the table. "He also said that he is interviewing several people who wish to claim Grace."

"Then they will need Grace's DNA to prove or disprove those claims."

"Exactly. I had no idea that my article would bring so many people to see if she is their missing child. One of the callers on the answering machine said her granddaughter disappeared six years ago and wanted to know if it was possible that Grace is older than four."

"When someone you love is missing, you will grasp at any straw no matter how small, and follow any lead no matter how far it takes you."

"I think I'm beginning to understand what you went through searching for your sister."

"At least I found Rebecca eventually and saw that she was okay."

"It must break your heart that she turned her back on you."

When he didn't say anything, Ruth clenched her fingers together. "Owen, can I ask you something?"

"Sure."

"When we were dating, why did you leave without telling me goodbye? Was it something I did?"

"How could you even think that? Of course it wasn't anything that you did."

He crossed the room and dropped to one knee beside her. He laid his hands over hers. "The night I kissed you, I realized how unfair I was being to you. I had nothing to offer. I knew I had to find my sister before I could think about settling down. I wasn't brave enough to tell you goodbye to your face."

His expression softened. "And for your information, it was the sweetest kiss I have ever known." Owen rose to his feet. "Clearly it was *Gott*'s plan for you to wed Nathan. Over the years I came to know that he loved you very much."

"As I loved him," she said, trying to reconcile what she knew now with what she had always believed.

"It's getting late. Would you like me to drive you home? I can get Grace up."

She shook her head and got to her feet. "Let her sleep. I'd rather walk."

He accompanied her to his front door.

She paused to face him. "Thank you for telling

me why you left. I was hurt by it for a long while. I should have asked sooner."

"*Nee*, I should have had the courage to face you and tell you myself instead of running off. I wasn't much of a man back then. None of it was your fault. It worked out for the best. Nathan was a *goot* man."

She reached out and laid her hand against Owen's cheek. "He was and I think you are, too."

OWEN COVERED HER hand with his and turned his head to kiss her palm. She didn't jerk away. She stared at him with sad eyes. Was it pity or understanding?

He stepped away and managed a smile. "Good night. I will see you in the morning. At least we are done with the shearing."

"There's still a lot of work to do to get ready for lambing. *Guten nacht*." She turned and walked away.

He closed the door and went back into the kitchen. He stood by the sink, staring out into the darkness.

The damage had been done and the past couldn't be changed. He was grateful that they had finally been able to talk about that time in their lives. Maybe they really were becoming friends. He smiled at the thought and waited to see her light. When it came on at last, he went to bed content for the first time in a long, long time.

The next morning found him working alongside Ruth as they dismantled the panels for shearing and reassembled them into numerous small pens for mothers and their newborns.

In the new addition at the back of the barn Ruth

stockpiled milk replacer and colostrum along with vitamins and iodine. To Owen it was beginning to look more like a pharmacy than a barn.

Grace was determined to make a pet out of Polkadot. Owen had separated her from the rest of the flock and placed her in her own stall. Grace brought her hay and grain, and soon the sheep was following her around the small enclosure when Grace took her out for exercise. Ruth's suggestion that Grace keep a little grain in her pocket did the trick.

It was nearly one o'clock when Owen heard a car pulling up outside. He walked to the front door and opened it. The sheriff stepped out of his SUV and walked around to the passenger side. The car door opened, and the bishop stepped out. Owen had a sinking feeling that this visit wasn't going to end well for him. He prayed he was wrong.

"Is it them?" Ruth asked from the kitchen.

"I see the sheriff, the bishop and a young woman in a gray suit with short brown hair."

Ruth came out of the kitchen holding her arms across her middle. "I don't know why I'm so nervous. What if they don't think an Amish home is appropriate for her?"

"I reckon we'll find out." He held open the front door. "Afternoon. Won't you come in?"

"Thanks." Sheriff McIntyre stepped in. Owen couldn't read anything in his expression.

Ruth nodded to the bishop. "Thank you for coming. Have you any news of Grace's mother?"

The sheriff shook his head. "We haven't learned anything new."

"That is a shame. Come into the kitchen and have a seat," Ruth said. "I just finished making some apple strudel, and I have coffee if you would like some."

"Sounds good. Thank you." The sheriff headed into the kitchen. The bishop and the social worker followed and sat at the table.

Owen decided to stand by the counter instead of taking a seat. He declined Ruth's offer and waited until she had served the others. "So what have you come to tell us?"

The sheriff turned in his chair to face Owen. "Grace has been declared an abandoned child and has been made a ward of the state, pending the discovery of any relatives who can care for her. We have been contacted by several people who believe Grace may be a missing member of their family. Then there are several people who wish to adopt her."

"She's not going to be put up for adoption," Owen said, trying to keep his annoyance in check.

"I certainly hope it doesn't come to that," the sheriff said. "That's why we are here. Ruth, Owen, this is Miss Terry Landry. She's a social worker with our Child Protective Services."

Miss Landry held out her hand to Ruth. "I've never met an Amish person before. Please excuse my ignorance if I do or say something inappropriate."

Ruth chuckled and took her hand. "Please don't be nervous. We are just people with Plain ideas. We don't expect those not of our faith to understand our ways."

"I'm glad to hear that. I'll get right to business. Because Grace has no parent or legal guardian to speak for her, it leaves us with a dilemma. As an abandoned child, she could be placed in the foster care system until a relative who is willing to take her and has the means to care for her is found. Because she's Amish and we have no Amish foster care parents, the consensus at our department is that she should remain in an Amish home. Mr. Mast, I understand Grace is living with you."

"You could say that, but she spends most of the day with Ruth."

Miss Landry gave him a perplexed look. "I don't think I understand."

Ruth leaned forward. "I'm like her *kinder heeda*."

Miss Landry looked to the bishop. "What does that mean?"

"A *kinder heeda* is someone who looks after the children."

"Like a nanny or babysitter?" Miss Landry scribbled a note.

"Ja." The bishop grinned and nodded.

Miss Landry paused in her writing. "Is there a married Amish couple who might be willing to foster Grace?"

Ruth glanced at Owen and then back at the social worker. "That might prove to be difficult."

Miss Landry tipped her head. "Why is that?"

Ruth sighed. "Grace is very attached to Owen.

It took some time for her to be comfortable having him out of her sight. She still becomes upset if she doesn't know where he is. I don't think taking her away from him is a good idea."

The woman tapped her pencil against her pad. "My understanding is that Mr. Mast is only here temporarily."

"I'm looking after my uncle's farm and helping Ruth until he returns."

"Do you have employment? Are you able to financially care for Grace?"

Owen could see where this was leading. She didn't think he was a suitable guardian.

The bishop leaned forward and laced his fingers together on the table. "Something you must understand about us is that we, our Amish community, care for our widows and orphans. A man never has to worry that his family will suffer if something happens to him. Grace will be clothed and fed, housed and educated by us."

Miss Landry put her pencil and pad aside. "I was not aware of your community's commitment. Thank you for explaining it. Ruth, if you could show me through your home I would appreciate it. After that I would like to visit with Grace and then I would like to tour the home where Mr. Mast is staying. And, Ruth, your apple strudel was yummy."

Ruth stood up. "*Danki*, thank you. Come this way."

As Ruth walked past him, she leaned close. "Did you clean those dirty dishes?" she whispered.

"I did."

She smiled and followed Miss Landry into the living room. Owen went outside to find Grace. He found her in the barn peeking out from the storage room. "What are you doing in there?"

"It's a safe place," she whispered.

"You don't have to hide from the sheriff or anyone else today. They are all safe people. There is a lady here who wants to talk to you. I hope you will answer her questions and be polite."

She stepped out of the storage room and closed the door. "Will you be with me?"

He dropped to one knee in front of her. "I won't be in the same room, but I will be close by."

"Promise?"

"I promise. Come up to the house. I would like you to meet her." He stood and held out his hand. She grabbed him and hung on. He knew she was worried even though she had no idea what was going on. Inside the house he helped her out of her coat and hung it up. Miss Landry came down the stairs with Ruth. "Hello. You must be Grace."

"I'm Grace." She stepped closer to Owen.

Smiling, Miss Landry leaned down and held out her hand. "I'm delighted to meet you. Let's go over to the sofa and sit down. I hear that you have a new pet. Can you tell me about it?"

Grace looked at Owen. "It's okay. Ruth and I will be in the kitchen. Just holler if you need something."

Grace reluctantly followed the woman into the living room. Ruth and Owen returned to the kitchen. Ruth sat at the table, where the sheriff and the bishop remained. Owen paced back and forth across the room. He stopped and turned to Ruth. "What did she say to you upstairs?"

"She said she didn't think she could live without electricity in her home."

He started pacing again. "The *Englisch* all feel that way. They think we are backward." He knew he sounded churlish, but he didn't care. The woman had the power to take Grace way and he didn't like it. What was the child telling her?

What were Miss Landry's real intentions?

CHAPTER SEVENTEEN

RUTH WAS RELIEVED when Miss Landry left Grace's side to come back to the kitchen. "Were you able to find out anything?"

"Not much. What do you know about her safe places?"

"She seems to need one wherever she stays. Apparently, her mother taught her to hide. We have wondered about it, but Grace would not explain it further."

"It leads me to believe her home life was not happy."

Ruth shrugged. "I can't speak to that. I never met her mother."

"Of course. She wouldn't answer some of my questions about her father, except to tell me that she can't say. Is that because she doesn't understand? I've read that Amish children don't learn English until they start school, yet Grace speaks English very well."

"We noticed that," Owen said. "She is fluent in Pennsylvania Dutch but seems to prefer to speak English. There are some Amish who believe teaching their children to speak English before school is important. Or it could be that she has family members who aren't Amish and she would have been exposed to the English language early on."

"I see."

"Would you like me to ask her your questions in *Deitsch*?" Ruth offered.

"Thank you. Let's try that."

Ruth translated Miss Landry's questions into the language spoken by the Amish, but Grace wouldn't supply any new answers. Ruth finally gave up. "I'm sorry. She insists that she can't say."

Miss Landry looked disappointed but seemed to take it in stride. "Thank you for your help anyway. The last thing I need to do is to get a DNA sample from Grace. I can explain what it is and that it isn't harmful in any way."

"We were expecting you to do this," Owen said. "We understand how it's done."

Miss Landry appeared surprised once again. "Excellent."

She reached into her bag and pulled out a small plastic package, put on a pair of blue plastic gloves and withdrew the swab. "Grace, I need you to open your mouth so I can touch the inside of your cheek with this. It won't hurt."

Grace clamped her mouth shut and frowned at Owen. He smiled to reassure her. "It's okay. Let the woman do her job."

She transferred her scowling gaze to Miss Landry, but she opened her mouth. Miss Landry swabbed Grace's cheek, put the swab back inside a plastic tube and placed it in a red plastic container. "Sheriff, I would like to visit Mr. Mast's home now."

"Sure thing." He settled his trooper hat on his head and led the way to his SUV. Owen went with him. Ruth stayed behind with Grace as Miss Landry gathered up her things.

Ruth was afraid to ask but she had to know. "Is there a chance the child won't be able to stay with Owen?"

"I'm going to file my report and my supervisor will make the final determination. You will get a letter from us in about a week. Grace is in no imminent danger. I don't see a reason to remove her at this time, but I will have some recommendations for you. She needs to be seen by a pediatrician and I feel counseling for her should begin as soon as possible. This is clearly a very traumatic situation for her. The abrupt loss of her mother can have long-term effects on the child's mental health."

Her answers didn't make Ruth feel any more positive.

Sometime later Owen returned alone. Ruth and Grace were spreading fresh straw in the pens that had been readied for the new lambs. Ruth left Grace to finish up and went to speak to Owen. Once they were out of earshot, she questioned him. "How did it go? Did she say anything?"

"Nothing more than what she said here." He looked angry and that worried her.

"I am sure that they will let you continue to care

for her. Grace adores you. Anyone can see that."
Ruth tried to reassure him, but her words fell flat.

"I got the feeling that Miss Landry didn't really trust me."

"We will leave it in *Gott*'s hands then, and pray for a just outcome."

"I reckon that's all we can do."

Ruth rubbed her hand up and down his arm. "I'm going to check the pasture for any lambs. Why don't you and Grace spend some time together? At least we can give her fine memories to take with her if she leaves."

OWEN KNEW RUTH was right. If Grace was to leave them, he wanted her to have fond memories of him. Unlike his sister, who didn't remember him at all. He walked toward the barn, where Grace was finishing her task. "Let's see if we can get Polkadot used to a halter."

Grace's eyes lit up with excitement. "Are we going to teach her to pull a cart?"

Her joy touched his heart. Perhaps it was because he never had a chance to do things with his sister that he became determined to help Grace enjoy the time they had left together.

He found several small halters in Ruth's tack room. He was able to modify one to fit Polkadot. Getting it on her the first time proved to be a bigger challenge than he'd expected. She was harder to hang on to with her short wool. He had made the mistake of trying to do it in her exercise pen but that left her too much room to dodge him without any other sheep around her.

He managed to get an arm around her neck, but she lunged forward and pulled him off his feet. He hung on as she made a full circuit around the pen, dragging him along. He had to let go when he realized he was accomplishing nothing but grinding dirt into his clothing. He finally backed her into a corner, grabbed her and sat her on her rump as he'd done when he was shearing her.

With all four feet off the ground she became instantly docile. He was able to get the halter on her head. Grace clapped in delight. He hadn't realized that Ruth had returned until he heard her speak. "That was very entertaining. How often do you give shows?"

He was panting with exertion, but he managed to smile. "I hope this was a onetime demonstration."

She grinned and chuckled. "That's a shame. I think people might pay good money to see sheep wrestling. It could be a way to supplement my farm income."

"The next time I put a halter on a sheep, it's going to be on a very small lamb. Would you be so kind as to fetch me a lead rope? I think letting her go would be a mistake."

Ruth disappeared into the barn and returned a few minutes later with an eight-foot length of rope. "Will this work?"

"That will be fine." He attached one end to her halter and made a loop on the other end, which he then slipped over the top of a nearby fence post. He stepped back and let Polkadot regain her feet. She stood, shook her head and tugged at the rope several times but soon realized she couldn't get loose. Grace climbed through the fence and offered the sheep a handful of grain. She munched it happily with her short tail wagging.

Owen came to stand by the fence where Ruth was watching him. "The next step in her training is to get her used to being around a cart. I seem to remember you had a pony cart for the children when they were little. Would you like to loan it to us?"

"I think it needs some repair."

"Let's go see if it will work for Grace?"

They found it under a blue tarp, backed into the corner of the machine shed, where her corn picker, bailer and wheat combine took up most of the space. She pulled the tarp aside. The cart was black with a red stripe down the side with a bench seat across the front and a box for hauling things on the back. Owen remembered one like it from his childhood when he and his brothers had taken produce to sell in town. There were missing boards in the bottom of the box but that would be an easy fix.

He looked at Ruth. "Do you think it will haul a pig?"

Her expression said maybe, maybe not. "If the pig isn't too large and doesn't jump out."

"I guess we will cross that bridge when we come to it." He would fix up the cart and teach Polkadot to pull it so Grace might remember her time here fondly, but what she really needed was for someone to locate her mother. "Do you mind if I leave Grace with you for a while this evening?"

"Of course not. Are you going somewhere?"

"I'd like to search along the lake road."

"Owen, I know that area has been searched several times."

"I realized that. It's just the most logical place for Grace to have come from. Her back would've been to the wind. She would've come along the sheep pasture fence and that might be how Meeka found her. Now that most of the snow is gone there may be tire tracks showing what people couldn't see before. I need to go look. I owe it to Grace."

Her sympathetic expression let him know she understood. "She can stay here as long as you want."

He rubbed his hands on his dusty pants. "I just feel she is still out there."

"If she is after all this time, I don't think she will be found alive, do you?"

"I don't. But if I can locate her maybe it will give Grace some comfort in the future to know that her mother didn't abandon her."

GRACE HELPED RUTH make cookies in the early afternoon. It was past time for her nap when Granny Weaver drove her buggy into the yard.

Grace clutched Ruth's dress. "Should I go to the safe place?"

"It's only Granny Weaver. She's a safe person. You met her at the bishop's home and saw her at church." Ruth still didn't understand why Grace needed that reassurance when she met someone she didn't know but she continued to use the phrase to make the child feel better.

Grace relaxed and went to the window. "It's an old woman. I remember her. She gave me a cookie. Maybe she wants a cookie."

"We will certainly ask her." Ruth opened the door and Granny Weaver tottered in on her cane in a wave of black shawls that swirled about her form.

"I don't think this cold snap will ever break."

Ruth smiled. "I think it's almost forty degrees outside today."

"Not warm enough by half in my book. How are you, child?" She began peeling off her shawls. Ruth hung up three of them, but Granny Weaver insisted on wearing one in the house.

"I'm fine. My knee is completely healed."

Granny grabbed her arm. "What's under this bandage?"

"It's nothing serious. I burned myself on a hot pan. Stupid really."

"There must've been a man in the kitchen," the older woman said with the waggle of an eyebrow. "That's what you get for paying more attention to him than to your stove."

Ruth knew better than to try to explain. Granny saw the world as she wished and often took steps to tell others what she saw. "Grace and I just finished making oatmeal raisin cookies. Would you like some?"

"*Danki*, don't mind if I do. Have you *kaffi*?"

"There is a pot of fresh-made coffee on the back burner."

"*Goot*. I'll have milk."

Ruth was confused. "Milk and coffee?"

"Just milk and cookies. Come out of hiding, child. I may look like an old crow, but looks often deceive one."

Grace peeked around the doorway. "Come, come," Granny said, crooking her finger at her. "Let me look at you."

Grace stepped into the room. "I like milk and cookies."

"Then you are my kind of people. The Amish drink way too much *kaffi*. Morning, noon and night. Bah! Gives me a sour stomach."

"I never have a sour stomach." Grace seemed intrigued by the older woman.

"I imagine you don't drink *kaffi*."

"*Nee, Mamm* and Ruth and Owen say I'm too young for it."

"Never start drinking the stuff. Stick to water and milk. Bring me one of your cookies."

Ruth stood back and watched as Grace carried the plate from the counter to the table. Granny Weaver patted her head. *"Danki."*

Grace grinned. "I helped Ruth. She made them, and I put them on the pan."

"They're *goot*. Are they as *goot* as the ones your *mudder* makes?"

"*Mamm*'s are better."

"Do I know your mother? When you live to be as old as I am, you know just about everyone. What's her name?"

"Becky." Grace slapped her fingers over her mouth. "I can't say. She'll be mad."

Her mother's name was the first thing the child had told them about her mother. It was a small step, but it was a start. Maybe Grace would tell them more as she grew less fearful.

"*Nee*, your *mudder* won't be angry. Ruth, how are you getting along with Owen?"

"Well enough."

"Still squabbling, I see."

"*Nee*. Not at all. We've discovered some common ground."

"Have you now? That's intriguing."

"I can't imagine why you'd think so." Ruth turned away and busied herself at the sink. "Owen was my husband's cousin, and there are many traits that they share."

"You speak of him much too often, Ruth."

Ruth bowed her head. She knew what Granny Weaver was referring to. "Nathan was everything to me. I miss him as much now as the day he died."

"Do you doubt that his death was part of *Gott*'s plan?"

"Of course not." It was the right thing to say, but did she believe it?

"I miss my husband, too. But I know he waits for me in heaven. I do not need to remind myself and others of our life together. Doing so shows you question *Gott*'s will. To mourn is a human thing. But we must also rejoice that our loved ones are with the Lord."

"I try. I do try. I pray often that I can find acceptance."

"Prayer is always a good first step to overcoming any problem. Don't hoard the love you have in your heart for your husband. There are better uses for love in this world. After all, there is no end to it. A mother knows this. A mother of fourteen loves each child as much as the mother who has only one. My grandmother had three husbands. I asked her once which one she had loved the best. Do you know what her answer was?"

"I can't imagine."

"She loved each one of them the best. I will never forget that. To her, each husband was the best husband until *Gott* took him home. Then the next became her best husband until *Gott* took him home. The last one she loved was my grandfather and I can remember how happy they were together. There is plenty of room in your heart for more love if you don't hoard what you already have."

Granny Weaver levered herself up off of the chair. "Grace, fetch my shawls for me."

The child returned with an armload of woolen garments and handed them to her. Granny Weaver put them on one at a time until she resembled a padded woolly black sheep. "*Danki* for the cookies. When Ernest returns, tell him I'd like to see him. I haven't enjoyed a good laugh in a long time."

Granny Weaver waddled toward the door. Ruth rushed to open it for her. "Is there some reason that you came by today?"

"I wanted to see the child for myself. She reminded me of someone when I saw her at church, but I can't quite put my finger on who. I thought seeing her again might jog my memory, but it hasn't. At my age memory is a fickle gift. Sometimes I see the past as clear as day and yet I can't recall what I needed at the grocery store ten minutes after I've left my house."

"That's not just age. It happens to me, too."

Granny's expression soured. "You aren't as old as I am, but you're no spring chicken."

Ruth snapped her mouth shut until she caught the twinkle in the old woman's eyes. "A mature hen is what I am."

Granny laughed. "Ernest is rubbing off on all of us. Grace is a sweet child. I hope you find her family. The bishop tells me he has had several couples in mind that might be willing to take her in."

"I'm afraid the *Englisch* law will have the final say in that."

"I prefer to think that *Gott* has final say in everything. Sometimes when He speaks we are simply too busy to listen."

After Granny Weaver left, Ruth asked Grace to sweep the front porch and steps. It was an easy task for a child her age and it left Ruth time to consider what losing Grace would mean to Owen when her family was located. For him, it had to be like losing his sister all over again. But instead of moving away from that hurt, he was embracing Grace with love and kindness while she was with him. He would be happy to hear Grace gave them her mother's name. He made Ruth ashamed of her resistance to loving someone again. Was Granny right? Could she love another man as much as she had loved Nathan?

It was easy to think she could open her heart, but she feared it would be much harder to do it. She had years of practice at keeping men at arm's length. Few of them wanted a bossy, determined, independent woman as a wife. She had cultivated those traits unconsciously but now she saw she had used them to protect herself from a new relationship. Owen had breached the outer walls of her heart's fortress, but she would have to open the last gate and ask him in. Was she ready to do that? She wasn't sure.

The front door swung inward as Owen walked into the house with Grace in his arms. "Who was that in the buggy?"

"Granny Weaver," Ruth said quickly, trying to gather her wits.

"What did she want?"

"She came to see Grace. Granny thought Grace reminded her of someone last Sunday, but she couldn't place her. She came today to see if she could jog her memory."

"And?" he asked hopefully.

"Nothing, but Grace let slip that her mother's name is Becky. I think we should let the sheriff know."

"I agree."

Ruth heard someone shouting for Owen. He heard it at the same time. They stepped out on the porch to see who it was. Peter Troyer came running up to the house. The winded boy leaned forward, bracing his hands on his knees as he struggled to catch his breath.

A few seconds later he looked up at Owen. "We found her."

CHAPTER EIGHTEEN

OWEN'S HEART BEGAN thudding in his chest. He knew exactly what the Troyer boy meant. He was also aware of the child he held. "Where?"

"On the rim of the stumbling blocks." A swath of rugged county with deep canyons and rock-strewn hillsides at the south end of the lake and less than a mile from Ernest's farm.

Owen handed Grace over to Ruth. "I think she's ready for a nap."

Grace shook her head. "I don't want a nap. Who did he find?"

Ruth took her from his arms. He saw Ruth's eyes were wide and filled with concern. "A lost sheep. Owen will tell us about it later."

"That's right," he said and tried to smile. He didn't want to alarm her.

When Ruth had taken Grace upstairs, Owen turned back to the boy in front of the steps.

"Is she alive?"

He shook his head sadly. "*Nee.* Andy and I were rabbit hunting with Wayne Zook. Andy spied a rabbit that darted into a clump of cedars about fifty yards from where the road turns and goes down to

Harold Miller's place. Wayne crawled in under the branches to try to scare the rabbit out for us. He came back white as a sheet and told us there was a dead woman in a car wedged in between the tree trunks. I didn't go look. Andy went to get our *daed*, and I came straight here. Wayne stayed out there. He's the bravest of us all."

She had been so close and yet no one knew it. Poor Grace was never going to see her mother again. Owen knew exactly how it felt to hear such news and he dreaded trying to make the child understand. He thought he knew the spot the boy was talking about. "Go down to the phone shack and call the sheriff. Tell him exactly what you told me. Wait at the phone in case he doesn't know where he should go."

"What are you going to do?"

"I'm going to go see if there's anything I can do. Get going. The sooner the sheriff gets here, the sooner we will all have answers."

The boy took off at a run. Owen turned toward the house. He considered telling Ruth what the Troyer boy said but he would wait until he was sure Grace couldn't overhear. He retraced Peter's steps back to the site as quickly as he could.

Wayne Zook was standing near a clump of cedar trees just as Peter Troyer had said. Wayne was pale and visibly shaken. "I went in just to look for a rabbit. I've never seen a dead person up close before."

"Are you okay to wait until the sheriff comes?"

The boy took a step back. "The sheriff? Why? We didn't do anything wrong."

"Don't worry. You aren't in any trouble. I'm sure he'll have a few questions for you and then you can go home. It was good of you to wait here."

"I didn't think she should be alone, you know? What with her being Grace's *mamm* and all."

"Danki." Owen gathered his courage and crouched low to get under the low thick tree branches. Inside he found a triangle of trees grown close together. The dense shade had kept the snow inside from melting completely. In the gloom he saw a green car with its hood wedged against the center tree. He couldn't be sure, but he thought it was the car that had hit Ruth's sleigh. The passenger-side door was open, but the driver's-side door was still closed. It didn't seem as if the woman had tried to leave the vehicle.

It was easy to see why the searchers had over-looked the spot. The evergreen branches laden with snow swept the ground around the outside and had several feet of snow drifted on top of them. Some-one passing by wouldn't realize there was room for a car in between the trees.

Through the frost-covered windows he could see a woman resting with her head against the seat back. She wore a white *kapp*. The driver appeared to be Amish, which didn't make sense. Why would an Amish woman be driving a car? He couldn't make out her features. The glass was coated with ice. He rubbed his gloved hand against the glass to clear a spot.

If not for the glaze of ice on her eyelashes and skin, he might've thought she was asleep. Her skin was as pale as porcelain. She had blond hair beneath her *kapp*. She wasn't wearing a coat. He started to open the door when he recognized the woman. His legs gave out and he dropped to his knees on the snowy ground. A roar filled his ears.

"Oh, dear *Gott*. Not little Rebecca. *Nee, nee*. Not like this." He buried his face in his hands and wept.

That was how Sheriff McIntyre found him twenty minutes later, mourning the little sister who had been snatched away from him years ago and for the young woman who had been afraid of him when he'd finally found her. He would never close his eyes without seeing her like this. Waiting to be found.

"Owen?" He felt the sheriff's hand on his shoulder and realized McIntyre had been calling his name.

He looked up at the man leaning over him. "It's my sister. Her name is Rebecca Mast. No, she went by Stoltzfus, our aunt's name, and I have no idea why she's here."

"You didn't recognize your niece when you met Grace?"

Owen shook his head. "I didn't know Rebecca had a daughter. Grace has dark curly hair while Rebecca is blonde. I should've seen the resemblance. I should have."

"Don't beat yourself up over it. I need you to step away from the car."

"I have to take care of her."

Sheriff took his elbow and helped Owen to his feet. He staggered as his vision reeled before settling down again.

"Our coroner will take care of her. You should go back to Ruth and let her know what you discovered."

"I can't go. I can't leave my sister. I couldn't do anything for her while she was alive, but I will see her properly taken care of in death."

The sheriff moved to stand in front of Owen, blocking his view. "I know you want to help, and I promise you can stay with her after we get her out of the car, but I need you to step outside with that boy and make sure he is okay."

Owen nodded. He heard the car door open and the sheriff's sudden intake of breath. Owen turned back. "What?"

The sheriff sank on his heels beside the open door and pulled his hands away. "I'm going to have to take back that promise, Owen. You can't stay with her. This is now a crime scene."

"What crime? A car accident isn't a crime."

The sheriff rose and laid a hand on Owen's shoulder. "Your sister was shot."

Owen stared hard at him. "Why do you say this?"

"I'm going to have to ask you to move away from the car and not touch anything. Did you touch the car?"

"I used my hand to clear away the frost to see inside. Who would shoot her? Why?"

"That's what I intend to find out. Now, please, do as I asked and go out the way you came in. Then I want you to go home, but don't leave the area. There's nothing you can do here."

Owen opened his mouth to argue but realized

there wasn't anything he could say that would make a difference. His sister was gone. He would never know the meaning behind the words in her letter to him. *I need your help. Don't tell anyone.* What kind of trouble had she been in?

Grace was without a mother, but at least they knew who she belonged to. Owen now had the right to care for her. She was his niece. There wouldn't be any more talk of adoption or placement in foster care. He would see to her needs for the rest of her life if need be.

After crawling out from under the low-hanging cedar branches, he rose to his feet and walked over to Wayne. "You said you were hunting rabbits. Is there any chance one of you fired a shot in the direction of the trees?"

"*Nee*, none of us got a shot off."

"Okay. You can go on home."

The boy looked uneasy. "What about the sheriff?"

"He knows where to find you."

"Be sure and tell Grace that I'm sorry about her *mamm*."

"I will do that." As soon as he figured out how he was going to tell Grace she would never see her mother this side of heaven.

He walked back to the road and saw Thomas Troyer coming his way on his tractor. Peter and Andy were with him. He stopped beside Owen. "Is it true?"

"Your boys found a car. The woman inside was dead. It's my sister Rebecca. I spoke to her a few months ago. I have no idea why she is here…"

"Wow. I'm sorry for your loss, Owen. We cannot understand *Gott*'s plan, but your sister is at peace."

"Danki." He climbed on the tractor and stood behind the driver while the boys each sat on one of the broad fenders. When they stopped in front of Ruth's house, Owen got down.

"I appreciate the ride."

"What can I do for you? My boys will take care of the chores at Ernest's place. They have done it before, so they know what to do. I will let some of our friends know and I will tell the bishop that you will be over to see him about the funeral when you can. Do you need help with the sheep here?"

Owen couldn't remember what needed to be done. "Ask me again tomorrow."

"Ja, I will do that. Seek the comfort of your friends, your family and *Gott*. They will see you through difficult times."

Owen nodded but didn't reply and went into the house. Ruth was waiting. She sprang up from her chair in the living room and hurried toward him. "Grace is sleeping. Is it true? Did they find her?"

He walked over to the chair his uncle preferred and sat down. "It's true that she has been found. The unbelievable thing is that Grace's mother is my sister Rebecca." He still couldn't grasp that she was gone.

Ruth pressed her hands over her heart. "Owen, I'm so very sorry. She must've been on her way to visit you. There's no other reason for her to be here, is there?"

"I did leave her Ernest's address, so perhaps she

was coming here to see him. But why? Why seek him out after all this time?"

Ruth sat down beside him. "You didn't know she had a child?"

He shook his head. "She never mentioned it, but our conversation wasn't that long. I didn't see the child with her when I met her."

"We will contact the bishop tomorrow about the funeral."

"We may not be able to hold one soon. The sheriff was with me. He says that my sister died of a gunshot wound."

Ruth's eyes flew wide. "Gunshot? Does he think it was an accident?"

"He said the car was a crime scene and that the coroner would take care of her body. I won't be allowed to stay with her."

"What are we going to tell Grace?"

"I was hoping you could tell me what to say." He needed her help.

RUTH SAW THE look of pleading in his eyes and she had to do all she could for him. "I think what you say must come from your heart. There is no way you can prepare for such a conversation. She will be heart-broken, but she has to know."

He closed his eyes. "At least we know where she belongs now."

"You are her nearest relative until we find her father."

"I've been thinking about that. What if he was the one Rebecca was afraid of?"

"Unless Grace can tell us, we may never know."

He looked at the ceiling overhead. "I think I will go sit with Grace until the sheriff comes."

"Of course. I should let those who worked so hard to find her know about this. I will go see the bishop and make some calls. I'm sure people will begin coming by as soon as they hear. Would you and Grace like to stay here tonight?"

"I appreciate the offer, but I think we would rather be alone for a while."

She smiled sadly. "I understand. Go ahead and sit with Grace. I will come get you if you are needed."

She watched him climb the stairs with slow, almost painful steps. She grabbed her shawl and headed toward the phone shack. She needed to let her family know. She had the number for her father's business and one of his *Englisch* neighbors. She hated to see Ella and Zack cut short their wedding trip, but she knew Ella, Faron and Ernest would want to return. They might not have known Rebecca, but they would want to support Owen. She wanted to ease Owen and Grace's pain but nothing she could do would truly help. Grief had to be endured.

OWEN STEPPED INTO the bedroom and saw Grace wasn't asleep. She sat up in bed. "Did you find the lost sheep?"

His eyes filled with tears. For a second he couldn't speak. He nodded and swallowed against the tightness in his throat as he sat in the rocker beside the bed. "I found her."

Grace crawled out of bed. "Are you crying?"

He straightened her *kapp*. "I am. Something very sad has happened. I have to tell you about it."

"Okay," she said in a tiny worried voice.

He lifted her onto his lap. "First I will tell you some good news. I found out that I'm your *onkel*. We're related. That means I can take care of you for always. Now, you will have to be brave. Can you do that?"

She nodded. He stroked her cheek. "We found your mother, Grace, but she won't be coming to take you home."

"Why not?"

"Remember when you told me your mother was sleeping?" Grace nodded. He drew a deep breath and pulled her close to ease the ache in his heart, but it only hurt worse. "She wasn't sleeping, honey. She has gone to be with *Gott*."

"Won't she come get me after she sees him?"

"*Nee*, she can't. Your mother is dead, Grace. Do you know what that means?"

She grasped the ribbons of her head covering and began to wind them together. Her lower lip trembled. "I had a kitten that died. We buried her in the garden." Tears began trickling down her cheeks. "Are you going to do that to *Mamm*? I don't want her to be in the ground."

His heart broke into small pieces at her words. How could he make her understand? "I know you will miss her, but she is with *Gott*. She doesn't feel any pain. She will never be cold or tired or frightened. She will always be watching over you."

Grace pulled back and hit his chest with her fists. "She's not dead. She's sleeping. Don't lie to me." Her voice broke as she threw her arms around his neck and began sobbing.

"I'm sorry, honey. I'm so sorry." Tears coursed down his cheeks as he began to rock her. His heart was breaking from the weight of her sorrow. Why had God allowed this? When Grace had cried herself out, she remained in his arms, limp and exhausted. "Will you take me home now, *Onkel*? I want to go home. Please?"

"*Ja*, I will take you home—as soon as I know where your home is."

"Promise?"

"I promise, *liebchen*. I will take you home as soon as I can."

Owen spent the rest of the afternoon with Grace. He had told Ruth he wanted to be alone but that wasn't the truth. Ruth's presence was comforting even if she wasn't in the room with them. He knew she was steps away waiting and wanting to help. She brought them up something to eat but Grace refused it. Owen couldn't blame her. His appetite was flat, as well. Grace clung to him and wouldn't go to sleep until he finished the song she liked so well three times. When she finally drifted off, he sat in the rocker, watching her sleep and wondering why he had let the chance to be a father slip away.

He was forty-three, late in life to be starting a family. Especially since he didn't have a mother in mind for the children. It didn't seem right to let Grace grow up without a family around her. Without a mother. She would need someone to help her grow into womanhood.

His driving desire to find his sister had prevented him from having a life of his own. He couldn't see that at the time, but he saw it now. His need to reunite what was left of his family had stopped him from marrying and having children of his own. It was useless to blame his aunt. She had never married. Rebecca must have seemed like a gift from God to her. A child to cherish, raise and love. If she had only expressed those things, he might have been able to accept Rebecca staying with her. Instead, his aunt's fear had left him to wonder for years what had happened to his sister.

Now Rebecca was dead, and he would never have the chance to learn the stories and experiences of her life. Had she been happy growing up? Did she have a pony like the one Grace spoke about? Was her faith strong? Had she trusted in the Lord? Who was the man she had married? He couldn't even be sure she had married.

This time spent with Ruth and Grace was certainly making him rethink his decision in the past. There was nothing to say that Ruth would've preferred him over Nathan if he had stayed in Cedar Grove. He and Ruth had been teenagers just beginning to look for a potential spouse when he'd left.

They might have found that they didn't suit each other after a few more evenings together. He liked to think he had been in love with her, but the emotions of an eighteen-year-old boy were different from the emotions of a man past forty.

He had grown to care deeply for Ruth in the past weeks, but he wouldn't allow himself to fall in love with her. She had already told him there would never be a place for him at her side. Owen saw nothing but heartache in store for him if he remained in Cedar Grove. Loving someone who couldn't love him in return was a poor way for him to spend more years of a life that had already seen too much time wasted. It could be that he was never meant to fall in love and marry, but maybe it was time he started looking for someone to love since he no longer had to look for his sister.

Grace was his niece, and he already loved the child. Ruth once asked him if he had room in his life for a child. Raising Grace alone would require him to be both mother and father to the girl. It was an enormous task and one he wasn't sure he was ready for. And there remained the unknown question of her father. Did she already have someone who would love and cherish her? Or was he the one Rebecca feared?

He glanced at the sleeping child. What did he do now?

The soft knock at the door made him look up. Ruth peeked in. "The sheriff is here to see you. I will sit with her if you'd like."

"That would be nice. Did the sheriff say anything more about how Rebecca died?"

"He didn't mention it. He did say he will need to question Grace again. I told him not tonight and he agreed."

Owen rose from the chair, feeling old and stiff in every joint. It was as though grief had aged him a hundred years in a few hours. "I appreciate you looking after her, Ruth."

She laid a hand on Owen's shoulder. "Caring for one another is what friends do. I'm sorry for your loss and for the grief you and Grace must endure."

"You have been a very good friend to both Grace and me. I thank you for that."

Downstairs he found Sheriff McIntyre at the kitchen table. He had a pen and tablet in front of him and was writing something down. Owen took a seat across from him. "What have you learned?"

"It appears that your sister was shot in the abdomen. The bullet went through the car door first. We will know more after the autopsy. You said you had been trying to track down your sister for a long time and you found her several months ago. Is that correct?"

Owen nodded. He relayed the story of how he and Rebecca had been separated and how he had spent years trying to locate her.

"Do you know why your sister might have been in this area?"

"When I found her, she was working in a small town in Indiana with a fairly large Amish community.

I gave her Ernest's and Ruth's addresses in case she ever wanted to get in touch with more family."

"Do you own a gun?"

"*Nee*, not even one for hunting."

"Does Ernest own a gun? Does he have one at the house where you are staying?"

"Ernest loves to fish not hunt. He may own a gun, but I have never seen it."

"I am going to get a search warrant to look for one."

The implication of what he was saying finally sank in. Owen looked at him in shock. "Do you think I killed my sister?"

CHAPTER NINETEEN

THE SHERIFF DIDN'T blink as he stared at Owen. "Did you kill her?"

Outrage replaced Owen's shock. "*Nee*, how can you think such a thing?"

"I wouldn't be doing my job if I dismissed someone as a suspect simply because I find him likable. The car was reported stolen by an elderly couple in St. Louis, Missouri, four weeks ago. Where were you before you came to Cedar Grove?"

"I was in Shipshewana, Indiana."

"Who can vouch for when and how you left?"

"Several people."

"Good. I'd like their names." The sheriff handed him a pen and slip of paper.

Owen wrote out the names of his boss and a co-worker. Was he going to go to jail?

The sheriff got to his feet and gathered up his notes. "I'd advise you not to leave the area. I intend to get to the bottom of this and find out why your sister— if she is your sister—was here when you claim you didn't know she was coming. The fact that you didn't know she had a child is troubling, too. Maybe Grace isn't her daughter. DNA will answer that question, but

I have more. I want to see you at the station the day after tomorrow. Make it early afternoon."

"My sister wrote to me a few months ago. She said she was coming to see me in Shipshewana on April 15. She also said she was in trouble and asked me not to tell anyone." His throat tightened. The note was the only connection he had to Rebecca besides Grace. He wasn't sure why he mentioned it now.

"Do you still have the letter?"

"In my coat pocket."

"I'll need to see it."

Owen got it for him. The sheriff held it by one corner and slipped it into a plastic bag he had produced from a pouch on his belt. "Do you know what kind of trouble she was in?"

"I don't. When will you bring my sister's body back?"

"That's up to the coroner. When he has finished his examination and issued a report, the body is usually released to the family." He went out the door, leaving Owen reeling in disbelief.

The bishop came in just as the sheriff went out. Bishop Weaver had his mother with him. He tipped his hat to the sheriff, but McIntyre didn't seem to notice as he walked by. Bishop Weaver came directly to Owen. "I'm sorry for your loss, Owen. May *Gott* bring you comfort."

"We should pray that the Lord reveals the truth. The sheriff seems to think I killed my sister."

"What? Has he said this?" Ruth was halfway down the stairs. Her shock echoed Owen's own.

"He asked me point-blank."

Granny Weaver banged her cane on the floor. "That's horrible."

Ruth stood beside Owen. "Perhaps we should visit Joshua King and ask him what he knows about a situation like this. He's had dealings with the *Englisch* law in the past."

"That is a fine idea, Ruth." Bishop Weaver looked to Owen. "Would you like me to conduct the funeral service?"

"*Ja.* I'm not sure when we will have Rebecca returned to us. I will let you know as soon as I can. Is there a funeral home I should use? One that understands our traditions?"

The bishop laid a hand on Owen's shoulder. "There is one we normally deal with. I will speak to them and let them know what to expect."

"The women of our church will come to prepare the house. Do you wish the funeral to be held here or at Ernest's home?" Granny Weaver asked.

Owen looked at Ruth. "What do you think?"

"I believe here would be better. I have more room and a bigger kitchen for feeding people after the funeral."

The bishop put his hat on. "I will return tomorrow. Until then may *Gott* be with you and comfort you." He and Granny Weaver left.

Ruth laid a hand on her forehead. "There is so much to do. Who will you ask to be pallbearers?"

Owen knew he needed four men for the task. "Joshua King and Thomas Troyer are the two men

I know best. Ernest and Faron if they're able to return in time. If they can't be here, then who would you suggest?"

"Ben Zook and his son William. Wayne is William's boy. I had better get started on Rebecca's burial dress. I will need to pick up some white material. I don't think I have enough. Grace will need a black dress. What about you? Do you have funeral clothes?"

The mundane things that needed to be done seemed too mountainous to Owen at the moment. He was glad that Ruth was here to take charge. "I do have funeral clothes. I will go start on her coffin. I want to have it finished before I go in to see the sheriff." In case he wasn't able to return.

He looked at Ruth. "Is it all right if Grace stays here tonight?" It was already getting dark outside.

"You should both stay. Take Faron's room. That way you'll be close if Grace wakes up and wants you."

"*Danki*, Ruth. I don't know what we would do without you."

"I wish I could do more."

Owen went out to Faron's workshop and began selecting pine boards to fashion into a six-sided box that would be his sister's final resting place.

OWEN WAS ALREADY up early the next morning when he heard a horse whinnying outside. He walked to Ruth's front door. Three buggies were coming down the lane. He recognized both Joshua and Thomas, but not the third driver.

The men and women got out of their carriages. None of them had children with them. Abigail came up the steps with a large basket over her arm. "My condolences, Owen." She turned to the couple behind her. "This is William and Jenny Zook. You met their son Wayne."

Owen nodded to them. Joshua came up to him. "The bishop stopped in last night. He told us what has been happening. Don't worry about the sheriff. He's just doing his job and that's to find the truth. If you were a serious suspect, he would've taken you into custody. Asking you to come to the station means he's trying to gather as much information as he can. It also means he trusts you will come of your own free will. I'll come with you if you like."

"That makes me feel better." If he didn't have to worry about being thrown in jail, he could concentrate on the things he needed to do. "Won't you come in?"

Ruth came downstairs. Thomas took his hat off. "Which room, Ruth? And where shall we put the furniture?"

"We will have the coffin placed in the living room. The furniture can all go out onto the back porch."

Abigail lifted the lid of her basket. "I brought some white dressmaking material. I didn't know what you had."

Ruth looked at it and smiled at her friend. "This will work. You've saved me a trip into the fabric store."

The men got to work clearing out the room. Laura Beth and Ruth went up to Ruth's sewing room while Jenny Zook and Abigail began cleaning the house.

After the furniture had been moved, Owen stood looking at the empty room. He would need sawhorses to hold the coffin. A memory of his childhood home emptied of furniture with five coffins lined up made him flinch.

Joshua came to stand beside him. "Do you want help making the coffin?"

"I'm almost finished with it and I'd rather do that myself." He'd never imagined making one for his sister.

"I understand. Thomas, William and I will start digging the grave."

"You have my thanks for that." It would be a hard job with much of the ground still frozen.

"No thanks are needed. It is our way to take care of our own."

The men left, and Owen went to check on Grace. He found her sitting in the rocking chair beside the bed looking lonely.

"Come down and eat something, *liebchen*."

"Okay." Her voice was small and sad.

He took her hand and they walked downstairs together into the kitchen, where a heaping plate of cinnamon rolls sat waiting for them on the table.

"Do you want to talk about the things I told you yesterday?" he asked gently.

"Nee." She took a roll, slowly pulled it apart and nibbled at it.

"I have to go feed the animals. Do you want to come with me?"

"Nee."

He hesitated to leave her, but the chores had to be done. He opened the front door, and Meeka pushed her way in. She went straight to Grace and laid her huge head in the child's lap. Grace threw her arms around the dog and laid her cheek against Meeka's soft fur.

"My *mamm* died," she whispered. "It's okay if we are sad."

Owen went out with a lump in his throat, but he was glad she had someone to talk to.

RUTH USED ONE of the dresses she had recently made for Grace as a pattern to cut out the black material. She had enough fabric left over from her own funeral dress to piece one together.

The women worked quietly. Grief was a private thing among the Amish. Ruth knew that Owen and Grace would be visited by members of the church soon, and again on Sundays for many weeks to come. She was almost finished with the dress when Grace crept into the room. She scooted her chair away from the sewing machine and held her arms out to the child. Grace climbed into her lap. The other two women rose and left the room.

Grace touched the fabric. "This is for me?"

"It is. Can I have you try it on?"

"I don't like the color. I like blue better. Did you make it black because I get dirty too often?"

"*Nee.* I made it black because that is the color of sadness and mourning among our people."

Abigail poked her head in. "I put the dog out. I hope that's okay."

Ruth nodded, and Abigail left.

Grace said, "I told Meeka that my *mamm* has gone to heaven to be with *Gott* and her family. Owen says he's my uncle now. Is that true?"

"It is. Owen would never lie to you. Your mother was his sister, but they were separated long ago when they were children. That's why we didn't know you were related to him."

"Can I go to heaven to be with *Mamm*? I miss her."

"*Gott* will call you to heaven when He knows your time on earth is over. You will not know when that day is coming, but never fear it. We will rejoice, for your mother is safe and happy now. She has no more pain."

"She's safe? Heaven is a safe place?" she asked hopefully.

"It is a wonderful safe place. Do you know why your mother wanted you to hide?"

"Because of a very bad man. She was scared he would take me away."

"Do you know the name of the bad man?"

"I'm supposed to tell you I can't say, but I saw him once. The night we left in the car."

"If you don't want to say, you don't have to. We must forgive the bad man for making your mother afraid. Always we must put forgiveness first." Ruth realized she was being something of a hypocrite. She hadn't put Owen's forgiveness first. She believed he had to earn it and that was wrong.

"How can I forgive him if I never met him?"

"Well, we will just say that we forgive the bad man and we pray that he will become a good man with *Gott*'s help. No man is all bad. He had a mother. Once upon a time he was a baby and then a little boy. The Lord puts goodness in us all when we are made. We may choose or reject that goodness, but salvation is waiting for anyone who seeks it."

"I forgive the bad man," Grace said solemnly.

Ruth knew the child was too young to fully understand what she was saying but it would become the building block of her faith as she grew older. "*Goot*. Now, we should have you try on this dress."

AFTER THE MEN and women who had come to help had gone home, Ruth gave Grace her supper, read her several stories from the Bible and then put her to bed. From the kitchen window she had seen the lights on in Faron's workshop. She poured coffee into a large mug, took a plate of baked chicken and went out to see Owen.

He was using a plane to smooth the sides of the coffin. He set down his tool. "Is it suppertime already?"

"Long past."

"I should get Grace and take her home. I didn't realize it was so late."

"Perhaps it would be best to leave her here again tonight. You are welcome to stay, as well."

He nodded. "I would like to finish this. I can use

the cot in the room at the back of the barn. That way I won't disturb you when I come in."

"As you wish."

He rubbed a hand across his brow. "How is Grace?"

"Sad, lonely, confused. She was able to tell me that her mother taught her to hide from the bad man who wanted to take her away from her mother." She handed him the mug of coffee.

He stared into the dark depths. "Did she know his name?"

"I don't think she does. She said she'd never met him but if anyone asked she was to tell them that she couldn't say."

"What a tangled life my sister seems to have led. I wish I'd found her sooner. I wish I could've done more to help her. Anything would've been better than the way it turned out." He put the coffee aside without tasting it.

"You did more than many people would have done. You searched for her tirelessly until you found her. How could you have done more than that?"

"You're right. I shouldn't punish myself for things out of my control."

"You have Grace now. Your sister left you a wonderful gift."

"I promised Grace I would take her home when I find out where my sister was living." He picked up the plane and began working. Ruth knew he was done talking. He had a huge responsibility that he was grappling with as well as grief. She wanted to help but she knew Grace's future was something he had to figure out by himself.

"You will make the right decisions, Owen. Don't be afraid. What a child needs most is love."

She spared a moment to admit she was suffering, too. Owen would be leaving again, and he would take Grace with him. She turned away before he saw the sorrow in her eyes.

GRACE WAS SUBDUED the following morning. She barely touched her breakfast. She sat with her hands folded on the table. Suddenly she looked at Owen. "Am I going to stay with you for always?"

"I'm not sure, Grace. We must see if you have other family members. We have to try to find your father. Do you know who he is?"

Grace shook her head. "*Mamm* told me he was gone before I was born."

"Maybe we can find a grandmother or grandfather. Would you like that?"

"Maybe. Can we stay with Ruth until you find my home? I haven't learned to drive Polkadot yet."

He smiled. "We're going to stay at *Onkel* Ernest's farm for a while until the sheriff finds out where your home is, but we will come over to see Ruth every day. And Polkadot." It suddenly occurred to him that Ernest and Faron would most likely be returning for the funeral and he wouldn't be needed anymore. It was a sobering thought.

Ruth looked at him over the edge of her coffee mug. "Are you going in to see the sheriff alone?"

"Joshua King is coming with me."

"He may be able to explain things in a way you can understand."

"I trust he will help all he can. If I can't return—"

Ruth stopped him by holding up her hand. "We will not consider such a thing. Don't worry. I know what to do."

"Danki."

Owen drove Ernest's tractor over to Joshua's farm. Together they drove the twenty miles into the county seat, where the sheriff's office was located beside the local police station.

"One bit of advice," Joshua said as they paused outside the door to Sheriff McIntyre's office.

"What is it?"

"Don't let your feelings of guilt do the speaking. Only answer the questions they ask you."

Owen pushed open the door. The sheriff was conferring with a man in a dark suit. He looked up and saw Owen. He broke into a smile when he caught sight of Joshua.

"Don't tell me you are involved in this case, Joshua."

"Nope. I'm here for moral support."

The sheriff gestured to the man beside him. "This is Agent Robert Morgan with the Kansas Bureau of Investigation. They are helping with the case. Agent Morgan, this is Owen Mast and Joshua King, both members of our Amish community."

Agent Morgan extended his hand. "Please accept my condolences on the loss of your sister."

Owen began to feel better about being under such

scrutiny. "I thank you for that. Sheriff McIntyre suggested that I killed my sister."

The sheriff managed an embarrassed smile. "Sometimes we say things to see how people will react. Not necessarily because we believe what we are saying or because it's true. Officers of the law are allowed to lie to get information."

"That may explain why there are no Amish policemen," Joshua said.

McIntyre indicated two chairs. "You are no longer a suspect, Owen. You have a solid alibi. Please have a seat and I will tell you what we know so far."

Owen and Joshua sat down. The sheriff sat behind the desk but the KBI agent remained standing by the window. "Our medical examiner has finished a preliminary investigation. Your sister died from a single gunshot wound to the abdomen. We were able to recover the bullet and it is a forty caliber. A semiautomatic pistol is most likely the weapon we are looking for. I know this is going to be hard for you to hear, but your sister did not die instantly. The bullet went through the car door and into her. It didn't come out. She bled to death in the car."

Owen closed his eyes to squeeze back the tears. "Did she suffer much?"

The sheriff's eyes filled with sympathy. "It is very likely that she did. It would've taken several hours for her to pass out from loss of blood."

Owen knew he would never forget those words. His fingers clenched into fists. He knew forgiveness should come first before anger. He prayed that God would remove the anger from his soul.

Agent Morgan crossed one foot over the other as he leaned against the windowsill. "It's possible she could have driven the car for an hour or two, maybe more. We have video from a traffic camera in Ottawa, Kansas, that shows her running a red light at 1:31 in the afternoon. There's no way you could have gotten to Ruth's place ahead of your sister."

"Why didn't she stop and get help?" Owen knew he might never have that answer.

"We haven't figured that part out yet," Agent Morgan said. "We think we have located Grace's birth certificate. The age is right. The father is listed as unknown. The mother's name is listed as Rebecca Stoltzfus. I understand you believe your sister voluntarily moved frequently. That might indicate she was afraid of being found by someone."

"I searched for her for many years. When I finally found her, she seemed afraid of me and did not remember that I was her brother. She was only three when we were separated. When I went back to see her the next day, she had packed up and left."

The sheriff and agent looked at each other. "That fits with our theory that she was on the run," Morgan said. "Now all we have to figure out is where she came from and where she was shot. Given the timeline the medical examiner estimated, I think we have about a two-hundred-and-fifty-mile radius to narrow down. That's a lot of countryside to cover."

Joshua turned to the sheriff. "Owen's sister was

dressed in Amish clothes, as was Grace. You should start looking in Amish settlements."

"Grace told me they lived on her grandmother's farm. If her father is listed as unknown that might mean my aunt Thelma Stoltzfus was the farm owner before she passed away five years ago."

Agent Morgan rose and went to a map on the wall. He made a quick circle around Cedar Grove with a pencil. He looked over his shoulder at Owen. "We will find who did this and bring him to justice."

Owen shook hands with the sheriff and left. He wasn't paying attention when he walked out into the bright sunlight. There were several people standing on the lawn nearby. They rushed toward him. "Are you the Amish man who discovered the lost child?"

"What is your connection to the woman found murdered?"

"Sir, can you give us a statement?"

He took off his hat and held it in front of his face as they pointed cameras at him. "I can't answer your question. Leave me be."

"Where is the child? Is this some kind of Amish cover-up?" a woman shouted.

CHAPTER TWENTY

OWEN TOOK A longer route back to Joshua's place but there were still two cars of reporters following him when he turned off the county road onto Joshua's lane. The road dipped down over a low water bridge and then climbed steeply to end at Joshua and Laura Beth's farm.

Laura Beth and Sarah came out of the house but stayed on the porch. Joshua got down from the tractor. "Don't worry, Owen. I know how to speak to them."

Owen stayed where he was. Joshua approached the two cars where both drivers were quickly getting out. One held a microphone, the other a video camera. Joshua held up one hand. "No pictures, please. My friend's grief is private. We kindly ask that you leave us in peace."

"This is an unusual human-interest story. We're just trying to find out the truth," the woman with a microphone said.

"I will be happy to grant you an interview for... let's say one hundred thousand dollars."

She almost dropped her microphone and juggled it a moment. "A hundred thousand dollars! Are you kidding? I didn't know the Amish were so greedy."

"It's not greedy to ask. It's only greedy to accept. I have requested that you leave my property. Please do so or I will summon the sheriff."

"I can't see how. The Amish don't use phones," the man with the recorder quipped.

Sarah sashayed off the porch to stand beside Joshua. She pulled a cell phone from her apron pocket. "Unbaptized members of the community don't have to abide by church rules during our *rum-springa*. Sheriff Marty McIntyre is a friend of ours. I have his personal cell phone number if you wanna discuss trespassing laws with him?"

The reporters exchanged looks and returned to their cars.

Owen got down off the tractor. "I couldn't believe my ears, Joshua. Why would you ask for money?"

"To give them pause for thought. Because the Amish are gentle, simple people, some outsiders think we aren't smart. I would not do an interview for any amount. If they trouble you, let Sheriff McIntyre know. Marty will see that they leave you alone." Joshua exchanged a high five with Sarah. "Way to go, sis."

Laura Beth approached the grinning pair with a stern face. "Sarah, where is your *daymoot*?"

Sarah rolled her eyes. "I knew you were going to say that. I will practice humility in the future. I beg your forgiveness for my bold behavior."

"You have my forgiveness." Laura Beth leaned back and crossed her arms. "It was very quick thinking, but I don't want to see anything like that from you again."

Owen watched the cars turn around and go down the lane, across the bridge and up the road on the other side. "Do you think they are waiting at the county road to follow me?"

"I wouldn't put it past them. Now, if you want to go home and not be followed there is a cow path that goes across the stumbling blocks. Your tractor could make it. A car couldn't. You can see where it starts just beyond the end of the stone wall. You'll end up at the Troyer farm."

"*Danki*, I appreciate all your help today."

"It was nothing. Sometimes I think about my old life and I miss things like television and rock 'n' roll music. Today was just a reminder that I am glad not to be a part of that world anymore. There are many, many good people of all faiths in the world. Some I call my friends, but a few believe that goodness is weakness and they try to take advantage of that. We will see which group those two reporters fall into."

Owen started his tractor again, waved at Joshua and followed the stone wall to the path his friend had indicated. It was a rough trip. At one point he feared he would become stuck in a muddy gully. The hillsides were steep and strewn with boulders, but he made it out the other side without tipping over. The Troyer twins were busy cleaning out the barn when they heard him coming and ran to greet him.

"Wow. Did you come all the way across the stumbling blocks? You've got mud everywhere," one twin said.

Owen smiled at him. "I did. Which one are you?"

"I'm Andy, and he's Peter." He pointed to his brother. "*Daed* is in his shop if you want to talk to him."

"I do. *Danki*. As for crossing the stumbling blocks on tractor, I don't recommend it."

He drove on to the steel building where Thomas had his engine repair shop. The large front door was open. Thomas came out, wiping his hands on a red rag. "Did you just come from that way?" He pointed toward the pasture.

"It was Joshua's suggestion. I think he was trying to give you more business."

"Now I'm curious."

Owen sighed and stepped down from his tractor. "I went to speak to the sheriff today and I was confronted by several reporters when I came out of the building. They followed us to Joshua's place. He had them leave but he was afraid they would follow me when I reached the county road. He told me about a cow path that led here. I would like to see the cow that could make that trip. I'm more inclined to think it's a mountain goat trail."

"What did the reporters want?"

"They knew about Grace being found and about Rebecca's death. They want details. Joshua said if they trouble me again I'm to let the sheriff know."

"I will keep an eye out for strangers and pass the word that they are not welcome."

"*Danki*. I had better get going. Grace may be worried since I've been gone so long."

"We'll come visit tomorrow. Having my daughter,

Harriet, and my boys to play with may make Grace a little happier."

"You'll be welcome."

He kept an eye out on the road behind him, but he never saw the cars again. He pulled up in front of Ruth's house feeling confident that he had not been followed.

RUTH STEPPED OUT to greet him. He looked tired and ready to fall over. "You were gone a long time. What happened?"

"I could use a cup of coffee and something to eat if you have it before I share my story."

And a hug, she thought but kept that to herself. She folded her hands in front of her and rocked back on her heels instead of drawing him into her arms. "There are cinnamon rolls, whoopie pies, brownies and three kinds of cookies for snacks. You may take your pick."

He looked impressed. "You've been busy today."

"I haven't. People have been bringing things by all day. Food, paper plates and napkins so I don't have as many dishes to wash, all delivered with kindness and condolences for you."

"I'm sorry I wasn't here to thank everyone. Your church has embraced Grace and me. I'm truly grateful."

"Half the people who came were not members of our church. They were the volunteers who were searching for Rebecca. You will know some of them. You went to school here for two years, didn't you?"

"I did. The seventh and eighth grade. Tell me, does Julie Temple still teach at the Cedar Grove school?"

"She does, and she was one who brought food today."

One corner of his mouth lifted in a half grin. "Let me guess, Miss Julie's famous macaroni salad. Am I right?"

Ruth laughed. "That is exactly what she brought."

He chuckled. "At every picnic and potluck that I attended while I lived here there was always a large green glass bowl full of green-colored macaroni salad. I'm glad to hear some things haven't changed."

"I hate to tell you, but one thing is different. The green glass bowl got knocked off the table and broke at the school Christmas dinner when Faron was in the fifth grade. She brings her salad in disposable plasticware now." They walked into the house together and Ruth realized how much she had missed him that day. How much more would she miss him when he left again?

Grace came running up to throw her arms around him. "Owen, I missed you."

He bent and picked her up in his arms. "You did? I'm sorry."

For a moment Ruth was jealous of the child. Grace had his unconditional love, and she was free to show him exactly how she felt.

"It was a long way into town, and it took me a long time to get back. Are those tears I see on your face?"

She sniffled and nodded. "I thought you went to

heaven, too." She threw her arms around him and pressed her face to his neck.

Ruth's heart contracted with pity for the child. She stepped close and laid her arm across the girl's shoulders. "Owen is right here. There's no need to cry."

"But he might not always be here," she muttered between a hiccup and a sob.

Ruth gazed at his face. She knew Grace's fear was as real as her own. He might not be around for long. Already the hole he would leave in her heart was growing larger. How did she stop it? How could she protect herself against that pain? *By not caring*, a small voice said at the back of her mind. She silenced it. She did care and there was no going back. All she could do was salvage what was left of her defenses.

His gaze locked with hers. "I'm here now and that's all that matters."

She turned away before he could see how much she wanted to believe his words, but she knew better. The future did matter.

He shifted Grace in his arms and used one hand to wipe her cheeks. "Dry your tears and let's go have a cookie."

"I'm not hungry."

"I am. Let's go watch me eat a cookie."

"I don't think so."

"Shall we take a cookie to Polkadot?"

"Sheep don't like cookies," she said solemnly.

"Wow, I'm glad I'm not a sheep because I love cookies." He bent his head down to see her face.

"Not even a smile? Not even a chuckle? Have I lost my funny?"

Grace nodded without speaking. He spun around, quickly making her grab his shoulders. "I have to find it. Here, funny, funny. Where did you go? We have to make Grace smile."

"I don't want to smile."

Ruth intercepted his desperate look. She lifted both hands, palms up. "If she doesn't want to smile. She doesn't have to."

Grace looked at her. "Ruth, will you read me a story?"

"I can read you a story," Owen said.

She pushed away from him and he lowered her to the floor. "I want Ruth to do it."

He rubbed his hands on his pant legs. "Okay. That's fine. Isn't it fine, Ruth?"

"It is. There is hot coffee on the stove and plenty of cookies to choose from. I'll come down and join you in a little while."

She read the confusion in his eyes and knew he didn't understand Grace's sudden rejection. Ruth understood. Grace was retreating behind her sorrow. She didn't want anyone to move it aside. While she loved Owen, he was also the one who broke her heart by telling her about her mother.

Upstairs Ruth sat in the rocker in her room and Grace crawled into her lap. She curled into a ball and began to suck her thumb. It was something Ruth had never seen her do before.

She patted Grace's cheek. "I know it hurts a lot now, but it will get better."

It wasn't the whole truth. The pain never really got better. A person just learned to live with it and keep going forward.

She got out the book about little kittens looking for their mittens and began to read. Ten minutes later Grace was sound asleep. Ruth moved her to the bed and pulled the quilts up over her shoulders as she had done for Ella and for Faron when they were Grace's age. She leaned over and kissed the top of Grace's *kapp*, then went out of the room, leaving the door open.

In the kitchen she found Owen staring into his coffee cup. A few crumbs and a half-eaten cookie decorated the table in front of him. He seemed every bit as sad and inconsolable as Grace. Ruth sat down across from him. "How did it go with the sheriff?"

"I'm not a suspect anymore."

"That's *goot* news."

"Apparently we are newsworthy now. There were reporters waiting outside the sheriff's department to ask me questions. They followed Joshua and me to his farm. He made them leave but I think they will be back."

"Why?"

"Because a lost child is a good human-interest story."

"Was it my article that brought them here?"

"Who can say? I don't want them upsetting Grace. She's been through too much already."

"She will recover with your love and understanding."

He raked a hand through his hair. "I hope so. She's tearful when I'm gone and pushes me away when I'm here."

"She needs time to adjust to her loss. It was the same way with Faron when his father died. One day he would be fine. The next day he was angry at the world."

"In the sheriff's office, I was so angry at the person who could do such a thing that I forgot for a moment I was Amish. I wanted him to suffer as she did. Then I remembered my vows and I was ashamed."

"For all we know it was an accident. If we forgive, then we have done what *Gott* asks of us. We are not to judge any man as good or evil."

"But is it enough? What if this person harms someone else because I didn't do enough? Wouldn't I be partly to blame for that?"

She reached out and took hold of his hand. "Only the man who does evil is responsible."

Owen seemed to realize that she was holding on to him. He was staring at her hand. He turned it over and grasped her wrist with his thumb resting on her pulse. She could feel the rapid beat as her heart sped up. He gazed into her eyes. "You are always ready to help. I can see why Nathan loved you so much."

She tried to pull her hand away, but he held on. "I care for you, Ruth. I'm sorry if that isn't what you want to hear. I wish I knew how to go back to the way we were when we squabbled with each other.

Now I just want to hold you close and breathe in the scent of you."

Didn't she want the same thing? Maybe it was seeing his raw grief that made her let down her guard. She rose and stepped behind his chair, wrapped her arms around him and laid her cheek against his head. She felt his body relax as he drew a deep breath. She stood with her arms around him for a long time. Neither of them spoke as they shared a moment that seemed frozen in time. She would always cherish the memory. He patted her arm. "Reckon I'd better get started on the chores."

She stepped away. He rose and headed for the door but stopped. He looked back. "Thank you for your kindness."

Should she admit her feelings for him had grown beyond friendship? She opened her mouth to tell him how she felt but he was already out the door.

Ruth carried his half-empty mug to the sink and poured it down the drain.

When he came in an hour later she had supper on the table. They sat across from each other and ate in silence. When he was finished, he reached across the table and took her hand. It was a simple gesture, but a rush of delight made her feel like a schoolgirl again. She squeezed his fingers. He smiled, his eyes never leaving her face. *"Danki."*

"For what?"

"For being you."

"You are welcome." He went upstairs and returned shortly with Grace asleep in his arms. Ruth opened the door for him. To her astonishment he kissed her cheek before he stepped outside. She pressed a hand to her face and watched until he was out of sight.

THE NEXT MORNING Owen saw a car parked in front of the house. He stepped out onto the porch and closed the door behind him. Grace wasn't up yet. The driver and passenger got out. It wasn't one of the reporters he had seen before. It was a middle-aged couple who approached his house. He heard the door open. He looked back to see Grace looking at him through a crack. "Do I go to the safe place?" she asked.

"*Nee*, there is no need of a safe place now. They are probably lost travelers and we can give them directions." Grace crept out to stand behind him. Owen remained where he was. "Good morning. Can I help you?"

The woman was trying to see around him. "Are you the man who found the lost child? Can I see her?"

"Lisa, it's not likely to be her," the man with her said. "I'm Eugene Page, and this is my wife, Lisa. We read about a little lost girl in an Amish newspaper. My wife likes to read about the Amish."

Grace peeked around from behind Owen. Lisa Page caught sight of her and her eyes widened. "Oh, Eugene, she looks just like our Carly, doesn't she? They could be twins."

"I see a little resemblance. The hair and the dark eyes maybe."

The woman walked up onto the porch and tried

to grab Grace's arm. Grace slipped around the other side of Owen. He frowned at the woman. "I don't know who you think she looks like, but she is my niece."

The woman had a strange, faraway look in her eyes. "Our daughter, Carly, disappeared five years ago. She always talked about joining the Amish. She wanted to live with God-fearing, simple people. She was pregnant when she ran away. I think this is her daughter. I'm sure this is my granddaughter."

Owen held out his hand to stop her. "Her mother's name was Rebecca and she was my sister. I don't know anything about your daughter, but this is not your grandchild."

Mr. Page took his wife by the arm. "It's not her, Lisa. We should go."

"He's lying, Eugene. That's Carly's baby. I would know her anywhere."

"I'm sorry we troubled you." Mr. Page pulled his wife away. "Let's get in the car, dear."

"But she looks so much like Carly."

"I know. I know. They all look like Carly." He helped her into the car, then got in himself and drove away.

Grace clung to him. "I didn't like those people."

"We must not judge them harshly. They have suffered a great loss. I think it has affected the woman's mind."

"That's sad."

"It sure is. Go in and set the table for breakfast."

Grace went back inside, and he watched the car

drive away. Hadn't he been almost the same? Looking everywhere for a face that seemed familiar? Asking about Rebecca everywhere he went. Had he looked as lost as Mrs. Page to the people who had answered his inquiries?

At least Lisa Page still had hope. His search had ended.

He turned back to go inside and saw Ruth standing at the corner of the barn. She held a basket over her arm. Her face wore a look of anguish. "It was my article that brought her here. I never meant to sow seeds of false hope."

"Our best intentions often fall short." He walked toward her and took the basket from her arm. "I hope you brought the cinnamon rolls."

She managed a half smile. "I did. How did you know?"

"Just a guess. Come in. A woman carrying a basket of cinnamon rolls is always welcome at my house."

He was relieved to see her smile widen. He couldn't believe how the sight of her raised his spirits. He was well and truly on his way to being in love with her. Did he dare hope that she might care for him?

CHAPTER TWENTY-ONE

GRACE OPENED THE door and peeked her head out. "Ruth, what are you doing here?"

"I thought you might like some cinnamon rolls for breakfast," she said, climbing the steps.

Grace shrugged one shoulder. "That sounds okay."

Owen stood behind Grace with his arms over his chest. "I can't believe she walked all that way just to deliver us fresh rolls. Isn't she nice?" He hoped she heard the challenge in his voice.

A faint blush brought the color to her cheeks. "That wasn't the only reason I was out this early."

"Aha!" He shook one finger at her. "The truth comes out. Why were you strolling through your pastures at dawn?"

Her blush deepened, and he tried not to smile. She was so adorable.

"The sheep are due to start lambing any day. I wanted to make sure we didn't have any early deliveries. I didn't find any. However, it's time we started checking daily."

"Do you hear that, Grace? We have been given a backseat to a bunch of baby sheep."

Ruth glared at him. "There is no front seat or

backseat. There are only the sheep to be taken care of. That is why you came here. Isn't that what you told me?"

"I came here to take care of Ernest's farm, and I got tricked into taking care of sheep for you. It took me days to get the smell of that lanolin off my hands."

She waved aside his comment. "Now you're being ridiculous."

"A little. It's better than being too serious, don't you agree?"

He detected a tiny twinkle in her eyes. She raised her chin. "Are you saying I've been guilty of being too serious?"

"I'm saying perhaps we both have."

She gazed at him for a moment and then nodded once. "We have been. It's not unusual for me, but it must have been a stretch for you."

His grin widened. "Oh, how I have missed this."

"I didn't realize my seriousness was making you miserable."

"Not miserable exactly."

"Then what exactly did you mean?"

"It was like that time when you were being nice to me."

Her jaw dropped. "Try to be more specific. I have been nice to you many times."

"Actually, you haven't."

"You make me sound like some kind of cruel boss."

"There now. Take that statement for example. How did you become the boss of me?"

She rolled her eyes. "It was easy. I tell you what to do. And you do it."

He pointed a finger at her. "I can see this conversation isn't going anywhere. I say we declare a truce. If you'll stop telling me what to do, I will stop making fun of you. It will be hard, but I will try."

She thought it over for a minute. "That's not a bad idea."

"What do you say, truce?"

"Agreed." She smiled and held out her hand.

He gave it a quick shake and held on to it longer than necessary. She looked down as a blush stained her cheeks.

Grace disappeared back into the house. He released Ruth's hand and held the door for her. She was staring across the field toward the county road. "Do you see someone parked along the road? I can't tell if it is black or a very dark blue."

He looked in that direction. "I wonder if it's a reporter?"

"I think there is a man looking this way. He had on a dark baseball cap and sunglasses."

Owen stepped onto the porch and stared in the same direction. "I see the car driving away."

He shook off the sense of unease. "It was probably someone picking up aluminum cans or bird-watching."

After breakfast Owen took them all back to Ruth's on the tractor. The rest of the day passed rapidly as more people came to drop off food or simply visit briefly. Grace remained quiet and sullen. Even a visit with Harriet and Caleb didn't cheer her. Late in the afternoon the sheriff pulled in. Ruth invited him in. Grace gave him a sour look and raced upstairs.

He nodded toward her retreating form. "She's taking it hard, isn't she? Can't say that I blame her. Bad business all around."

He turned to Owen. "The medical examiner has released your sister's body to the mortuary recommended by Bishop Weaver. They will bring her here tomorrow if that is acceptable."

A chill ran up Owen's spine. Was he ready for that? Was Grace? A wave of grief brought sudden tears to his eyes. He blinked hard to hold them back. He felt Ruth take his hand. He gave her fingers a gentle squeeze and looked at the sheriff. "That will be fine." His voice didn't crack, and he was glad.

"We've had a couple of persistent reporters asking about attending the service. I thought I'd ask you before I told them no."

Owen cleared his throat. "Tell them it is a private service."

The sheriff settled his hat on his head. "I'll see that they understand. The story made it into a few of the local papers. I'm sorry we couldn't stop it."

"I understand."

"You can expect a letter from Miss Landry soon. You'll have to make a court appearance to be appointed Grace's legal guardian if we can't locate her father."

Owen shifted from one foot to the other. "I had the feeling that Miss Landry didn't approve of Grace staying with me. Will that be a problem?"

"I don't think so. You are her next of kin until we can locate her father. We've had no luck with that. There is a chance her DNA will provide us with a match. What my office did learn from researching land records is that a Thelma Stoltzfus purchased a small farm outside Columbia, Missouri, ten years ago. Her daughter, Rebecca Stoltzfus, inherited the place. It might be Grace's home. The sheriff there agreed to investigate further for us."

Owen was happy to hear what the sheriff had learned but Columbia was a long way from Cedar Grove. He had promised Grace he would take her home and he meant to keep that promise, but maybe they could return to Cedar Grove to see Ruth when Grace was ready.

"When will this court appearance happen?" Ruth asked.

"I'm sure that'll be in the paperwork she'll be sending. Oh, and tell Joshua I think he should split his interview fee with me."

Owen chuckled. "I'll do that."

The sheriff touched the brim of his hat and left.

Owen realized he was still holding Ruth's hand. He laced his fingers through hers. They fit perfectly. He gazed into her eyes. He'd never felt so connected to another person. Holding her hand in his made him believe he might one day have a place by her side. "I appreciate you helping me keep it together. We

Amish are supposed to be stoic, but I can't seem to manage that."

"We Amish are human. We deal with human emotions the same as anyone else. I hope you know you are not alone. You have friends standing by ready to help carry your burden."

He squeezed her fingers. "I'm very grateful for one special friend."

She smiled and pulled her fingers away.

He missed the warmth of her touch immediately and wished he had some reason to take her hand again. "Can I ask a favor? Will you talk to Grace about the funeral?"

OWEN TOOK GRACE down to the barn to visit Polkadot when the funeral home hearse drove up the next morning. Joshua, Thomas, William and Ben Zook, along with all the wives, arrived a short time later. Grace was busy petting Polkadot and didn't seem to notice the activity up at the house. He didn't want her to realize what was going on.

She discovered that one of the sitting hens had hatched a half-dozen chicks. Their peeping and yellow fluffiness drew Grace out of her shell for a little while as she watched them explore the new world.

About half an hour later, Ruth came down to the barn. She took a seat on a bale of straw and lifted the child onto her lap. "Grace, I have something to explain to you. We're going to have a funeral for your mother. Your mother's body is in the coffin in the house, but her spirit is not there. Her spirit is already with *Gott*. It will make you sad to see her, and that is okay. When you feel ready I want you to come into the house and see her. She looks like she is sleeping but she will never wake up. In a few days we will take her body to the cemetery and lay her to rest in the ground. It's important for you to remember that she isn't in pain or uncomfortable. She's with the Lord in heaven."

Grace nodded. She was having to grow up much too fast. "Can I see her now?"

"Owen will take you in." She looked up at him.

He nodded and took Grace by the hand. "This is the time that we say goodbye."

"Okay." She slipped off Ruth's lap and walked beside Owen to the house.

RUTH DREW A shaky breath. The task of hosting a funeral was a pointed reminder of the time Nathan died. Sadness enveloped her, but it wasn't as suffocating as it had been in the past. Perhaps she was growing accustomed to the weight of it at last.

Was it because of her time with Owen? He was so different than she had believed him to be. He was caring and kind. He had a sense of humor, thankfully not as overblown as Ernest's.

She had received a letter from Ernest the previous day. His mother's poor health prevented him from returning for the funeral. Zack and Ella were coming and should reach home tomorrow. Faron had gone on a fishing trip with several new friends and wasn't expected to return to Jamesport until the day after the funeral. Ruth was disappointed that more of Owen's family couldn't be with him but knowing Ella and Zack were on their way lifted her spirits.

Ruth got up from the hay bale and went into the house. Owen and Grace were sitting quietly beside the coffin. Grace was holding on to Owen and only peeking occasionally at her mother. Rebecca was dressed in a white gown with a white apron and a white *kapp*. She was a pretty woman, and it saddened Ruth to think how someone had cut her life short.

Ruth walked over to Owen and Grace. "We will expect visitors soon. It's time we changed into our black dresses."

Grace got up without a comment and went upstairs. Ruth took a good look at Owen. He appeared more composed than she expected. "How are you holding up?" She laid her hand on his shoulder. He covered her hand with his.

"Better now that you are here with me. You have a knack for raising my spirits." He looked up at her and smiled.

"I'm glad." Her heart seemed to turn over in her chest. Every minute they spent together was becoming more precious.

Zack and Ella arrived the following afternoon. Ruth hurried out of the house to meet the van the newlyweds had hired to drive them back to Kansas. Ella rushed to her mother and kissed her cheek.

"I'm sorry to interrupt your wedding trip, but I'm so glad you could return. You can *redd-up* before supper. I know it was a long drive." Ruth linked her arm through her daughter's as they went into the house together. Zack followed behind them.

Ella glanced at her husband. "I think we would like to pay our respects before we clean up."

Ruth smiled sadly. "Of course. Come into the living room."

Granny Weaver was seated beside the casket. The elderly woman was nodding off but perked up at the sound of voices. "Zack and Ella, how nice to see the happy newlyweds so soon."

Zack took off his hat. "It is good to see you, too, *Grossmammi* Weaver."

Granny stood and gestured to the coffin. "Ella, this is your poor cousin Rebecca Mast. She was the sister that Owen searched for far and wide. At least the good Lord brought her to him so she could be buried with some of her kin. Her grandfather, his *sohn* Karl and his wife lie there."

Zack and Ella stood quietly by the side of the coffin sitting on sawhorses in the center of the room. After several minutes, Ella glanced at Ruth. "Where is Owen?"

Ruth smiled at the mention of his name. "He's in the barn with Grace. They're cleaning the lamb nursery and making sure the warming boxes are all working before the lambs begin to arrive. He is trying to stay busy."

"And Grace? How is she taking this?"

"She is quieter, withdrawn, not eating well and

she's not sleeping well. She has been staying here, and Owen has been sleeping in the lamb nursery."

Ella sat down on a chair next to Granny Weaver. "I'd like to stay here for a while. Do any of my friends know I'm back?"

"Sarah, Melody and Angela have offered to be sitters. Sarah should be here soon to relieve Granny."

The outside door opened and Sarah Yoder came in, carrying a large box. Ella hurried to greet her. Sarah handed Ruth the box. "Laura Beth sent some food for the dinner tomorrow." The two young women then embraced.

Funerals among the Amish were a time to gather and enjoy the company of friends and family more than to mourn. Ruth's grief was still a part of her, but the wall it had created around her emotions was crumbling where Owen was concerned.

The funeral was conducted at Ruth's home on the third day. The room around the coffin was filled with benches and chairs as were other areas of the house that the bishop's voice could reach. Everyone wore black. Bishop Weaver spoke about the glory of being reunited with the Father in heaven. There was no mention of Rebecca's life because no one knew what it had been like, but also because the life of the deceased person wasn't to be celebrated, only the knowledge that they were now with God. The congregation was reminded that their earthly life was but a brief stepping-stone into eternity. One hymn was recited by the bishop but there was no singing. When the hour-and-a-half service finished, the mourners filed past the open casket and then out to their buggies and cars. Many of Ruth's friends and neighbors, both *Englisch* and Amish, were in attendance.

The coffin was loaded onto a black wagon. The line of black horse-drawn buggies stretched for a quarter of a mile behind the wagon carrying Rebecca Mast to her final resting place in the small Amish cemetery outside Cedar Grove.

Behind the buggies came a slow procession of cars. Sheriff McIntyre in a patrol car with flashing lights brought up the rear. Several cars joined the procession behind the sheriff when they turned onto the highway.

It was something the community had never seen before. Dozens of the people were *Englisch* neighbors and even folks from towns far away who had braved the cold and snow to search for the missing mother. Now they joined the Amish to show their respects. Only Grace and Owen had known Rebecca in life, but she had captured the hearts of the community in a poignant way that left few untouched.

Owen had chosen to drive the hearse. Grace sat beside him on the wagon seat, a small lonely figure in a black bonnet and a black coat huddled beside her uncle on a cold gray morning.

A reminder that life went on elsewhere was driven home to Ruth when she saw two tractors with loaded hay trailers stopped at a crossroads to let the procession pass. She happened to glance in her rearview mirror and saw the tractors pull out across the road once the sheriff's car passed. They stopped, completely blocking the road to three trailing cars. The road curved and she couldn't see anymore.

Zack was driving her buggy. "The sheriff's idea seems to have worked."

Ruth leaned forward to see him around Ella. "What idea?"

"He said he couldn't ban people, even reporters, from using a public road but there was no reason a couple of farmers couldn't stop and visit for a spell in the middle of that same road."

"Those were reporters behind the sheriff?" She wished she had taken note of the colors of those cars. Was one of them the car she had seen stopped near Owen's place?

The Amish cemetery was enclosed by a split-rail fence approximately five miles from Cedar Grove. All the tombstones were small and simple. A name and the dates of birth and death were the only inscriptions. The newly dug grave smelled of freshly turned earth. The smell of spring and the season of new beginnings.

Peace belonged to Rebecca at last. As a mother, Ruth knew Rebecca could rest knowing Grace was safe in the arms of people who loved her.

Ruth helped Grace down from the hearse's wagon seat and led her to the open grave.

Quietly everyone gathered around as Rebecca's coffin was removed from the wagon bed by the pallbearers. The men carried it on their shoulders across the grass and placed it on a small mound of dirt beside the grave. Bishop Weaver gave a short service in Pennsylvania Dutch and in English, and then the coffin was lowered into the ground.

Ruth turned Grace over to Owen. He smiled his thanks but didn't say anything. She left him and walked across the grass between the headstones. She noticed a small toy horse leaning against the headstone of a child who had passed away two years before. The couple behind her stopped and pulled a few weeds away from the stone. They were the child's parents.

Ruth walked on until she came to Nathan's stone beside his mother's and father's graves. She cleared away some of the old leaves and ran her fingers over the edge of the stone. Time had dulled the edges of her grief so that her heart no longer cried out in pain. Her husband's passing was part of God's plan. That she remained behind was also part of His plan.

"I wish I could talk to you, Nathan. There are so many things I would like to tell you. Owen is here, and you were right all along. We were meant to be friends."

Maybe more if he keeps chipping away at my resistance.

"I still miss you. The children have grown so much. Ella and Zack are wedded. I know you are happy for them. Please keep an eye on Faron until he comes home." She wasn't surprised when Owen appeared at her side. He dropped to one knee and ran his fingers across the top of the headstone as she had done. "It's tilting a little."

"I noticed. I'll have the caretaker reset it before it gets worse. I'm ready to go if you are."

He stood and offered her a hand to help her to her feet. She laid her hand in his and realized how often they seemed to touch these days. It was a small thing but somehow it made a difference. It made her feel cherished. His eyes held a soft light as he gazed at her face.

She glanced down to the stone. "Nathan, you were right. Owen and I should have become friends long ago. He might have come to visit us more often."

She drew a deep breath and smiled at Owen. "He spoke about you often with great affection. He truly felt you were his brother and best friend. I can't tell you the number of times he made me laugh at stories of your boyish pranks." She looked at Owen and saw the light fade from his eyes. Why? What had she said?

He released her hand. "You still love him, don't you?"

"Of course I do."

He turned away, leaving her struggling to make sense of his withdrawal. "We should get back to the house. People are starting to leave. Will you take Grace with you?"

Grace came running over to them. Her face was pale, and she was panting. "I need a safe place. Where's a safe place?"

Ruth picked up the panic-stricken child. "Grace, what's wrong?"

She hid her face in her hands. "I saw the bad man."

CHAPTER TWENTY-TWO

OWEN SWEPT THE cemetery and surrounding area, looking for anyone out of place. "Where did you see him, Grace?"

"By the trees." She pointed over her shoulder.

"I'll go take a look." Zack strode in the direction Grace had indicated. He stopped and got Joshua and the sheriff to go with him.

Sarah came over. "What's going on?"

"A man frightened Grace." Ruth was trying to get her calm.

Sarah looked around the gathering. "I see a few unfamiliar faces. Grace, what did the man look like?"

"He had black bug eyes and spiders on his neck."

"Bug eyes. You mean sunglasses?" Sarah asked.

Grace nodded and wrapped her arms around Ruth's neck. "I wanna go home."

Ruth patted her back. "We will. We'll go home soon."

The men came back from checking the tree line. Joshua held his hands wide. "I didn't see anyone."

Sarah rubbed Grace's back. "Maybe she's just overwrought. It wouldn't be surprising."

Ruth bounced her gently. "You are probably right.

I will ask the bishop to start the procession back to my house."

No one they talked to had seen a man in dark sunglasses until Granny Weaver spoke up. "I saw him. Back by the trees before the service got started."

"What was he doing?" the sheriff asked.

"He was just watching us. I thought he was one of those reporters or something."

Owen looked around. "That would explain it. He seems to be gone now."

"I'm going to do a little more looking around." The sheriff started to walk off but stopped. "Owen, I got word this morning that the Columbia property did belong to your sister."

"I appreciate your checking it out." Now he knew for certain that he could take Grace home.

Ella took her husband's arm. "Would you drive the wagon home, so Owen can ride with us? I think it will make Grace feel better."

"Sure, I can do that." Zack climbed onto the wagon and started down the road. Owen got in the buggy with Ruth, Grace and Ella. As the procession started back to Ruth's farm they came upon the two farmers still visiting in the center of the road. On the other side of them several cars remained. One had attempted to go down into the ditch and up into the wheat field. The melting snow had left it as saturated as a sponge. The car was bottomed out. The other cars resorted to honking their horns every few minutes.

The farmers backed their vehicles to clear the road

and took their hats off as the procession went by. Owen stopped his horse in front of one and nodded toward the stuck motorist. "Will you help that fella get his car out of there?"

"I reckon. If I don't he's just gonna tear up more of my field. Hey, maybe I can sue him for the damage. Or maybe I'll offer him an interview for a hundred thousand bucks." He chuckled and slapped his knee.

Grace was huddled beside Owen. "That man thinks he's as funny as Ernest?"

Ruth gave her a small squeeze. "Nobody is as funny as Ernest or as funny as he thinks he is."

That made Grace giggle. It didn't lift Owen's mood. He glanced toward Ruth. She would never belong to him the way she had belonged to Nathan. The ache in his chest went so deep it was hard to draw a breath.

Ruth was still in love with her husband. While he had realized that before, he didn't fully appreciate the extent of that love until he saw her talking to the tombstone as if she were talking to the man. The gentle smile on her face and the sadness in her voice left him with no doubt.

While Ruth might care for him, Owen would never be able to replace her Nathan in her heart. Any hope of winning her love died a slow and painful death as he drove the buggy toward her house.

He had come to Cedar Grove to help and to make amends. That was still his intention. When Ernest and Faron returned, Owen would take Grace home as she had asked. He couldn't bear the heartbreak of loving Ruth and knowing she couldn't be his. With some time and distance perhaps he could learn to accept it.

He bowed his head as the truth sank in. He was in love with Ruth Mast. Hopelessly in love and nothing was going to change his feelings.

When they arrived at her house, Ruth carried Grace inside and Owen took the horse to the barn. He unhitched and unharnessed Licorice, giving her a rubdown before returning to the house. A half dozen of the younger boys were parking the buggies and unhitching the horses from them. Leaving their harnesses in place, the boys tethered them to the fence. They brought water to each animal in turn, then put on their feed bags.

The meal was being served cafeteria-style. Men and women moved in and out of the house with plates and drinks. Sarah and Ella were at a large tub washing the dirty dishes as they were brought out. William Zook and his sons were carrying clean plates back around to the kitchen.

Owen spoke to several of the men and women who approached him. He commented on the weather and talked about the places he visited. He wasn't asked about Rebecca.

Several women offered to bring him a plate of food, but he declined. He wasn't hungry. Grace's scare at the cemetery had him on edge. He scanned the road repeatedly for lurking cars.

"Aren't you going to eat?" Julie Temple asked as she approached him with an empty plate in hand.

"I'm not really hungry." It was good to see his grade school teacher. He remembered her fondly. She hadn't changed a bit.

"I'm sorry for your loss, Owen. I kept the paper you wrote in the eighth grade about being separated from your sister. It was very poignant."

"It was a sad time for me."

"As today must be."

He nodded. She laid a comforting hand on his arm. "In your paper you said your only wish was to find Rebecca and make sure she was safe and happy. God has answered that prayer even if not in the way you wanted."

Miss Julie was right. He knew where his sister was. He knew she was safe and at peace. "Thank you."

Another of Miss Julie's former students approached. Owen reached for Julie's empty plate. "Let me take that for you." He carried it to where Sarah and Ella were washing dishes and handed it to Sarah.

"What do you make of Grace saying that she saw a bad man?" Sarah asked as she took the plate from him and slipped it into the sudsy water.

"I believe she saw someone."

"A stranger with spiders on his neck. I wonder. Was he a curious onlooker, a sneaky reporter or someone more sinister?"

Ella frowned at her friend. "Those reporters are rubbing off on you."

Owen's gaze snapped to Sarah's face. "Have they been back to your farm?"

"Once when Joshua wasn't there. Laura Beth

loaded them up with a bushel of last year's dried lavender harvest. At a significant markup. She was so polite and talkative they couldn't get a question in edgewise. I think they thought if they purchased her goods, she would give them an interview. Nope. But they went away smelling sweet."

"Thanks for telling me." Owen let his temper cool. He didn't like that Grace's situation was putting his friends and neighbors in awkward situations. The best that he could hope for was a more interesting story to come along and draw the reporters away. Rebecca was dead. He didn't want Grace's grief spread across newspaper pages or television screens. At least when he and Grace left, he doubted the reporters would follow him out of state.

Two DAYS AFTER the funeral Zack and Ella were getting ready to continue their wedding trip. They would be back at Christmas and perhaps even once before that, but Ruth knew that would be much too long. Sarah came to see Ella off. The two women embraced, and both wiped the tears from their eyes.

"You come visit!" Ella pressed a finger to Sarah's chest.

"I promise I will. After the lavender season is over. I'll even bring you some of Laura Beth's goat milk soap. I know how much you like it."

Zack held open the door of the van they had arranged to take them back to Jamesport. "We need to get going."

Ella looked around. "I haven't taken my leave of Grace. Where is she?"

"Under the sink in the bathroom. She can't give up her safe place for long. I'm worried about her."

"Poor child. Give her some time. She's been through a lot. Tell her I said goodbye."

Ruth nodded. "I will."

Ella hugged Sarah one last time. "Check on *Mamm* for me. She's going to be terribly busy when the lambs start arriving."

"I promise that I'll come over. I will even bottle-feed some of her adorable lambs if she will let me."

"Sarah, I'll cheerfully welcome your help." Ruth put her arm around Sarah and the two of them watched the van pull away.

Sarah leaned her head on Ruth's shoulder. "I miss her, but I'm glad she found the man that makes her happy."

Ruth gave her a quick hug. "It's a great blessing when the right man comes into your life."

"That's what Laura Beth says. She says she has been doubly blessed to love Micah and then to find love again after his passing with Joshua."

"I admire your sister. I think she was very brave to marry again."

"Don't you think that you will marry again some-day?"

"I don't know what *Gott* has in store for me. I used to think I wouldn't, but who knows?"

"At least you're not opposed to the idea. That

should make it easier for the Lord to find someone for you."

Ruth chuckled but she wondered how much truth there was in Sarah's words.

That evening the sheriff stopped in to see Owen. She sent him down to the barn where Owen was storing the recently delivered bales of hay.

Ruth hadn't had to purchase more. A trailer loaded with prairie hay had been dropped off in the yard overnight without even a note for an explanation, but Ruth soon figured it out. The trailer belonged to one of the farmers who had blocked the road during the funeral. He was a good neighbor, and she would return the favor one day.

Owen was the one puzzle she couldn't seem to solve. He had been withdrawn since returning from Rebecca's burial. She assumed it was because of his continued sadness over the loss of his sister, but a small part of her began to think that might not be all it was. Like Grace, she was willing to give Owen the time he needed to heal. That morning a letter had arrived from the social worker. The child custody hearing was set for two weeks from Monday. Faron and Ernest would be back by then.

She was sweeping the porch when she saw Owen walking toward her with the sheriff. Both men wore grim expressions. She went down the steps to meet them. "What's wrong?"

Owen looked toward the front door. "Where is Grace?"

"Frosting some cupcakes for me because my kitchen isn't messy enough."

The sheriff didn't smile at her joke. "I have some news about Grace's father. We have a DNA match. He's a man named Antonio Winters. He's an ex-con with a long history of violence, including domestic abuse, and he's wanted for questioning in a homicide investigation in Cincinnati. I have some questions for him about Rebecca's murder, too."

Ruth's eyes locked with Owen's. "Could he get custody of Grace?"

The sheriff held up one hand. "We haven't heard from him in that regard, but we do believe he's been in the area. We have surveillance footage from a gas station outside Ottawa showing someone who looks a lot like Winters driving a white Ford pickup. It's not far off the interstate so there could be any number of reasons why he was there, but the date stamp said it was two days before the funeral. I want you to keep an eye out for the man. He has a spiderweb tattoo on the right side of his neck."

Ruth crossed her arms as a shiver went down her spine. "Grace said the bad man she saw had spiders on his neck."

The sheriff nodded. "Exactly."

"Perhaps he only wanted to see his child's mother laid to rest," Ruth suggested.

"I don't think his motives were that pure. I'm going to have my men patrol this area much more frequently. I don't have the manpower to leave someone with you around the clock so I'd like the two of you to carry cell phones. That way you can let me know if you see anything suspicious."

"Cell phones are not permitted for baptized members of our congregation," Ruth said.

The sheriff pressed his lips together. "I'm hoping you'll bend the rules a little this time. He's a violent man."

"It is not our way to fear any man or any thing. *Gott* is our protection," Owen said.

"I was afraid you'd say that. I'm still going to keep up increased patrols for a few weeks. Maybe that will discourage a visit from him."

Ruth frowned. "You believe he will come here?"

"I do. It's my gut feeling that Grace was a witness to her mother's murder. Maybe she can't name him, but I'm pretty sure she could pick him out of a lineup. He could be thinking the same thing. I've got a call into Agent Morgan. I'm hoping he will loan me a few more men. Unless he does, I can't assure your safety out here."

"*Gott* is our assurance," Ruth said softly.

OVER THE NEXT few days the vehicles of the sheriff's department were seen frequently up on the county road. Several times a day a deputy drove into the farmyard and waved as he turned around and left. Ruth saw their lights at night and knew they were keeping a close eye on her. With no new reports or sightings of Winters, Ruth began to relax, but her concerns about Grace continued.

The child remained withdrawn and quiet, often

slipping into her safe place for several hours at a time. She only left the house to be with Owen. He had been as quiet and reserved as Grace.

Ruth wanted to give him room to grieve, but she couldn't help feeling that he was shutting her out. It didn't seem as though they were as close anymore. She couldn't put her finger on exactly what it was, but he hadn't taken her hand once since leaving the cemetery. It was amazing how much she missed his gentle touch.

Ruth carried her dust rag and furniture polish into her living room and started on the end table.

The outside door flew open with a bang and Grace went tearing into the kitchen. "I see one! I see a baby sheep!"

A second later she sped into the living room and skidded to a halt in front of Ruth, hopping up and down as she pointed out the front door. "I saw one! It's out there! I saw it."

Owen followed her in the open door with a huge grin on his face. "She saw one, all right. She sure did."

Grace's eyes were wide with excitement. "I did. There's a baby sheep in the pasture."

A slow smile spread across Ruth's face. This was the first sign of happiness she'd seen from Grace since she'd learned her mother had passed away as well as the first real smile from Owen.

"I'm sure I mentioned this is what happens in March, didn't I?" She went to the entryway and began to pull on her boots.

"I didn't see the ewe with it. What if she has abandoned it?" Owen asked.

"Then you will get to do Ernest's favorite job and bottle-feed it."

"Can I do it?" Grace asked. She clasped her hands together and continued hopping up and down.

Owen shoved his hands in his pockets and tapped his foot as he waited for Ruth. "Don't hurry on our account. Who knows how long the poor thing has been lying there."

She looked up. "This isn't my first lambing season."

"Well, it's my first. What should I be doing?"

She waved him out the door. "Go check and see if the mother is nearby and take this hopping child with you. I have to gather my supplies. It's exciting, but I dread it at the same time. I hope you are caught up on your sleep."

He went striding toward the pasture with Grace running to keep up. Ruth chuckled as she pulled the backpack she had loaded with supplies off the hook by the door. His excitement would wear off soon enough. It would be a long and tiring week or more.

When she met up with Owen in the pasture, she saw the lamb sleeping quietly in a patch of sunshine. The snow was long gone. The grass wasn't tall, but it was a lush green, making the pasture look more like a manicured lawn than an animal pen.

Grace squatted a few feet away from the lamb. "It's so small."

"Aren't they adorable?" Ruth opened her backpack. A bleating cry alerted her to the fact that the ewe was on the other side of a small rise. She walked over and saw the new mother's second lamb was nursing and twirling its tail happily. She turned to Owen. "It's twins."

"Twins. I hope she takes care of them both. I'm not sure I could manage to bottle-feed one. I've bottle-fed a couple of calves, but they weren't as delicate as these little creatures."

Ruth picked up the lone lamb. It was a male. He came awake and began bleating. His cries brought the ewe running to check on her babe, objecting loudly as she came. "You need to distract her, Owen."

His eyebrows shot up. "What? How?"

"Get between her and me and try to keep her back but be careful. That's number eighty-eight. She's a very protective ewe and can do some damage. Grace, I want you to stay behind me."

"What are you doing?" Owen asked, stepping between the irate mother and Ruth. He started clapping his hands to drive the animal back.

Ruth held the newborn up to her face and planted a kiss on his nose. "Hello, sweet *bobbli*. I don't think we've met. I'm Ruthie. Welcome to my farm."

Owen glanced over his shoulder. "Are you talking baby talk to a sheep?"

"We're just getting to know each other. When a lamb is born our work starts. First, we check to see if the lamb is healthy. Is it active? Are the eyes bright? Does it seem strong? This one appears to be fine.

After that, we dab iodine on the navel to prevent infection, give him some vitamins and band the tail."

"Are you about done? Because this mama is getting antsy." He snatched his hat off and waved it to keep her from getting too close.

"Not quite. I have to mark them with the ewe's number using waxy crayon sticks."

She demonstrated by marking the lamb's left side with two large yellow eights. "If it's a single birth, the lamb will get marked with one stripe across its back. Two stripes for a twin and so on. It doesn't matter if you mark them on the left side or the right side but it's best to always use the same side. I mark my lambs on the left side."

The ewe continued to announce her displeasure and lowered her head in a threatening gesture. Owen took a step back toward Ruth. "Are you done? She's very upset."

"Almost. I need to put a rubber band over the tail. The part below the rubber band will die and fall off in a couple of weeks. A shorter tail makes for cleaner sheep. Fortunately my Icelandic sheep have a naturally short tail and I can skip this step with them. That's another reason I like the breed."

"Just hurry up."

Ruth chuckled as she put the lamb on the ground and watched as it scurried to Mom. Owen wasn't as brave as she thought if a mad mother sheep frightened him.

The ewe stopped protesting and nuzzled her baby before moving away. "Catch the other lamb, Owen.

You take care of this one and I'll keep the mother busy. Grace, stay behind Owen."

He managed to go through the entire process quickly and confidently as he marked the other lamb and turned it loose. "Now what?"

"We go look for more lambs."

Grace went running ahead and came back in a minute with Meeka beside her. "Owen, I see another one with his mother over there. Come on."

He looked at Ruth and grinned. It warmed her heart. "I can't believe we've been worried about her. She's as happy as a lark."

"Now you know how I feel when I'm with my flock."

The morning went well with five mothers all delivering twins. Two males and eight new females. Two of the females were Icelandic sheep that Ruth would keep to increase her flock. When the last one was marked and treated, Ruth sighed with pleasure. "It is a good start to our lambing season. I just hope the weather doesn't get any colder."

Owen smiled at her. "Thank you for teaching me all about baby sheep."

"Thanks for being a good student. Is it as bad as you thought it would be?"

"*Nee*, I kinda liked it."

"I'm glad. I hoped you would." She walked toward the house with a light heart. Owen liked her sheep.

The following day was a church Sunday and while Ruth hated to leave the sheep unattended for even a few hours she joined Owen and Grace for the service at a nearby farm, but they left before the meal was served.

The weather turned cold and rainy the next day. It was a potentially devastating situation for all the newborn lambs.

Most of the recently shorn mothers sought the shelter of the barn, but others chose less suitable places to have their babies, such as dense thickets or draws in the pasture. Both Ruth and Owen tramped through the wet grass, slid down muddy embankments and pulled aside dripping branches to look for lambs in every nook and cranny.

Ruth and Owen worked long hours to move each reluctant mother with her newborns into the barn. Grace couldn't keep up. She often napped in the lamb nursery with Meeka beside her, a watchful and massive guardian. As the rain continued Ruth and Owen quickly ran out of room for the ewes and new lambs.

Owen built additional pens inside the barn and even moved Licorice to Ernest's place so he could turn her stall into a sheep maternity ward. Polkadot had to give up her private stall, as well. Owen put her out into the corral beside the barn and moved three new mamas and babies into it. Ruth divided her time between searching for new lambs and making sure Owen had food, hot coffee and dry clothes. She all but forgot about the threat to Grace except for the continued presence of the sheriff's officers stopping by.

Grace, on the other hand, was at her happiest. She stayed in the lamb nursery bottle-feeding a pair of orphans every three hours. Her giggles and delight in her new babies made Ruth and Owen smile no matter how tired they were. Ruth entered the nursery and found Grace pushing a lamb under the sink cabinet. "Grace, what are you doing?"

Grace spun around and kept the door closed with her hands behind her back. "Nothing."

The pitiful bleating of the lonely lamb was muffled but plain as the look of guilt on Grace's face.

Ruth walked over and moved Grace aside. She opened the door and the lamb sprang out. "Your little one doesn't want to be shut in a cabinet."

"I have to have a safe place for my babies. I have to teach them to go to the safe place."

Ruth sank to her knees and pulled Grace into a hug. "Our home is a safe place. *Gott* is watching over us. There is no need to hide. Not for you and especially not for your lambs."

Grace didn't look convinced, but Ruth didn't find any more lambs under the sink the rest of that day. Would Grace ever feel truly safe or would she constantly search for somewhere to hide?

As Ruth was returning to the house that evening, she caught a glimpse of car lights turning in at the end of her lane. She waited to see if it was one of the sheriff's cars, but the lights shut off. She waited a few minutes, but they didn't come back on. Out in the pasture, she heard Meeka barking ferociously.

CHAPTER TWENTY-THREE

OWEN SAW RUTH staring out into the darkness. It had stopped raining. He walked up beside her. "What are you looking at?"

She shrieked and jumped like a startled rabbit. Pressing a hand to her chest, she glared at him. "Don't scare me like that."

He held up both hands. "Sorry. I didn't mean to frighten you. What's so interesting?"

"I saw lights turn into our lane and then they went out. They haven't come back on."

"Probably an *Englisch* teenage couple looking for a little privacy."

"Maybe." She kept gazing out into the night.

"Do you want me to go check it out?"

She shook her head as she turned to him. "*Nee*, you are probably right and it's nothing. What are you up to now?"

"I'm actually headed for bed. You should be, too."

"I am. Check under your cot for any lambs."

"Grace?"

"Yep. I found her today trying to make a lamb stay under the sink. She said her babies need safe places."

Ruth clasped her upper arms and hunched against the chill. "I wish she felt safe here."

"You're cold. Take my coat." He took it off and laid it across her shoulders.

His hands lingered there and then slid down her arms. This was what she wanted, to be close to him, but she wasn't close enough. She leaned back against him with a sigh. He was so strong, and she needed his strength.

IT FELT RIGHT to hold her this way. Owen didn't want the moment to end. "You smell *goot*."

She chuckled. "Like a sheep?"

"More like a flower garden. Soft, sweet, like spring flowers."

"It's my shampoo. I couldn't find my usual unscented one, so I picked up this discount brand without realizing it was heavily scented. I know it's too fancy, but I haven't gotten back to the store this week and I had to wash my hair."

She was so dainty, so delicate. How had she managed to run a farm, raise children and not crumple beneath the weight of it all? He fought the urge to slip his arms around her and hold her tight, but knew he was about to lose the struggle. He abruptly stepped away. "Good night."

"Good night, Owen." The confusion in her voice shamed him. Should he tell her how he felt and be done with it, or should he continue hiding his love for her, knowing she couldn't return it?

He could only keep his secret if he avoided being

alone with her. He both longed for and dreaded the return of Ernest and Faron.

The next morning Sarah showed up to help as promised. Owen could have hugged her. She took over the cooking and watching Grace, giving Ruth a much-needed respite.

Owen saw how exhausted Ruth was as they walked in from the pasture. "Take a break for a few hours."

"Me? I'm fine."

"You should be sitting down with your leg on a pillow. You're limping worse now than when you first hurt your knee. Did you hurt it again?" He closed the pasture gate behind them as they headed to the barn.

"An ewe with an attitude tried to knock me down, and I twisted it getting away."

"Unbelievable. You are done for today. Do you hear me?"

"Owen, you know how I hate being told what to do."

"I have no idea how you have remained Amish. With your attitude you should have been shunned for pride ages ago."

She shrugged nonchalantly. "What can I say? The bishop likes me. I'm going to add fresh straw to the pens. You are going to go in the house and make me some hot cider and check on Grace. I'll be there in half an hour and then I will rest."

"See that you do."

It only took her twenty minutes to finish. She made her way to the house. The smell of hot spiced cider greeted her the second she stepped inside. Grace was sitting on the floor of the kitchen with two new lambs asleep in her lap and wrapped in her favorite quilt.

"Where did they come from?"

Owen stood at the stove. He turned around with a large white mug in his hand. "I saw number seventy-one had twins beside the barn, but she wouldn't nurse either of them. As soon as I'm done here I'll take them out to the nursery and get them into warming boxes. Sit. I will get you a pillow so you can put your leg up. And this time you are not going to object to being told what to do, because you know I'm right."

She sat down with a weary sigh. "Boss me all you want but that doesn't mean I'm going to obey you. Right now I'm going to sit down and put my leg up on a pillow. Could you fetch one for me, please?"

A tiny shake of his head showed his disbelief. "I see. It's only a good idea if you think of it?"

She smiled at him. "Now you are beginning to understand me. While I'm resting, can you check the temperature of number twenty-six's lamb? He wasn't nursing, and he looked weak."

"What's a normal temp?"

"Around 102 degrees. If he's colder than that move him to a warming box, heat some milk replacer and tube-feed him."

"Now who's being bossy?"

"This isn't about us. It's about saving as many of my lambs as possible."

"I'm sorry. You're right, Boss."

OWEN DIDN'T REALLY care if Ruth was being bossy. He just wanted her to take care of herself. The pace had been grueling for him and he knew it had to be tough on her. When she had her foot up and a mug of hot cider on the table in front of her, he left the house.

The lamb's temperature was low. Owen bundled him in a towel and carried him to the nursery. Ruth had set four boxes around the stove. Owen put the lamb in one and got the milk replacer out of the fridge. The old propane stove had only two burners, but it provided rapid heat to warm the water he set the bottle in. He had just finished putting a tube down the lamb's throat when Ruth walked in.

He scowled at her. "I thought you were taking a break?"

"I did. The hot cider was delicious, *danki*." She sat on a folding chair.

He finished tube-feeding the baby and put it in the warming box. He slanted a look at Ruth. "Did you have anything to eat today?"

"Of course I did. I had French toast for breakfast."

"That was yesterday."

She tilted her head to the side. "Really? Then I must have had some graham crackers."

"You can't work all day on a couple of graham crackers."

"Okay, what did you have to eat today?"

"The same thing Grace had. Church spread on toast. Church spread on white bread and church spread on celery."

Ruth chuckled. "I'm glad you were able to get

some vegetables in her diet. I'm glad Sarah is here. She loves taking care of Grace. Of course, so do I."

It probably wasn't the right moment but it had to be said. "Ruth, I've been wanting to talk to you about something."

"Okay." Her tentative reply almost made him change his mind.

"Grace has asked me numerous times to take her home. I promised her I would. When Ernest and Faron get back, she and I will be leaving for her mother's farm near Columbia after the custody hearing next Monday."

Ruth pulled her sweater tightly across her chest. "I see. Won't you consider staying in Cedar Grove? She seems to like it here and you and I are getting along."

If only she knew how much he wanted to say yes. How could he stay when simply sitting across from her in a barn that reeked of sheep left him wanting to take her in his arms and kiss her? How much harder would it become each day to pretend those feelings didn't exist?

"I'm hoping Grace will feel secure at the home she is familiar with. She needs that, and I need to take her there. Maybe I can learn something about Rebecca. She is still an unsolved mystery to me."

"When do you think you'll be back?"

"I can't say."

Ruth nodded slowly. "I understand." The disappointment on her face gave him pause. Did she want him to stay because of Grace? Or was there another reason?

He rose to his feet. She spun to face him. "I haven't thanked you for your help. I'm sorry I doubted your usefulness and your determination to see the job through."

"I've given you a few reasons to doubt me in the past."

"I won't ever again." She stepped close and laid her hand on his cheek. "I couldn't have done this without you."

"You're very welcome," he said softly. His resistance crumbled. He leaned down and kissed her.

Her lips parted as if in surprise, but she didn't pull away. Overwhelmed by the love in his heart he knew he should stop but he couldn't. He slipped his arms around her and pulled her close. It felt so right to hold her this way. One part of him said it was wrong. She still loved Nathan. Another part of him said that it didn't matter because he loved her even if she could never love him.

She flattened her palms against his chest, but she didn't push him away. He ended the kiss and saw her eyes flutter open. They widened with confusion. With all she had to worry about she shouldn't have to concern herself with his actions. It wouldn't happen again. Without a word he walked out of the barn, calling himself every kind of fool. But it had been worth it.

RUTH PRESSED HER hand to her lips. His kiss had been brief but tender. Why had he walked away without saying anything? What did it mean? It wasn't a kiss between friends, she was sure of that. Maybe it was a goodbye kiss. Her heart sank.

Ernest and Faron would be back in a few days. What would life be like without Owen? Without Grace? She didn't like to think about it. That goodbye was going to be almost too much to bear. She sank onto a chair and covered her face with her hands, determined not to cry.

She heard the door open. Owen came back in with something buttoned up inside his coat. Crossing to the stove, he knelt there. "I need your help."

He opened his jacket enough for her to see he had two tiny wet lambs bundled against his body for warmth. They didn't look good.

Ruth sprang into action. She pulled towels from the supply closet. Returning to Owen side, she waited as he extracted one black-and-white lamb and handed it to her. "Dry her good. She might make it. I'm not so sure about her brother."

"Did their mother reject them?" She wrapped her baby in a towel and handed a second towel to Owen.

"*Ja*, they belonged to Polkadot. She had triplets, but she would only nurse one."

Ruth put the little one she was drying down and stuck several towels in the oven to warm. She continued to dry her charge as best she could. The vigorous stimulation seemed to help. When the towels in the oven were warm, she wrapped both lambs in them and put them in the warming box.

"They'll need colostrum," Ruth said. The first milk the ewes produced was essential to the newborns' health. Ruth kept a supply frozen in the freezer section of her refrigerator.

"I'll get some heated up." He headed to the fridge.

She grabbed his hand as he went past her. He stopped. She didn't understand the pain in his eyes. "I'm glad you found them. Grace will be heartbroken if anything happens to Polkadot's babies."

"You're an amazing woman, Ruth. I don't know how you do it. I admire your dedication, your skill, your selflessness, your faith. This has been a time I will never forget."

Then why leave? She couldn't bring herself to ask the question, because she already knew the answer. He cared about her. But he didn't love her enough to stay. She was the one in love, and she didn't know what to do about it.

The silence stretched between them as they fixed bottles for each lamb and began to feed them.

Owen cleared his throat. "Ruth, about that kiss."

"What about it? You surprised me, but it was a sweet kiss." She tried to sound nonchalant. Her heart began pounding so hard she was afraid he must hear it. What if he had meant something other than goodbye? Was she ready to take that next step in their relationship if that was what he wanted? She was.

"It was a mistake. I'm sorry."

She blinked hard. "A mistake?" She hadn't expected that.

"You know what I mean." He put his lamb in the warming box.

She carefully placed her lamb in beside his. "Actually, I don't know what you mean. Did you want to kiss me or didn't you?"

He stared at his feet. "A man shouldn't kiss a woman unless he is prepared to marry her."

"And?" She held her breath as she waited.

He looked at her then. "And you aren't—I mean, I'm not prepared to marry you."

A rush of hot tears filled her eyes. "Oh."

"Not that you aren't a fine woman."

"But not fine enough to marry! Too old? Too set in my ways? Give me a hint." She sniffled and brushed at her cheeks.

"Don't twist my words. It's none of those things. I know you are still in love with Nathan, and I respect that."

"Nathan has been gone for four years."

Owen slipped his hands in his pockets. "I know."

She waited for him to say something, anything. He stood staring at the floor.

"Owen Mast, you must be the blindest man I've ever met." She whirled on her heels and left the room.

CHAPTER TWENTY-FOUR

OWEN SAT DOWN on his milk crate with a heavy sigh. The lambs bleated at him. He gazed at their cute faces. "That didn't go well."

What did she mean that he was blind? He had seen the tears in her eyes. Should he follow her and ask what it was he should have seen? She was in love with Nathan, wasn't she? She'd said so at the cemetery. He fed the last crying lamb, rose and walked slowly up to the house.

Inside he saw Sarah in the kitchen. She scowled at him. "What did you say to Ruth?"

"Why?"

"She's upstairs crying."

He never wanted to hurt her. He rubbed his palms on his pant legs. "Do you think I should go talk to her?"

"Not if you want to live to be a day older."

"Maybe I'll wait until later. Where's Grace?"

"She went out to see her lambs. It's almost time for their feedings."

"I was just in there and she wasn't anywhere around."

"That's odd." Sarah put her dish towel on the countertop.

"Do you have any idea where she might be?"

"My first suggestion would be one of her safe places."

He looked around. "I know about the one in the house. Are their others?"

"I'm not sure." She went out onto the porch. "Grace! Where are you?"

It was already getting dark. Together they walked to the lambing nursery. Grace wasn't there but Owen noticed one of the lambs was missing. "She's taken one of Polkadot's lambs."

Sarah went to the door and began shouting, "Grace, answer me!"

Owen walked over and opened the cabinet under the sink. It was empty. It was then that he noticed two of the drawers beside the refrigerator had been opened partway. He checked the countertop and sure enough, there was a small footprint with the toes pointing toward the refrigerator. Relief made his knees weak. "Come out wherever you are, Grace. It is safe now."

The door of the cabinet above the refrigerator opened a crack. He glimpsed four tiny fingers clutching the panel.

The outside door opened, and Ruth rushed in. "I heard you shouting for Grace. Is everything okay?"

Her eyes were red and puffy. He wanted to kick himself for making her cry. He took a step back. "Okay, come down. That is an excellent hiding place, but I don't ever want you taking the lambs up there. We don't want Ruth mad at both of us."

The door opened wider and a lamb hopped onto the top of the refrigerator. It looked over the edge and seemed prepared to jump but Owen caught it and handed it to Sarah, who looked as relieved as he was.

Sarah shook a finger at Grace. "Do you know how much trouble you would be in if one of these lambs gets hurt?"

Grace crawled out carefully. "A lot?"

Owen held up his arms to the child. "I'm very disappointed in you."

"But I found a good safe place." She allowed Owen to lift her off the top of the refrigerator.

Sarah put the sheep back in the warming box and closed the lid. "That's a pretty weird game unless you just wanna do nothing for an hour."

Ruth took Grace from Owen's arms. "You shouldn't scare us like that."

"I'm sorry."

"I'm sorry, too," Owen said quietly.

Ruth gave a deep sigh. "I forgive both of you."

Meeka began barking ferociously outside. It wasn't her coyote-warning bark. It was her this-is-serious-business bark. Owen took a flashlight from their stock in the drawer. "I'd better go see what's wrong."

He heard a loud thud followed by a pain-filled yelp from Meeka and then silence. He looked at the women and the child waiting for him to tell them what was going on.

"You in the barn. Send out the kid, and nobody's gonna get hurt."

Ruth stepped close to Owen and grabbed his arm. "Who do you think it is?"

"I think it's Grace's father."

"What do we do?" Sarah asked.

He thought for a second. There was only one way out of the nursery. They were trapped. "Do you have your cell phone?"

Sarah shook her head. "It's in the house." She looked around and then up. "Owen, help me get out of the skylight. I think I can cross over the top of the barn and stay out of sight."

"I'm waiting! I'm not a patient man. Send out my daughter," the intruder shouted.

Owen picked up Grace and set her on the countertop. "Go to the safe place."

She jumped to the top of the fridge and disappeared into the cabinet. Ruth used her apron to wipe away her footprints.

Owen looked at Ruth. "Where is the ladder to open the skylight?"

"Faron keeps it in his workshop."

Owen tried to judge the distance. He piled two milk crates on top of each other and stepped up. "Sarah, climb onto my shoulders. When you get out the window be quiet. We don't want him to know that something is going on."

Ruth walked toward the door. "Sir, I'm coming out so that we may speak face-to-face. We Amish are pacifists. I am no danger to you."

"That ain't a good idea, sister."

Sarah gave a nervous giggle as she climbed up Owen's back. He steadied her. "Are you okay?"

"Sure. This isn't the first time I've done this. I'll fill you in later."

"We don't know who your child is," Ruth shouted.

"Don't give me that. I read about the woman and kid found out here. I know she's staying with you. I saw her go in the barn just a little bit ago. You can't keep me away from my kid!" The man's voice was growing increasingly angry.

Owen heard a slight grating sound as the window opened. Sarah levered herself off his shoulders and out the opening. He knew she would have to drop from the low side of the barn into the corral. It was at least a ten-foot drop but it was on the opposite side from the man outside.

He moved to stand beside Ruth. "The woman was my sister Rebecca. How do you know her?"

"She was my wife, the lying tramp. I want that girl and I want her now. She's my daughter and I keep what's mine. Nobody makes a fool out of me."

"The child is in a safe place. You cannot harm her." They needed to stall for time. How long until Sarah got to the house? How long before the sheriff came?

Ruth clutched Owen's arm. "What are we going to do?"

He looked into her eyes. "'But I say unto you, That ye resist not evil: but whosoever shall smite thee on thy right cheek, turn to him the other also.' I'm going out to speak with him."

She drew a deep breath. "It is my faith also. I will go with you." She took his hand. He wanted to dissuade her, but he knew the choice was hers. He slowly opened the door. If he faced death on the other side, he would not fear it.

He stepped out into the darkness and scanned it for the man who had been talking. He saw only a white bundle of fur on the ground and he knew it was Meeka. He couldn't tell if she was alive or dead. Nor could he see the man speaking. He and Ruth walked to the dog. There was a bloody gash on her head, but she was breathing.

"Stop right there. Bring the kid out here."

Owen faced the darkness. "I will not aid you to harm a child. She is an innocent in the eyes of *Gott*."

"I'm not going to hurt the little lady. Don't you Amish have to believe I speak the truth?"

"If you mean no harm, then show yourself," Ruth said. The intruder stepped out of the shadows with a gun pointed at Owen. He was tall with a shaved head and a long blond mustache. A tattoo of a spiderweb covered the right side of his neck. The barrel of the gun shifted between Owen and Ruth. "Now that you've seen my face, this may not have such a happy ending." He started laughing.

Ruth pressed close to Owen's side.

"Grace! Grace, honey, come out here and meet your papa or your friends are going to end up like your mama."

"Are you the one who killed my sister?" Owen heard his voice crack. He needed to be strong.

"I can't admit to that. I don't know if you're wearing a wire and the cops are listening."

"I am not. I have no connection to the police. If she did die by your hand, I want you to know that I forgive you as I know she would have done."

"Mighty nice of you, but for someone with no connection to the law you've had them crawling all over this place. I didn't think I'd ever find a way in. But here I am. Patience and planning. That's what pays off. I wouldn't let a few country-bumpkin cops keep me from taking what's mine. Becky tried, but I knew I'd find her sooner or later. Grace? This kind man and his pretty lady will end up like your mama if you don't come out."

"Winters, this is Sheriff McIntyre. Drop the gun."

The man swung his pistol toward the sheriff's voice and fired twice.

CHAPTER TWENTY-FIVE

RUTH THREW HERSELF into Owen's embrace and held
on tightly. She sobbed as more gunfire erupted and
Owen pulled her to the ground. The echoes faded
away and the frantic bleating of the sheep filled the
night. Sheriff McIntyre and two of his men, including Agent Morgan, climbed the fence of the corral.

Owen searched her face and her arms with trem-
bling fingers. "Are you hurt?"

"I think I'm okay."

Sheriff McIntyre came up to them as Agent Morgan checked the man on the ground. He gave a slight
shake of his head. Ruth knew the man was dead. The
sheriff helped them up.

"You gave me a mighty big fright when you
walked out of that barn toward a man holding a gun.
What possessed you? No, don't tell me. God was
your protection." Sheriff McIntyre gestured toward
the barn. "Let's step inside. Where is Grace?"

Owen went in and crossed to the refrigerator. He
opened the cabinet above it. Grace was huddled inside. "You can come out now, sweetheart."

"Is the bad man gone?" Her voice trembled and
there were streaks of tears down her cheeks. Owen

handed her to Ruth, who held her tight and consoled her.

"He will never trouble you again," the sheriff said.

Owen left Ruth's side to speak to the sheriff quietly. "How did you get here so fast?"

The sheriff's grim expression eased. "You have the KBI to thank for that. They've staked out the place for the last week. I was on my way to check in with Agent Morgan and his partner when I got the call from Sarah. That is one gutsy gal."

"*Danki*, Marty," Sarah said as she came in. Both Owen and Ruth pulled her into a fierce hug. "Ella would never forgive me if I let something happen to you," Sarah muttered.

Ruth patted her back. "Of course she would forgive you. You were very brave to escape through that skylight."

Sarah laughed. "It was a tight fit. I tore my new dress."

Ruth hugged her. "I'll make you a new one."

"I can help," Grace said.

Sarah kissed her forehead. "I would love that."

Agent Morgan came inside. "I'm sorry he got by us undetected. He must have come across the pasture, because we were watching the house and the road."

Sarah drew back and looked at the sheriff. "How did Rebecca get mixed up with a fellow like that?"

"I can answer that," Morgan said. "Rebecca's aunt passed away about five years ago. Rebecca took a job in a diner outside Akron. It appears she had left the

Amish at that point. They may have met at the diner. We don't know. Winters had just finished a five-year stretch for assault and robbery. Maybe he was trying to go straight or maybe she thought she could fix him. They were married within a few months. Almost immediately there were reports of domestic violence. After one incident Winters was arrested but Rebecca disappeared before the case went to trial. There were rumors that she went into hiding among the Amish."

Ruth handed Grace to Sarah. "Why don't you take her to the house? We'll be there soon."

Once they were out of the barn, Ruth turned to Agent Morgan. "Why would he kill her?"

"Revenge. Winters was obsessed with making her pay for getting him tossed back in jail and for hiding his child from him. We really don't know much else about her movements until you mentioned seeing her in Indiana. After that she apparently went back to her farm in Missouri. According to a neighbor, she would come and go from the farm every few months when she needed money. She worked as a waitress in a number of places but never for long. It seems Winters found her there. She was able to escape in the car he'd stolen but not before he got off a shot. He then stole the neighbor's pickup and tried to follow her. The storm stopped him. You pretty much know the rest. We believe she was trying to reach you or your uncle."

Ruth held on to Owen's hand. "Rebecca must have

been afraid of him for a long time. Grace has never known anything but hiding from strangers."

Owen glanced at Ruth and squeezed her fingers, then looked at the two officers. "We are grateful for your intervention. The Lord used you as His instrument to save us."

The sheriff's smile faded. "I'm sorry it turned out this way. I would've much rather sent him back to jail."

"He is facing his maker and answering for all that he has done. That is the true justice," Ruth said softly.

Owen kept his arm around her as he escorted her back to the house. She leaned into him, never wanting to move away from the comfort he gave. Owen left her side when he entered the kitchen and sat down. Grace crawled onto his lap. "Can we go home now? I want to go to our farm."

He held her close. "Soon, *liebchen*, soon."

Ruth steadied her nerves by performing the mundane tasks of making coffee and getting cinnamon rolls out of the freezer to be warmed up. Doing something always made her feel better.

Sarah started laughing hysterically. Ruth and Owen looked at her in concern. "What's so funny?" Owen asked.

"Faron," she croaked and started laughing again. "Faron wanted more excitement in his life. So he went on a fishing trip to Arkansas while down on the dull old farm there was a shoot-out with a criminal. He's gonna kick himself for weeks that he missed this."

Ruth looked at Owen and they started chuckling.

A few minutes later the sheriff came in. "My people will have a few questions for you and then we will get out of your hair."

"But I have cinnamon rolls warming in the oven. You can stay another ten minutes, can't you?" Ruth asked.

He broke into a wide smile. "For some of your cinnamon rolls, Mrs. Mast, I could stay the week."

Ruth dished up pastries and hot coffee for all of the men. Agent Rankin, Agent Morgan's partner, was particularly impressed with her baking skills. "These are the best rolls I've ever had."

"I'm glad you enjoy them."

"Tell me something. I saw you walk out in front of that killer and I was sure he was going to kill you before we could stop him. Why did you do it?"

"We hoped we could convince him to leave us alone. The Lord was protecting us."

"I think the sheriff and I were protecting you."

She chuckled. "How does it feel to be an instrument of the Lord?"

"Scary. What are your plans now, Owen?" the sheriff asked.

"I'm taking Grace home as soon as I can."

Ruth wasn't going to beg him to stay. He was still searching for something. She prayed he would find it and know contentment at last.

Don't go, Owen. You're breaking my heart. I can see the love in your eyes, but why can't you say it? Why can't you tell me? Can't you see it in mine?

Ruth wanted to run to him and grab onto him like a terrier and shake him until he came to his senses.

She stared at him a long moment, then she rushed out of the room.

AFTER THE SHERIFF and his men left, Owen took Grace and returned to Ernest's farm. He continued to wrestle with his decision to leave. As much as he wanted to stay, he knew leaving, while painful, would not be as torturous as remaining. He needed to keep his promise to Grace to take her home. He hadn't been able to keep his promise to her mother. He hoped by being among Rebecca's things and talking to people who knew her that he might gain some insight into who his sister had become. In his mind she would always be the little girl crying out for him as she was taken away.

Ernest and Faron returned two days later, in time to help with the last days of lambing. Sarah was right. Faron was fit to be tied that he had missed the excitement of a police shoot-out in exchange for a few black bass. Ernest was soon recounting the tale in the community as if he had been one of the sheep in the warming box while it was all going on.

Following a quick hearing on Monday afternoon Owen was granted full custody of Grace. He made arrangements to leave two days later.

Faron came over to Ernest's place to say goodbye before Owen left. Owen couldn't believe how much the boy was growing to look like his father. "What was the best part of your trip, Faron?"

He blushed. "You'll laugh."

"I won't."

"Okay, it was fun to get away and see new things, but the best part was coming home. Seeing the green pasture full of sheep and the dark earth waiting for me to plant corn. I might travel again, but it will be a long time before I leave home."

"Your mother must be thrilled."

"She says she is, but she's been crying a lot lately. That isn't like my *mamm*. You're going to stop in before you leave, right?"

"We will." Owen picked up his duffel bag. He had left Ruth without a word once before. He wouldn't do it again no matter how painful it would be to say goodbye. He found Grace carefully doctoring the cut on Meeka's head. She was following the veterinarian's recommendations to the letter. Meeka wore a long-suffering face while the child wrapped a bandage around her head with a long piece of gauze and lots of tape. Meeka's gash was healing well thanks to Grace's tender care.

"I'm taking you home, Grace, to your mother's farm. Meeka will be fine."

Grace frowned. "You said *Mamm* isn't at home. She's with *Gott*."

"That's right but I hope to get to know your mother by talking to some of her friends. You want to see them, don't you?"

"I miss Mr. Clayton. He looks after my pony when we're gone."

"Okay, then, are you ready to go?" He held open the car door.

She left the dog and climbed into the backseat of the car he had hired to take them to Columbia.

As they drove into Ruth's farmyard, she came out of the house to meet them. She avoided looking at Owen and focused her gaze on Grace. "You must be excited to be going home."

"Sure, but don't we need to check on all the lambs first?" Grace gazed longingly at the pens.

Ruth pulled her into a tight embrace. "Faron and I will look after the lambs. You look after Owen for me." Owen heard the catch in her voice and knew he was breaking her heart by taking Grace away.

"Can't you come with us?" Grace asked.

She sank to her knees in front of the child. "I have all my lambs to look after. I can't leave them. Goodbye, Grace." Ruth rose to her feet and held out her hand. "Goodbye, Owen."

He grasped her fingers gently. "Goodbye, Ruth. May *Gott* bless you and yours." Letting go of her hand was the hardest thing he'd ever done.

THE TRIP TO Rebecca's farm took three and a half hours. Owen was plagued by the thought that his sister had made the drive while she was dying. Grace remained quiet the entire trip, but she sat up to look out the window when the car turned down a gravel drive and stopped in front of a small neat house with a large flower garden out front. The door of the home opened, and an elderly couple came out.

Grace pushed open her car door and ran to the woman's welcoming arms. "Mrs. Clayton, I'm back."

"My little Grace, I've missed you so."

"This must be the place," Owen muttered as he got out and paid the driver. The man unloaded their suitcases.

The elderly man came forward with his hand outstretched. "Welcome. You must be Owen Mast. The sheriff said you'd be the one who came to look after Rebecca's estate. Not that she had much, but she never complained. Let me take your bags in. I assumed you'd want to stay in her house. The wife and I live just down the road."

"Thank you."

"Come in," Mrs. Clayton said. "I've got lemonade and gingersnap cookies."

Owen lagged behind as the others went in the house. He studied the house, the garden and the small stable. It was all in fine shape with fresh red paint on the stable and white trim.

In the garden he saw his sister loved irises. They bloomed along the white picket fence in a dozen colors from pale yellow to deep purple. Their mother had loved the stately iris, too. There were other flowers, some he didn't know the names of. It felt good to admire something she must have loved.

In the house he found the Claytons waiting for him at the kitchen table. Mrs. Clayton poured him a glass of lemonade. "Grace has gone to see her pony. Sit. We know you must have questions for us. We have some for you."

He sat down and spread his hands on the tabletop. "I don't know where to start."

Mrs. Clayton smiled at him. "Then I'll tell you a little about your sister. She was so excited to meet you. You can't believe how happy she was to have found some family. After Thelma died, Becky thought she was alone in the world."

"I have to say she didn't seem excited when I spoke to her." Had she really been happy that he'd found her?

"That was her way. Always cautious. The same with Thelma. She was more than cautious, she was paranoid that someone was coming to steal Becky. We didn't understand but maybe now we do. How sad that she couldn't share her child with you and your family."

"What was Rebecca like when she was little? Did she talk about her family at all? Did she mention me?"

Mr. Clayton shook his head. "We didn't meet her until eight years ago. She never mentioned you."

Mrs. Clayton held up one finger. "Now, maybe she did. She told me once she had a recurring dream about a young boy who saved her from terrible danger and promised to take care of her forever. She never had a name to put to him, but I think it might have been you."

Some of the tension drained from Owen's shoulders as a weight lifted from his chest. She hadn't completely forgotten him. "She wrote to me and said she needed my help. Do you know what that was about?"

They exchanged sad glances. Mrs. Clayton sighed deeply. "She knew Antonio would find them someday. She wanted Grace in a safe place. She was going to ask you to take the child. Isn't it strange how things worked out?"

He shook his head. "She didn't even know me."

"I think maybe she did. I think she saw the boy in her dreams in you."

He smiled at the couple. "Tell me everything about her."

Hours later, he was outside petting Rebecca's pony when Grace came around the side of the house. He finally thought he knew who his sister had been. A proud mother, a sweet friend, a member of the faithful, a sad woman trying to protect her child from her own worst mistake. That child came toward him, but she wasn't smiling as he had expected her to be.

"What's the matter, Grace? Isn't it *goot* to be home? Pansy has missed you."

The pony put her head over the fence so Grace could rub her forehead. Grace complied. "*Mamm*'s not here. I thought she might be. Whenever she went away she always came back here. I looked everywhere."

His heart ached for her sadness. "She isn't here but all the things she loved are here. Her flowers, her house, her friends. They are here to remind you of her. I'll never let you forget her."

"I won't forget her, but what if Ruth forgets about me?"

He smiled at the thought. "I doubt Ruth will forget you. She's more likely to forget the sun rises in the east."

"Meeka is going to forget me. Who is changing her bandages?"

"I'm sure Ruth will." It hurt to talk about her not knowing when he would see her again.

"I miss her. Don't you miss her?"

Far more than he cared to admit. "We can go visit her someday."

Grace's eyes lit up. "Tomorrow?"

"We just got here. I thought you wanted to come home."

"I did, but I don't think this is home anymore. *Mamm* used to say home is where your heart is happy."

"That's something our mother used to say."

His heart wasn't happy. He loved Ruth. He would never be truly happy without her.

Grace narrowed her eyes as she stared at him. "I think home is with Ruth and Polkadot and Meeka now because they love me."

"I love you."

She grinned at him. "I love you, too, and so does Ruth. Can we go back? Ruth is missing us an awful lot. She's crying."

"We'll see, but not tomorrow. We only just got here." The child would change her mind again, he was sure of it.

She folded her hands together. "Please?"

"Definitely not tomorrow."

"Why not? Don't you miss Ruth and Meeka and the sheep?"

"I do miss her," he said softly. So why was he trying to talk himself out of going back?

He loved Ruth. Even if she couldn't love him he could at least be near her. He thought it would be less painful staying away, but he had only been fooling himself.

He shook his head. "I don't think Ruth wants me hanging around the place."

"Did you ask her?"

It couldn't be that simple. Could it? Was he brave enough to ask her how she felt or was he going to keep running away?

He looked into Grace's hopeful eyes. "Okay, you win. We're going home."

SHE WASN'T GOING to cry anymore. Ruth rubbed her scratchy eyes and opened the front door two days after Owen and Grace had left. She stood staring out across the pasture, wondering if she would ever see them again. If she had just told him how she felt. If she could have made him see that loving Nathan didn't mean she couldn't love him. She should have tried, but women didn't propose to men. Not in her community. The Amish took their modesty seriously.

The sun was barely over the horizon. The warm golden light radiated in bright rays above and below a solitary gray cloud promising a gorgeous spring day. She had learned that life went on even in the face of unbearable sadness. The sun always rose. And the sun always set.

She didn't know how long she stood staring out the door until she noticed a commotion in the pasture. The flock was breaking in two and running in different directions as a child came barreling through them. The lambs darted away and then came back to leap beside her.

Ruth couldn't believe her eyes. It was Grace. She rushed down the steps, through the gate and out into the field.

Grace skidded to a halt in front of Ruth and struggled to catch her breath. "I need to ask something."

"What are you doing here?" She gathered the child in a tight embrace not certain she wasn't dreaming.

"I missed you. *Onkel* Owen doesn't think you want him to live here. Can I tell him this is his home, too, so we don't have to leave and our hearts can be happy?"

She brushed a few stray strands of hair from Grace's face. "If only it were that simple."

"What's hard? Tell him you want him to stay." Grace pushed against Ruth. "Tell him this is a safe place."

Ruth looked up to see Owen walking toward her. "I think Owen is looking for his own safe place."

"Our home is a safe place. You said so."

"Oh, Grace, it's my fondest hope that Owen will realize that someday."

"I'll go tell him." Grace squirmed out of Ruth's

grip and took off running across the grass with the ribbons of her *kapp* streaming behind her.

"Owen! *Onkel* Owen! Ruth says we can stay." Grace didn't slow down but plowed into Owen and almost knocked him over as she wrapped her arms around his leg. "Ruth wants you to stay. Her home is a safe place. You don't have to look for another one. Our hearts can be happy here."

Owen gazed at her upturned face so full of hope. Suddenly his jumbled world clicked into place and he knew exactly what he had been searching for and never found. A safe place. A home. For his body and his heart. Ruth was his safe place. The place where his heart longed to rest. He hadn't seen it before because the shadow of Nathan obscured it. He wasn't half the man his cousin had been. How could Ruth settle for less?

"Please stay, *Onkel* Owen. Ruth wants us to stay. She said it was her fondest hope."

"She did?" For the child, he understood that, but for him?

Grace nodded vigorously. "It's Meeka's fondest hope, too. And Polkadot's."

He looked toward the house. Ruth was running toward him. She didn't slow down. She slammed into him, too, and threw her arms around his neck.

"I can't stand it. I can't watch you walk away from me again. I love you, and you are an idiot if you don't know that. This is not the proper way for a woman my age to behave. Forgive me but I can't lose you."

Owen held her tight as despair gave way to happiness. He had found the home he'd been searching for and never knew it. He rocked back and forth with her in his embrace.

Ruth pulled back. "You can tell me that you don't love me, and I'll go back to the house."

"Stop talking."

"Just know I'm going to love you for the rest of my life even if you don't love me."

He pulled her close and laid a finger on her lips. "Stop talking so I can kiss you."

"Oh. Okay."

"I love you. Of course I love you. I love you more than my life, you sweet, darling woman." He bent to kiss her and she rose on tiptoe to meet him. It wasn't simply a sweet kiss. It was a kiss filled with tenderness and the promise of a future together. His head reeled as his pulse thundered in his ears. No more waiting and wishing. She was his.

"Are your lips stuck?" a little voice asked by his side. He had forgotten about Grace.

He pulled back but didn't let Ruth out of his arms. "I love you."

"Why didn't you say so?" she muttered against his chest.

"Because Nathan was your soul mate. How can I compete with that?"

She reached up to cup his face in her hands. "You don't have to compete with Nathan. I can love you dearly because you are Owen. There is no limit on how much love a heart can give."

"He was a better man than I am."

"That's not true. I did love him above all others. It hurt so much to lose him. I never wanted to feel that agony again. I couldn't risk loving someone so much it would tear my heart in two. I didn't plan to love you. I fought against it. The night Winters came after us, I saw what it would be like to lose you. When I saw Grace running to you the way I wanted to run to you, and I had to follow. I will love you for as long as *Gott* wills. I pray He gives us many years together. Never doubt that I love you most dearly."

"I love him most dearly, too," Grace declared, sandwiched between them.

Owen picked her up and kissed her cheek. "I love you the mostest dearly of all." He settled her on his hip with one arm and held his other out to Ruth. She slipped into his embrace without hesitation. Gazing into her eyes, he saw a future as bright as the rising sun.

"*Gott* has been good to me," he said softly.

"He has been merciful to all of us. I think it's time we went home, Owen Mast."

He kissed her forehead. "I'm comfortable right where I am. I could stay here all day."

Grace frowned at him. "But I'm hungry for breakfast."

He chuckled. "*Ja*, I can see the future clearly. I'm going to have to compete with pancakes for my little girl's love."

"I promise to share with you," she said.

"That makes me feel better." He lowered the

child to the ground and gripped Ruth's hand as they walked side by side. "Well, my future wife, what is for breakfast?"

Grace stopped in her tracks. "Ruth is going to be your wife?"

"I hope so. If she says yes. Will you marry me, Ruth?"

"I believe I must for I've never met anyone in more need of a home and a family."

"And love?"

"And lots of love." She smiled so sweetly, he almost took her in his arms again.

"Danki." He leaned over and kissed her instead.

"If we are going to be a family, can I be the daughter and you two be the *daed* and *mamm*?"

"That sounds like a fine plan. Don't you think so, Ruth?"

"I do. I think it's a very fine, very smart plan."

Grace stood beside them grinning. "See, I told you finding a wife is a lot smarter than doing your own cooking, *Onkel* Owen. I mean, *Daed*."

* * * * *

If you enjoyed this story, look for the next book in the Amish of Cedar Grove series, The Promise *by Patricia Davids, available May 2020 from HQN Books.*

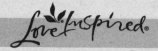
"Are the *kinder* okay?"

"Yes, they'll be fine." Uncomfortable with his small intrusion into her family, she said, "Kevin had a bad dream and woke us up."

"Because of the rain?"

She wanted to say that was silly but, glad she could be honest with Michael, she said, "It's possible."

"Rebuilding a structure is easy. Rebuilding one's sense of security isn't."

"That sounds like the voice of experience."

"My parents died when I was young, and both my twin brother and I had to learn not to expect something horrible was going to happen without warning."

"I'm sorry. I should have asked more about you and the other volunteers. I've been wrapped up in my own tragedy."

"At times like this, nobody expects you to be thinking of anything but getting a roof over your *kinder*'s heads."

He didn't reach out to touch her, but she was aware of every inch of him so close to her. His quiet strength had awed her from the beginning. As she'd come to know him better, his fundamental decency had impressed her more. He was a man she believed she could trust.

She shoved that thought aside. Trusting any man would be the worst thing she could do after seeing what Mamm had endured during her marriage and then struggling to help her sister escape her abusive husband.

"I'm glad you understand why I must focus on rebuilding a life for the children." The simple statement left no room for misinterpretation. "The flood will always be a part of us, but I want to help them learn how to live with their memories."

"I can't imagine what it was like."

"I can't forget what it was like."

Normally she would have been bothered by someone having sympathy for her, but if pitying her kept Michael from looking at her with his brown puppy-dog eyes that urged her to trust him, she'd accept it. She couldn't trust any man, because she wouldn't let the children spend their lives witnessing what she had.

Don't miss
An Amish Christmas Promise *by Jo Ann Brown,*
available December 2019 wherever
Love Inspired® books and ebooks are sold.

LoveInspired.com

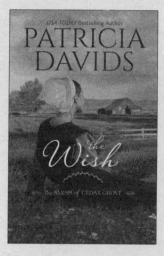